"You're exactly who scares the like me."

"What kind of woman do you think I am?" Grace asked, her voice soft and a little breathless.

"You're a nester." Travis smiled to show her he meant no insult. "The kind of woman who can make a shack into a home with nothing but her hands and her smarts. The kind who makes a man feel so at ease, he never wants to leave."

"And you're a rodeo man, terrified of a nester 'cause she might tie you down?" Her lips curved into a wry smile. "And here I thought you crazy bulldoggers were so brave."

Travis shrugged, but didn't smile back at her. "Everybody's afraid of something...." *And he certainly was afraid of the way she was making him feel!*

Dear Reader,

Back by popular demand, MONTANA MAVERICKS: RETURN TO WHITEHORN reappears in Special Edition! Just in time for the Yuletide season, unwrap our exciting 2-in-1 *A Montana Mavericks Christmas* collection by Susan Mallery and Karen Hughes. And next month, look for more passion beneath the big blue Whitehorn sky with *A Family Homecoming* by Laurie Paige.

Reader favorite Arlene James makes a special delivery with *Baby Boy Blessed*. In this heartwarming THAT'S MY BABY! story, a cooing infant on the doorstep just might turn two virtual strangers into lifelong partners...in love!

The holiday cheer continues with *Wyoming Wildcat* by Myrna Temte. Don't miss book four of the HEARTS OF WYOMING series, which features a fun-loving rodeo champ who sets out to win the wary heart of one love-shy single mom. And you better watch out, 'cause *Daddy Claus* is coming to town! In this tender tale by Robin Lee Hatcher, a pretend couple discovers how nice it might be to be a family forever.

Rounding off a month of sparkling romance, *Wedding Bells and Mistletoe* by veteran author Trisha Alexander launches the CALLAHANS & KIN miniseries with a deeply emotional story about a forbidden passion—and a long-buried secret—that can no longer be denied. And dreams come true for two tempestuous lovers in *A Child for Christmas* by Allison Leigh—the next installment in the MEN OF THE DOUBLE-C RANCH series.

I hope you enjoy all these romances. All of us here at Silhouette wish you a joyous holiday season!

Best,

Karen Taylor Richman,
Senior Editor

Please address questions and book requests to:
Silhouette Reader Service
U.S.: 3010 Walden Ave., P.O. Box 1325, Buffalo, NY 14269
Canadian: P.O. Box 609, Fort Erie, Ont. L2A 5X3

MYRNA TEMTE
WYOMING WILDCAT

Silhouette®

SPECIAL ▼ EDITION®

Published by Silhouette Books
America's Publisher of Contemporary Romance

SILHOUETTE BOOKS

ISBN 0-373-24287-5

WYOMING WILDCAT

Copyright © 1999 by Myrna Temte

This edition published by arrangement with Harlequin Books S.A.

Visit us at www.romance.net

Printed in U.S.A.

Books by Myrna Temte

MYRNA TEMTE

grew up in Montana and attended college in Wyoming, where she met and married her husband. Marriage didn't necessarily mean settling down for the Temtes—they have lived in six different states, including Washington, where they currently reside. "Moving so much is difficult," the author says, "but it is also wonderful stimulation for a writer."

Though always a "readaholic," Myrna never dreamed of becoming an author. But while spending time at home to care for her first child, she began to seek an outlet from the neverending duties of housekeeping and child-rearing. She started reading romances and soon became hooked, both as a reader and a writer. Now Myrna appreciates the best of all possible worlds—a loving family and a challenging career that lets her set her own hours and turn her imagination loose.

McBride Family Tree

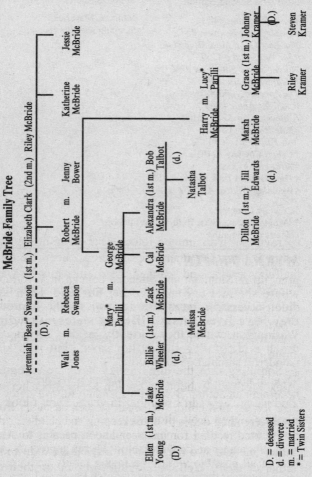

Jeremiah "Bear" Swanson (1st m.) Elizabeth Clark (2nd m.) Riley McBride
(D.)

Rebecca Swanson — Robert McBride — Katherine McBride — Jessie McBride

Jenny Bower m. Robert McBride

Walt Jones m. Rebecca Swanson

Mary* Parilli m. George McBride

Ellen (1st m.) Jake McBride
(D.)

Billie (1st m.) Zack McBride
Wheeler
(d.)

Melissa McBride

Cal McBride

Alexandra (1st m.) Bob Talbot
McBride
(d.)

Natasha Talbot

Harry m. Lucy* McBride Parilli

Dillon (1st m.) Jill McBride Edwards
(d.)

Marsh McBride

Grace (1st m.) Johnny McBride Kramer
(D.)

Riley Kramer

Steven Kramer

D. = deceased
d. = divorce
m. = married
* = Twin Sisters

Chapter One

Travis Sullivan ambled into the bar of an upscale motel in Billings, Montana, and ordered a beer. He turned halfway around and scanned the room while he waited for the bartender to deliver it. At a table near the dance floor a feminine hand shot up and waved vigorously. Since he didn't know a soul in Billings, he allowed his gaze to drift past the hand, then jerked it back when his brain registered a familiar face.

Squinting into the dim, smoky haze, he recognized Alex McBride…shoot, he couldn't remember her married name. He hadn't seen her in years. Didn't look like she'd changed a bit, though.

He hastily paid for his beer and carried it to Alex's table. She had two friends with her, but he didn't know either of them. Well, he wouldn't intrude on their evening. He'd just say hello and move on.

Alex jumped to her feet as he approached, took the

beer out of his hand and set it on the table, then held out her arms for a hug. "Travis Sullivan, what are you doing here? Is there a rodeo in town?"

"I don't think so." He gave her a quick hug and stepped back. "Didn't your cousin Dillon tell you I've retired from the circuit?"

"No. Are you all right?"

"I am now. Messed up my right shoulder at the finals last year. I'm all healed up, but my bulldogging days are over. It's a kid's game."

She pointed at his championship belt buckle and grinned. "You made it all the way to the top, though. Congratulations."

"Thanks. Hey, I saw Dillon and your brother Jake in Cody last week. Starting Monday I'll be spending the next three months at the Flying M, filling in for Dillon while he's in California."

"That's great. I knew they were looking for help, but I didn't realize they'd found someone."

One of the other women cleared her throat. Alex glanced down and her eyes widened as if she'd just remembered her friends were there. "Ohmygosh, where did my manners go? Travis, grab a chair and I'll introduce you to my new sisters-in-law."

He snagged an empty chair from the table to the left and smiled at the other women. Alex introduced the one with long, light brown hair as Cal McBride's wife, Emma. The one with the darker brown hair and the soft, southern accent was Zack McBride's wife, Lori.

"Sounds like there's been some hot romancin' goin' on at the Flying M," he said with a chuckle.

"That's not all," Emma said. "Alex is a newlywed, too."

"Whoowee." Travis fanned himself. "What are you gals doing up here all by yourselves?"

"Why does anybody from northern Wyoming come to Billings?" Alex said. "Shopping. It's only sixteen days until Christmas. Grace is here, too, but she's up in our room calling home to check on her kids. She should be here any minute."

Travis stared at her. "Little Gracie has kids?"

Snickering, Alex rolled her eyes at him. "She's thirty-one, Travis. All grown-up. Wait'll you see her."

Travis shook his head, shocked and a little saddened at the realization that life was passing so quickly. The last time he'd seen Grace, she'd been a skinny fifteen-year-old with gangly arms and legs and braces on her teeth.

"She's had a rough time lately," Alex continued. "Why don't you ask her to dance?"

"Be glad to," he said.

"There she is now," Lori drawled with a smile. "Doesn't she look gorgeous?"

Travis spotted a tall, curvy woman with the McBride family's strong features and raven hair curling around her shoulders hesitating in the bar's entrance. She was all gussied up for the evening in a white, long-sleeved Western blouse, a short denim vest with lots of fancy stitching on it, a swingy little denim skirt and a pair of short blue boots that were cute but hardly practical. Those boots showed off a long, smooth stretch of leg between them and the hem of her skirt. Lord, have mercy, her legs looked long enough to wrap around a fat horse and then some.

Little Gracie had grown up, all right. When she stepped into the room and walked toward the table, the gaze of every man in the place followed the gentle swing of her hips. The instant stirring of attraction going on below his own belt buckle made Travis feel guilty. The woman was his buddy's baby sister, for God's sake, and she was married, too. He shouldn't be having such a lusty reaction to her.

Unfortunately the closer she got, the stronger that lusty reaction was, and he had a suspicion that it wasn't going to go away any time soon.

Oh, Lord, what am I doing here?

Grace McBride Kramer hesitated in the doorway to the bar. She was supposed to meet her cousin Alex and her two in-laws to celebrate the new-and-improved Grace. Fifteen minutes ago it had sounded like fun, but now... Well, now she wasn't sure she wanted to step inside the place.

There was nothing "new and improved" about her. Nothing that really mattered. Oh, she'd had about a foot of her hair cut off, so it fell to a couple of inches below her shoulders. Rather than twisting it into her old, no-fuss, no-bother braid, she was wearing it loose and had even let its natural curl do whatever it wanted for a change. That much was new.

She'd also had a facial and a makeover, a manicure and a pedicure, not to mention a shopping spree that would give her heartburn when the bills arrived. But all of that was just window dressing. While she undoubtedly looked better than she had before, inside she was still the same old insecure, scaredy-cat Grace, who would rather spend a quiet night at her family's ranch than walk into this bar.

Not even the sparkling Christmas decorations made the place look any more inviting. Stepping back out into the real world and facing the prospect of dating again terrified her. She'd already made one doozy of a mistake in that arena. She would be damned if she'd make another one.

Come to think of it, she wasn't too sure she liked men all that much anymore. Considering the horrendous secret her dumb brothers had kept from her—for her own good, of course—it would be a mighty long time before she ever trusted anyone with a Y chromosome again. Her sons, Riley and Steven, might be an exception, but they'd spent so much time hanging out with their idiotic uncles, she was reserving judgment on them for the present.

So what was she doing here now? Her self-image, her memories of courtship and marriage, her whole blessed world had been shredded four short days ago. She was still bleeding inside from the betrayals of the last man she had loved. What was the rush to spruce her up so she could go out and find another one?

On the other side of the dance floor, she saw an arm go up and wave vigorously in her direction. And there, in the flesh, was the answer to her question—her dear cousin Alex, the first person she'd called after learning the truth about Johnny. Alex had listened to Grace's sob story, shared her indignation at the behavior of all the males involved and immediately started planning this women's weekend out in Billings.

There'd been no stopping her after that, so here was the new-and-improved Grace, ready or not. Oh, not. Definitely not. But, according to Alex, she had to start living again sometime.

Inhaling a deep breath, she straightened her spine, lifted her chin and walked around the dance floor to join the others. Alex and Emma toasted her with their margaritas. Lori held up what looked like a plain old glass of orange juice. Oh, no. There was a man at the table, too.

A big, good-looking man with dark hair and a sexy smile. Where on earth had Alex dug him up? If she was matchmaking again, Grace just might have to hurt her this time.

Always dramatic, Alex leapt from her chair and hugged Grace halfway to unconsciousness.

"Gracie, you look absolutely smashing," she announced with a huge grin. "I can hardly believe it's really you."

"Alex, you're too kind," Grace muttered. "And too loud."

"Huh?"

"Pipe down, will ya? People are staring."

"Well, of course, they are," Alex said with a laugh. "They always stare at gorgeous women. You know, if you were just an inch taller, you could be a supermodel." To Grace's horror, Alex turned to the stranger at the table and said, "Don't you think she could be a model?"

He pursed his lips and gave Grave the most thorough once-over she could remember. Her neck and cheeks grew warm, but she refused to give him the satisfaction of looking away. He looked familiar, somehow, but she couldn't place him. His lips curving into a devilish grin, he slowly shook his head.

"Nope," he said. "She's not nearly scrawny enough to be one of those models, thank God. She's lots prettier this way."

Grace's face felt so hot she was afraid it might ignite. Making her tone as dry as the alkali flats east of the ranch, she said, "Gee, thanks, mister. Your approval makes my whole darn day shine."

The man chuckled. Emma spilled half of her drink and started coughing as if she'd laughed in the act of swallowing and choked herself. Lori thumped Emma on the back and kept her own head lowered. Grace figured she was probably laughing as hard as Emma. Alex confiscated a chair from another table, waved Grace toward it and cocked her other thumb toward the stranger. "Don't you remember this fella?"

Grace lowered herself onto the chair as gracefully as she could manage with the man watching her every move. She didn't care who he was, she just wanted him to stop staring at her. Staring right back at him, she shook her head. "Can't say that I do."

The man clutched his chest with both hands. "Ouch! And here I thought I was *unforgettable.*"

She smiled at him, showing lots of teeth. "Sorry."

Alex swatted her arm. "Oh, stop. This is Travis Sullivan, Grace. He's one of Dillon's rodeo buddies."

The instant she heard his name, Grace remembered a lanky, laughing young man who had taken turns with Dillon teaching her fancy new dance steps they'd learned on the rodeo circuit. She'd loved the attention he'd given her and a safe opportunity to practice her fledgling flirting skills on an older man—who must have been all of twenty at the time.

He gave her a broad wink and pointed a teasing finger at her. "It's coming back to you, isn't it?"

Grace slowly nodded, then had to chuckle at his obvious delight in her admission. "Vaguely."

"Can you still do any of those dance steps I taught you?"

"I can keep up with Dillon. I imagine I can keep up with you, too, Mr. Sullivan."

"Mr. Sullivan?" He flinched as if she'd whacked him. "Cruel woman. You tryin' to make me feel old?"

"Is it working?" Grace asked.

He let out a loud laugh, then shook his head. "Not hardly. Sullivans usually live into their nineties. By those standards, I'm just headin' into my prime right now."

Grace had no desire to argue with his statement. He had a new scar over his right eyebrow, a bump on the bridge of his nose and crow's feet at the corners of his eyes that gave his rugged face a comfortable, lived-in look to it. The maturity of sixteen years had erased the lankiness of his youth and improved his looks altogether. The cocky glint in his eyes told her he knew it, too. Not that he seemed conceited, exactly.

As far as she could tell, he was the same old charming, fun-loving Travis he'd been before. But she felt oddly uncomfortable in his presence. He reminded her too much of her big brothers—well, Jake, Zack and Cal were cousins, but her family and Alex's were so close, they rarely made a distinction between cousins and siblings.

The problem was, Travis wasn't looking at her as if he felt brotherly toward her. She didn't feel any sisterly fondness for him, either. Instead, there was a strong man-woman sort of chemistry going on between them. Just like the instant attraction she'd had with Johnny. Even the idea of it was unsettling.

A five-piece band suddenly climbed onto the stage and tuned up their instruments. At the same time, the barmaid delivered a fresh round of drinks for the table. Grace grabbed her margarita and downed a third of it in one swallow, gasping softly at the icy bite of tequila, salt and lime in her mouth. Travis raised his eyebrows at her. Emma, Lori and Alex chattered and giggled like a bunch of adolescents until Grace wanted to kick all three of them under the table.

The band launched into a toe-tapping, hard-core, country song that drew couples from all over the room to the dance floor. Taking another long drink, Grace settled back in her chair to watch the action. Two minutes later Travis offered his big hand across the table in invitation.

"Dance with me, Grace?"

She wrinkled her nose at him. "I don't know, Travis. To tell you the truth, it's been a long time since I danced."

"Don't worry about it, kid. I'll take it easy on you."

Alex elbowed Grace in the ribs so hard, she nearly fell off her chair. "Go on. You love to dance."

Knowing she would have no peace until she gave in, Grace shot Alex a filthy look, then walked around the table, slipped her hand into Travis's and strolled out onto the dance floor with him. When he turned her to face him, her mouth dried out, her heartbeat sped up and she felt as awkward and bashful as she had when she'd been fifteen. Luckily he didn't give her much time to get nervous.

The band swung into a fast song with a driving beat, and in thirty seconds it was all Grace could do to keep up with him. He had a rodeo cowboy's perfect sense of timing and balance, and another sixteen years' worth of Saturday nights to practice since the last time she'd danced with him. Unwilling to risk goofing up in front of him or the group of women she'd left behind at the table, she focused her entire attention on following his lead.

They were both smiling and breathless when the song

ended. With only a chord change for warning, the band ripped into another tune.

Travis raised his eyebrows in query. She nodded. He laughed out loud, spun her away from him, then yanked her right back with a hard flick of his wrist.

It was fun in its purest form, something she'd had far too little of for too many years. At the end of the last number in the set, he held on to her hand instead of releasing it. "Could I buy you a drink?"

Grace hesitated. It was one thing to share a few dances with Travis. It was something else to sit down with him away from the others. Of course, she'd probably never see him again, and it might be fun to practice her flirting skills on him, but he didn't seem all that safe anymore.

Glancing over her shoulder at her table, she spotted Alex, Lori and Emma all making shooing motions at her. Travis chuckled, and Grace's neck and cheeks heated again. She looked up at him and saw a sympathetic interest in his eyes that eased her embarrassment.

"Sorry," she said with a rueful laugh. "They're probably telling newlywed secrets, so they're dumping me on you."

"I'm glad they did." He placed one hand at the small of her back and escorted her to a table for two on the opposite side of the dance floor. When he'd ordered a beer for himself and the cola she'd requested, he leaned forward, braced one forearm on the table and grinned at her. "You're still one heck of a dancer."

"Thanks," she said. "You, too."

"What's your husband like?"

She held up her ringless left hand. "I don't have one."

"Oops. Sorry about that. Grace said you have some kids and I just assumed—"

"Well, I did have one once." She looked away so he couldn't see the bitter fury that might show in her eyes. "He died in an accident five years ago. It was the same wreck that messed up Dillon's face so bad."

Feeling like a jerk for bringing up what was obviously a painful subject, Travis reached across the table and clasped her hand between his palms. "Damn, Grace, I'm sorry to hear that. He couldn't have been very old."

"He wasn't." She retrieved her hand, then admitted, "I'm just starting to think about dating again."

"How do you like it so far?"

"This isn't a date."

"Feels like one to me," he said. "Close enough, anyway."

She grimaced, then shook her head. "It feels weird. Johnny and I were high school sweethearts before we got married. I haven't had much experience with other men."

His heart contracted at the brittle smile on her lips and the anxiety he heard in her voice. "Is that why the newlyweds really came up here with you? To give you moral support?"

"Probably. They all spent a lot of money shopping today, but I'm sure they really came along for my sake."

"They must be good friends."

"They are." Glancing over her shoulder at them, she turned back to him and raised her glass in a toast. "Here's to good friends."

"Here, here," he agreed, lifting his beer bottle in

return. Sensing he'd better lighten the mood, he told a couple of bad jokes. She groaned at the appropriate moments and told him a couple he'd heard before, but he laughed at them anyway. He couldn't help it when she looked so pleased with herself.

"So what are you doing up here all by yourself?" she asked.

"Just getting away for a couple of days."

She absently tugged a small, silver locket out of her blouse. Rubbing it, she asked, "You're not married?"

"Divorced."

"Oh, I'm sorry," she said, sounding as though she really meant it.

He shrugged. "It was a long time ago. We were both young and stupid. At least we didn't have any kids."

"You don't like kids?"

"Oh, I love 'em." He lifted a corner of the label on his beer bottle and slowly peeled it off. "I'm just glad I didn't have to drag any through that divorce. So what do you have? Boys or girls?"

"Two boys. Riley's almost thirteen and Steven is ten."

"What are they like?"

"They're little cowboys," she said with a chuckle. "One minute they're sweet, the next they're a couple of knotheads. What one of them doesn't think up, the other one does."

"And you wouldn't trade 'em in for anything."

"No way." Her smile wobbled and then faded away. "They're my whole life."

Unsure what to say to a remark like that, Travis took a long pull from his beer. The band took the stage again. Grateful for the distraction, he took her hand and led her back into the fray of dancers.

The second set started with three hot and fast songs, just what he needed to reset the mood. Grace seemed young and innocent and free of the games so many women played in an attempt to appear sophisticated. He was tickled half to death that she wasn't overly impressed by his rodeo career. She was reacting to *him,* not some rodeo star, and he loved it, even though she still acted wary of him.

He was so used to women throwing themselves at him, her wariness amused and fascinated him. He loved seeing the glow on her cheeks, the light of pleasure in her eyes, the delighted smile on her sweet mouth when she forgot to worry about anything else but dancing. The band seamlessly slid into a slow, haunting ballad.

Panting slightly from the exertion of the previous song, she gazed up at him with renewed caution in her eyes. She reminded him of a little chicken at the low end of the pecking order, looking every which way, searching for any possible source of danger before stepping out of the coop. He opened his arms to her, holding himself still, silently telling her the decision was hers to make.

He imagined he could hear the wheels turning in her brain as she studied him. Then she slowly stepped into his embrace, resting her left hand on his shoulder and letting him cradle her right hand between them. She stiffly held herself away from him at first, making their steps awkward.

The music gradually came to the rescue. He moved with the rhythm of the song. She moved along with him, her feet again following his with unerring accuracy. During the second slow song, her posture softened; by the third one, she'd looped her arms around his neck and he'd crossed his wrists at the small of her back, holding her closer still.

She felt good in his arms. Better than good, if he was honest. She was tall enough—five-nine or five-ten—that he didn't have to bend down to see her face or hear what she said. Her breasts brushed against his chest and he enjoyed every motion her sweetly rounded hips made. She was incredibly sexy in a subtle, unstudied sort of way.

Grace floated along in Travis's arms, half fearing some cranky fairy godmother would suddenly appear and tell her she had to go home. She hadn't enjoyed a man's company like this since... Well, come to think of it, she couldn't remember ever having had such a nice evening.

Travis smelled wonderful and his shirt smelled as if it had been dried outside. There was immense strength in his heavily muscled arms and shoulders, and yet he held her as if she were some fragile figurine he wanted to protect at all costs. Thinking of herself as something fragile was ridiculous, but she liked it anyway.

She had to admit that, thanks to Alex's determination to get her a new "look," she felt less like a *mom* tonight and more like a *woman* than she had in years. An amazing array of fantasies were playing in her mind, some of them shocking in their boldness. Thank heaven Travis couldn't read her thoughts.

He pivoted, turning her to face Alex, Lori and Emma's table. The three of them raised their eyebrows, made fanning motions and heaved huge sighs, then broke up laughing.

Why *had* they all come with her? Grace supposed there was a skunk in this woodpile, but she didn't want to stop and find it. Besides, if there was one, the varmint undoubtedly had Alex's name written all over it. Lori and Emma were too new to the family to be pulling any matchmaking stunts yet, although it wouldn't take Alex long to corrupt them.

Travis turned her again. She closed her eyes and concentrated on how she felt in his embrace. Warm. Aroused. Safe. Amazingly safe considering how little she knew of him. Being in Travis's arms made her body...hum. He really seemed like a nice guy, more handsome prince than frog.

But then, so had Johnny.

A cold, clammy mist of insecurity settled over her at that thought. Shivering, she pulled back and studied Travis's face. She felt flattered by his attention, but the evening's magical glow had started to grow dim. She couldn't help wondering about his motives for suddenly appearing tonight and spending so much time with her.

Yes, they danced well together, but it really didn't make sense that he would keep dancing with her when he could have any of the beauties making eyes at him. Johnny must have gotten those same looks, but she'd never paid any attention to them. Funny how she noticed them now, even though she had no claim on Travis.

Now that she'd taken a moment to think, she supposed he was a very experienced man. She'd heard enough stories about the "buckle bunnies" on the circuit to know Travis would have had his pick of women at every rodeo he attended.

Oh, damn. Alex was going to get it when she got back to the table. It was just like her to find Grace a nice, "safe" guy so she wouldn't get involved with anyone as unsuitable for her as Johnny had been. Dillon was probably in on it, too. Her whole dang family had been doing stuff like this since Johnny's funeral, as if she were incapable of running her own life.

As if he'd sensed the negative direction of her thoughts, Travis asked, "Is something wrong?"

"No," she said, hoping her smile looked less phoney than it felt. "I was just wondering how well you know Alex."

"About as well as I know you. Why?"

Grace laughed without humor, then pulled away from him, planted both feet firmly on the dance floor and folded her arms across her chest. "Come on, Sullivan. I didn't fall off the hay truck yesterday. How much did Alex pay you to dance with me tonight?"

He frowned. "She didn't pay me a cent."

"Then I'll bet you owed her a favor," Grace suggested.

"Yeah, I owe her a big one, but—"

Grace turned away, paused and looked back over her shoulder at him. "Consider it paid in full. Thanks for the soda and the dancing, Travis. I enjoyed it." She tried to sound as pleasant as possible.

"I did, too." He gave her a lopsided grin that would have melted her anger under other circumstances. "Don't you want to dance some more?" he asked, looking confused.

"I need to have a little talk with Alex."

"It's not what you're thinking, Grace. You're making a mistake."

"I don't think so."

There went that grin again, and darn it, she really wanted to step right back into his arms and dance some more as if nothing at all had happened. But she couldn't do the denial thing anymore. If there were problems, she had to face them—to tackle them head-on—which was exactly the way she intended to tackle Alex right now.

By the time Grace reached the table, Alex was on her feet and looking oh-so-worried, Grace wanted to scream.

"Grace, honey, what's wrong?" Alex demanded. "Did he—"

For once in her life Grace couldn't have cared less about causing a scene. "He didn't do a damn thing you didn't tell him to do. And thanks for having so little faith in me."

"What are you talking about?" Alex asked.

"Don't play dumb with me. What do you *think* I'm talking about? I don't have a fancy college degree like some people, but contrary to popular belief, I'm not a complete idiot."

"I never thought you were."

"Ha! You set me up, and don't you try to deny it."

Alex winced, and she darted a quick look at Emma. "It wasn't like that—"

"Bull."

"Oh, Gracie—"

Grace leaned across the booth, grabbed her purse and tucked it under her arm, then turned back to face Alex. "You're no better than our brothers. I don't want to hear your lame excuses and I don't give a damn about your wonderful intentions. It's enough to know you didn't think poor, pathetic little Gracie could attract a man unless you provided one for her. From now on, butt out of my life."

"Stop." Alex grabbed her arm, but Grace wrenched it away.

"Stop?" Grace laughed and shook her head. "I just got started. You wonder why I'm always so rebellious?

Well, maybe it's because you all *treat* me like I'm a kid. Right now I'd rather have a mangy, flea-bitten dog in my bed than any man alive, but if and when I ever do want another man, I'll find him myself. I don't *need* your help and I don't *want* it, either. Is that clear?''

Eyes huge, Alex nodded. ''You bet.''

''Good.'' Grace whirled around and practically buried her nose in the center of a broad, muscular chest she'd seen up close only a moment ago. Tipping her head back, she stared at Travis.

''Well, hi there,'' she said, feigning such a sweet, perky smile, she could've made a whole room full of beauty pageant contestants weep with envy. ''Sorry I can't stay. I have places to go. People to meet. Things to do.''

Without giving him a chance to reply, she quickly stepped around him, strode out of the bar and kept right on going across the lobby and out the front door into the night. The sky was spitting snowflakes, and the temperature hovered below the freezing mark, making her new outfit woefully inadequate to keep her warm. But there was no way she was going back inside that building.

She'd rather die of exposure than have to face Travis Sullivan again.

Chapter Two

Grace looked around the dark parking lot. On the other side of a frontage road, she spotted a flashing neon sign for another motel chain. She had a credit card in her purse. Maybe she'd spend the night over there. She set off in that direction, her teeth already chattering.

Five minutes later she was still walking across the massive parking lot. Her toes were as cold as ice cubes inside the ridiculous fashion boots Alex had nagged her into buying. What she wouldn't give for one of her old flannel shirts, a pair of jeans and the ancient hiking boots that fit her feet as if they'd been custom made. The parking lot was a vast, frozen desert, the neon sign a mirage, but on she trudged.

Wait a minute. Was that the wind, or were there footsteps echoing her own? She stopped walking and listened, silently debating whether to run like hell or turn and fight. She hadn't quite made up her mind when a familiar male voice cut through the frantic pounding in her ears.

"Grace, hold on a second."

She groaned, then started walking again, faster than before. If not for the icy pavement and the slick soles of her boots, she would have run. Travis was the main reason she'd left her motel in the first place. So why did the big jerk have to go and follow her?

"Grace! Come on, now, honey. You'll freeze out here."

"So? What's it to you?" she said over her shoulder. "And I am *not* your honey."

With his longer stride, he soon caught up to her. She scowled at him, but figured her violent shivering must have dulled the effect. He now wore a black Stetson hat and a bulky, fleece-lined jacket. Before she could protest, he unzipped the jacket, pulled her against him and wrapped the open side around her as far as it would go.

The instant heat felt wonderful. Suddenly all she wanted in this life was to be somewhere warm where the icy wind could no longer whisper up under her short skirt. Travis hustled her along, forcing her to keep up with him.

He pointed toward the flashing sign. "You headed for that?"

She nodded. He smiled. "Good. We're almost there."

They weren't "almost" anywhere, but she was glad for the encouragement. Travis kept up a running line of patter until the other motel suddenly loomed in front of them. He yanked open the front door and rushed inside, practically dragging her because her feet were too numb to obey her brain's commands.

The lobby's Christmas lights became a red-and-green

blur in Grace's peripheral vision while Travis made a beeline for a grouping of sofas that faced a cozy fireplace. They collapsed side by side onto the sofa nearest the crackling flames. Travis peeled off his jacket, then took Grace's hands between his palms and gently rubbed them. The friction made blood flow into her fingers. She winced at the tingling, almost burning sensation in her fingertips.

Travis's eyebrows swooped together in a worried frown. "Are they that bad already?"

She grimaced. "They'll be fine in a minute. My toes are probably worse."

He glanced down at her boots and shook his head. "I'll bet they are. Those things wouldn't keep your feet warm in July."

"They wouldn't have to keep them warm in Ju—"

A startled screech cut off the rest of her sentence when he leaned down, grabbed her ankles and swung her feet up onto his lap. She yanked at the hem of her skirt, trying to preserve at least a hint of modesty while Travis wrestled off her boots. After dropping them onto the floor, he wrapped his hands around her left foot, then her right, then her left again.

It was one of the oddest experiences she'd ever had. Warming her feet didn't seem to bother Travis a bit, but to Grace, it seemed like an awfully intimate gesture for...acquaintances. After all, Travis was Dillon's friend, not hers. She could hardly protest, however, because she knew it needed to be done and he wasn't actually taking advantage of the situation.

The tingling and burning were twice as bad in her toes as he massaged the soles and balls of her feet. Still it felt fantastic—as if layer by layer, he was stripping away her tension with each strong sweep of his thumbs.

"Don't tell me, let me guess," she said, struggling not to dissolve into a pile of bones and utterly relaxed muscles. "You're really an alien with a foot fetish, cleverly disguised as a cowboy."

He tipped back his head and let out a gusty laugh. "Is that any better than a mangy, flea-bitten dog?"

Her neck and cheeks felt hot, and she knew it had nothing to do with the fireplace. "Sorry. If I'd known you were behind me, I wouldn't have said that. I suppose you heard the rest of it?"

"*Every*body heard the rest of it." His eyes glinted with unholy glee. "You were in fine voice and had yourself one heck of a tan—uh, I mean snit."

"No, you meant tantrum," she said with a wry grin. "That's probably what it sounded like."

She hadn't been able to see the color of his eyes before, but in this light they were a soft blend of green and brown, like a pasture sprouting new grass in the spring.

"Sounded to me like you might've had some provocation."

She gave a little shrug and grimaced. "You could say that."

"Well, I've got an idea. Let's go in the coffee shop and thaw out. When you're ready to go back, we'll call a taxi. How does that sound?"

"Sure you're not an alien cleverly disguised as a cowboy?"

He flashed his killer grin as she'd hoped he would, slid her boots back on and helped her to her feet. The coffee shop was small and quiet, the coffee strong and delicious. Conversation suddenly flowed as easily as the brew filling their cups.

Avoiding more personal topics such as families and

former spouses, they talked about everything and nothing. Movies, the weather, stupid Montana jokes, politics and religion gave Grace tantalizing glimpses into his personality. She saw a man with a gift for gab, a delightfully warped sense of humor and strong opinions. But he didn't try to force his opinions on her, and she found that a refreshing change from her relatives.

It was after one when she slid into the back seat of a cab and motioned for Travis to hurry up and join her. She sat close to him for warmth, realizing that somewhere between their frigid walk, his magical foot rub and the coffee, she and Travis had crossed the barrier that separated mere acquaintances from friends.

She smiled at the idea. She hadn't had a real friend outside of her family in years. She doubted anything would come of it, but it sounded nice in theory. By the time they arrived back at her motel, she felt pleasantly tired and delightfully relaxed. Holding her hand, Travis escorted her across the lobby. The sweet, melancholy notes of a country waltz came from the bar.

Turning to face her, he said, ''I don't want to let you go just yet.'' He inclined his head toward the bar's doorway. ''That's probably the last set. Want to finish it?''

''All right.''

She accompanied him onto the dance floor again. Stepping into his arms felt completely natural this time. Her body moved easily with his. She looked into his eyes and immediately felt eighteen again, as if she had a future with unlimited possibilities ahead of her.

He raised his eyebrows at her. ''What are you thinking?''

Smiling, she shook her head. ''Nothing important.''

It *was* important, but she couldn't explain it to him

when she didn't fully understand why she suddenly felt so optimistic. Or if any of these new feelings had anything to do with him.

Of course that was about the silliest idea she'd ever had. Travis had given her an evening of fun and helped her to realize the depth of the rut she'd been living in since Johnny's death. She appreciated that, but eight hours ago he'd only been a long-forgotten memory. After tonight she'd probably never see him again, and it was just as well.

Sighing softly, she rested the side of her head against his shoulder and closed her eyes. He tightened his arm around her, pulling her snugly against him. His heart thumped out a strong, rhythm beneath her right ear. Her breasts came into contact with his chest and her hips brushed against his with every step. His big, warm palm slowly stroked her hair and back.

She drifted along in his embrace, enjoying the sweet sensations of arousal she had thought were gone forever. Neither of them spoke again until the band stopped playing. Ignoring the other die-hard dancers, Travis raised the hand he'd been holding against his chest and kissed the backs of her knuckles.

A shiver of delight shimmied the length of her spine. She swallowed a heartfelt sigh and moved back a step. He smiled, laced the fingers of his left hand through the fingers of her right and walked her back to the lobby. Stopping beside the elevator doors, he gazed down at her, a half smile on his lips and a decidedly lusty glint in his eyes. Feeling incredibly awkward, she started to thank him, but he cut her off with a quick shake of his head.

"I'll see you to your room," he said.

"Oh, but—"

The elevator doors opened and he nudged her inside. "Relax. Mom taught me a gentleman always escorts a lady to her door."

Grace smiled. "I've been trying to teach my boys better manners, but they don't seem to be learning very fast."

"They'll get there," he assured her. "It just takes time and lots of repetition."

The elevator stopped, and the doors slid open with a loud ding. Holding hands again, they ambled down the hallway that led to the room she was sharing with Emma. Outside her door, Travis pulled her to him. Cupping one palm along the side of her jaw, he tipped back her head.

He was going to kiss her. She could see it in his eyes. It had been forever since her heart had thumped at her rib cage with this delicious sense of anticipation. But a kiss might not be enough, and she couldn't let this go any further.

Until she heard the results of her tests from Dr. Casale, she probably shouldn't be doing anything like this. The humiliation of it brought a vile taste to her mouth. Travis lowered his head. She turned her face to the side, wanting to curse and weep at the same time when his lips brushed over her cheek instead of her own lips.

He pulled back, giving her a rueful grin. "Don't like me enough to kiss me, huh?"

Unable to look at him, she studied his shirt and shook her head. "I like you fine. I'm just not ready for this yet."

Lifting her chin with one finger, he forced her to meet his gaze. "It's only a kiss."

"Maybe it is to you, but to me... Well, it's more than that."

"That husband of yours must've been quite a guy."

"Yeah. He was quite a guy." Her laugh held a bitter note she hoped Travis couldn't hear. She turned away, found her key and stuck it into the lock. He caught her arm and turned her back to face him.

"Dammit, Grace, we had so much fun together, I can't leave you like this."

His obvious irritation torched hers. "What did you expect? A romp in my bed? Sorry, you'll have to find someone else. I don't do that."

"I never thought you did." He studied her for at least an eon, then lowered his hands and stepped away from her.

"I'm sorry, Travis," she said quickly. "You didn't deserve that. My life's complicated right now, and I'm pretty confused."

He nodded solemnly. "I understand. I shouldn't have come on so strong, but... Well, don't worry about it. I'll see you around." Then he gave her a two-fingered salute and sauntered off toward the elevator.

More than a little bemused, Grace watched him until he was out of sight before stepping into her room. The connecting door to the next room banged open and light flooded in. Alex, Lori and Emma followed.

"Do you have any idea what time it is?" Alex demanded.

"If you want to live to see daylight, get away from me, Alex," Grace said.

"Oh, for heaven's sake, cut it out," Alex said.

"Down, girls. Both of you behave yourselves," Emma said with a laugh. She came across the room, took Grace's hand and dragged her over to sit on one of the double beds. Lori and Alex sat on the other bed and pulled their feet up under themselves.

"Okay," Emma continued, "inquiring minds want to know. Where did you go? What did you do? Is he a good kisser?"

Grace smiled and said nothing.

"Aw, c'mon. What good is having a single sister-in-law if you can't live vicariously through her adventures?"

"Not my problem, Emma. You and Cal will just have to cook up your own adventures."

Lori grinned. "Did you have a nice time?"

"Yes, I did," Grace admitted. "He's a lot of fun. He said he'd see me around, but I doubt it'll happen."

The other three exchanged startled glances, then burst out laughing.

"All right, what's so funny?" Grace demanded.

They just laughed harder. Grace snorted in disgust. It was late, she was tired and she wasn't going to take any more of their teasing. Grabbing her tote bag, she carried it into the bathroom. She'd had her fling in Billings. Now she was ready to go home to Sunshine Gap and be Riley and Steven's mom again.

"Travis, must you ruin everything?" Louise Sullivan said. "I work so hard to make Christmas perfect for all of you and suddenly you have to leave? I thought the rodeo part of your life was over now and we could finally have our whole family together for the holidays."

Travis looked up from his plate and forced himself to smile. "I'm only going to Sunshine Gap, Mom," he said calmly. "And I'll be sure to be here for Christmas."

"I'm glad you'll be able to do that, son, but I said the holidays. That includes Christmas Eve and it lasts through New Year's Day. How do you expect to have quality time with your family if you're never available to spend any quantity of time at home? You can't plan special moments. You have to be there when they happen."

"Yes, ma'am, I can see your point," Travis said. "But I gave Dillon and Jake my word that I'd fill in for Dillon, and I can't go back on it now."

"It doesn't have to be you. The McBrides can afford to hire five men to replace him."

Travis laid his fork along the edge of the plate. "I'm sure they can, but they asked me to do the job, and I said yes. There's nothing I can do about it now."

"Couldn't you at least wait until Dillon actually leaves?"

"He doesn't know exactly when he's going to leave. It could be next week or the week after that or even the week after that."

"Well, your sitting over there twiddling your thumbs while he figures out his schedule doesn't make any sense."

"I won't be twiddling anything," Travis said. "He wants to show me where everything is in case I end up having to do the work by myself, and it's been so long since I did some of that stuff, I'd like to see how he handles certain things. Take a little refresher course from him."

"Oh, that's right, I forgot you were never as good as Luke when it came to doing chores."

Travis inhaled a deep breath and promised himself he wouldn't let her drag him into an argument. Still, a trace of resentment slipped out in his voice. "No, I sure wasn't, Mom."

Travis's dad banged the side of his fist on the table. "Don't take that tone with your mother."

Louise rolled her eyes at her husband. "Nice one, Mike. You're good at showing our son your love and affection so he really wants to stay home."

Mike ignored her. "I'd like to know why you'd even want to work somebody else's place when we sure could use your help right here."

"You don't need me here, Dad," Travis said. "And while I'm over at the Flying M, I'll figure out what I want to do next."

Mike banged his fist again. "What's to figure out? You'll stay here and help your brother and me run this place. It's not like you've got any other job skills to turn to. I can't believe you had all those scholarships and you didn't even finish college."

Travis had heard this lecture so many times, he could deliver it himself. "Well, you never know. One of these days I might surprise the heck out of you and make something of myself."

"Yeah, right," Mike said. "And I've got a magic bean stalk out back."

"Please, Dad, stop it. I appreciate everything you and Mom have done for me since my last surgery, but we all know there isn't enough profit on this place to support another full-time salary. There's no point in trying to make me feel guilty about leaving. I'll find something I want to do pretty soon."

"Define *pretty soon,*" his dad groused. "You've been traipsin' around this country like a saddle tramp since you dropped out of college. It's time you settled down and stuck with something. Get married. Have some kids."

"I know he doesn't always say things in the best

way,'' Louise said, ''but your father has a point. You're not getting any younger. You should find yourself a nice young woman and start a family.''

Pushing his plate away, Travis looked from one sour, disillusioned face to the other. Oh, yeah, his folks were a living, breathing advertisement for the institution of marriage, all right. He'd sooner stick his head in a grizzly's mouth than wind up as disgruntled with life as either one of them.

''Oh, don't do that,'' his mother said. ''I spent all afternoon in the kitchen and you've hardly eaten a bite.''

''Sorry, Mom. I'm not very hungry.'' He stood, scraping the legs of his chair over the dingy tile floor. ''I've gotten everything pretty well packed up. I think I'll just head on over to the Flying M tonight.''

His dad flicked one hand, waving Travis off and writing him off as he'd done so many times before. ''Well, go on then. You're gonna leave no matter what anybody says.''

Travis went. It only took two trips to load his gear into his pickup. Knowing it was no use to go back in and say goodbye, he climbed in and drove out of his parents' driveway as fast as safety allowed. He didn't know why it always had to be this way, why they couldn't understand that there was nothing for him at the Bar S. Why they'd never really expected him to be successful at anything.

Furthermore, he was proud of what he'd accomplished with his life so far. He hadn't earned a bachelor's degree, but he'd finished three full years of college. He'd also won a Professional Rodeo Cowboys' Association World Championship in steer wrestling, or bulldogging as the old-timers called it. Most people he knew considered that plenty successful.

Unlike a lot of his pals, he'd saved most of his winnings over the years. By adding in his substantial earnings from product endorsements, he'd built himself a fat stock portfolio. He wouldn't have to work another day in his life if he was real careful. He couldn't see himself doing that, but it was an option his dad and brother sure didn't have.

Maybe he should take that job he'd been offered as a TV commentator. Knowing his folks would only scoff at the idea, he hadn't mentioned it to them. They didn't know about any of his assets, either. As long as he wasn't asking them to support him, his finances were none of their business.

He could afford to spend as much time as he wanted to decide what he wanted to do next, but he'd never get anywhere if he stayed at home. *Risk* was a four-letter word at the Bar S. Travis couldn't live without it. He'd be damned if he'd settle into a life of routine and boredom, which was exactly what he'd get if he stayed at home. The thought of it made him shudder.

Once he drove through Powell and turned south toward Cody, his spirits rose. He'd follow the original plan and stay in Cody tonight, then drive on to Sunshine Gap in the morning. Dillon had promised him a furnished, private guest house. Whenever he'd visited the Flying M, he'd had a great time with the McBrides. He was looking forward to spending some time with them now. Especially with Grace.

He'd thought about her all weekend. Well, *fantasized* about her was a more accurate description. He wanted the kiss she'd denied him. He wanted to hold her close again, to trace her luscious curves with his hands. Hell, he just plain wanted her.

Not that he really expected to have her in his bed. She wasn't the kind of woman who could enjoy having sex without a serious commitment. He wasn't ready to make one, and the last thing he wanted to do was hurt her.

But he could enjoy her company without getting into a hot and heavy relationship with her. Of course, he could. Without the challenge of her wariness, he probably wouldn't have been all that attracted to her in the first place.

When the storm door on the mudroom finally banged shut behind Dillon and Jake on Monday morning, Grace rolled her eyes and muttered, ''Alone at last.'' God willing, she would be blessedly alone for the next couple of hours while the men fed the stock and made sure the animals had an unfrozen supply of water to drink. She poured herself a mug of coffee and sat at the kitchen table to drink it in peace for a change.

The men were all in an uproar because she hadn't yet forgiven them for withholding the truth about Johnny's death. Well, tough. They'd let her make a fool of herself in front of the whole community of Sunshine Gap for five years; they could damn well wait as long as it took for her to get over her hurt feelings and wounded pride.

The back door opened with a blast of frigid air and a miniature flurry of snowflakes. Dillon stuck his head into the kitchen.

''Sis, I forgot to tell you our new hand is comin' in today.''

''What new hand?'' Grace asked.

"The one who's gonna take my place around here when I go to California. We talked about it at dinner last week. Don't you remember?"

"I was probably in the kitchen while you were talking. What time's he supposed to get here?"

"Before noon. He'll be stayin' in the guest house."

She glared at him. "Nice of you to warn me. Nobody's been out there since last summer, and it'll need a good cleaning before it's fit to live in. I think you should do it, Dillon."

"I've got hungry cows to feed." He gave her a coaxing smile. "Sorry. It just slipped my mind."

It took a lot of restraint to hold back a snide remark about the sorry state of his mind, but she managed it. Barely. "All right," she said. "I'll take care of it."

"Thanks, Gracie."

"Dammit, Dillon, don't call me—"

The back door banged shut before she could finish her sentence. The big coward. He hadn't even told her their new hand's name. Heaving a disgruntled sigh, she collected fresh bedding and towels for the guest house, packed some cleaning supplies and put on a heavy sweatshirt over her flannel one. They only heated the guest house enough to keep the pipes from freezing in the winter. It would take a while for the furnace to warm it up.

Without the usual layers of family clutter to contend with, Grace finished her cleaning in a little over an hour. She stood in the small living room for a moment, enjoying the satisfaction of a job well done. Her Grandpa McBride had built this house for her grandma back in the thirties. While it could use some serious updating, it was still solid and cozy, and it held a wealth of fond memories.

Well, she had other things to do today besides dwell on the past. Packing up her cleaning supplies, she hauled them out to her pickup and drove back to the main house. She put everything away, then stripped off her sweatshirt and draped it over the bannister so she'd take it upstairs the next time she went to her room.

She heard a door slam outside. She glanced at her watch, but it wasn't time for Dillon and Jake to be home yet. An instant later there was a knock at the front door. It must be the new hand, she thought, hurrying to answer it.

Smoothing her hair, she walked through the living room and unlatched the storm door. The man standing on the back steps was big, like her brothers. He'd been turned halfway around, probably getting the lay of the ranch into his head. When she opened the door, he turned back to face her and she felt as if she'd been sucker punched.

Giving her one of his delightfully wicked grins, Travis Sullivan pulled the door open wider and stepped inside, crowding her until she stepped backward, no doubt with her mouth still hanging open in shock. "Hiya, Grace. Got any coffee?"

"What…" She paused and cleared her throat. Lord, he was every bit as handsome and appealing as she'd remembered. "What are you doing here?"

He frowned. "You don't know?"

"Would I ask if I did?"

"Guess not," he said with a laugh. "I'm going to fill in for Dillon while he's gone."

"*You're* the new hand?"

"Yeah." His eyes narrowed and his grin faltered. "You got a problem with that?"

She didn't have *a* problem with that. She had a hundred problems with it. He was too sexy, too charming, too attractive to have around. He confused her. Her own reactions to him confused her. What in the world had her brother been thinking?

She sighed inwardly. Obviously, Dillon had been thinking about his friendship with Travis and Travis's experience with ranch work, not the possibility that his little sister might have a...well, for lack of a better word, a *crush* on his old buddy. Or maybe that had been the point all along, and this was just the second phase of the setup Alex had started in Billings.

Oh, that *had* to be it. She didn't believe in coincidences, and what were the odds of seeing him in Billings on Saturday and then finding him on the doorstep the very next Monday? And the whole damn family was probably in on the plan.

Well, she wasn't going to fall for it, and she wasn't going to let anyone know she was disturbed by the prospect of having Travis around. Better just to grit her teeth, put up with him for however long he stayed and keep out of his way.

Unfortunately, that wasn't going to be easy. She couldn't remember having many hired hands at the Flying M, but the extra men had always eaten their meals with the family.

"Grace? I asked if you had a problem with that?" he said.

She gave her head a hard shake and carefully avoided meeting his gaze. "No, of course not. I was...surprised, that's all."

He stepped closer again and tucked a finger under her chin, lifting it until she met his eyes again. "Was it a nice surprise?"

In spite of her misgivings, she couldn't stop herself

from smiling at him. He smelled just as good as he had on Saturday night, the spot he'd touched on the underside of her chin tingled and a pleasant, fluttery sense of anticipation filled her insides. Still, she refused to give him any false encouragement. With a noncommittal shrug, she said, "I suppose. We can always use an extra hand around here."

Chapter Three

"Are you sure, Doctor Casale?" Grace asked later that morning, clutching the phone so hard her knuckles ached. Dillon and Jake were both upstairs changing into dry clothes, and she was glad they weren't standing around drinking coffee and listening to every word she said for a change. "You don't need to do any follow-up tests or anything?"

"You're fine, Grace, and your boys are fine," the doctor replied. "Stop worrying and get on with your life."

Oh, man, the real reason for her trip to Billings had paid off in privacy about her medical problems and peace of mind. Blinking back tears, Grace nodded, then realized the other woman couldn't see her over the telephone and said, "I will. It's just such a huge relief."

"Of course it is. You were smart to have these tests done."

"I don't know how to thank you."

"No need. I'm as delighted with the results as you are. Take care of yourself, and drop in the next time you're here."

Grace hung up the phone and exhaled a deep breath. Arms wrapped tightly around herself, she rocked back and forth, closed her eyes and said a quick prayer of gratitude. She was healthy. Oh, thank God, she was healthy and so were the boys. Until this moment, she hadn't realized just how frightened she'd been that her test results would show that Johnny had given her some sexually transmitted disease and she had unwittingly passed it on to Riley and Steven. She could hardly bear to think about it. If Johnny hadn't already been dead, she cheerfully would have killed him for putting her through this.

"Gracie?" her brother Dillon said from the doorway that led into the back hallway. "You all right?"

She looked across the room, saw the new, deeper lines around his eyes and mouth, the worry in his eyes, and her anger at him wavered. But then she remembered his part in this fiasco. By keeping the truth about Johnny from her, Dillon had endangered her and her boys.

"Yeah, I'm all right," she said. "No thanks to you."

He grimaced as if her words caused him physical pain. "What do you mean?"

"I just heard from my doctor in Billings."

"Doctor? What'd you have to see a doctor up there for?"

"To find out if my dearly departed husband gave me any diseases before he died. You never thought about that when you decided to keep your secret, did you?"

Dillon's mouth dropped open and he gaped at her for a full thirty seconds before he muttered a curse and plowed furrows in his hair with his left hand. "No, I didn't."

"Considering the number of women he was fooling around with, you should have." She banged the side of her fist on the counter top. "Did you think I never had sex with my husband? Or that I was immune because I've always been a 'nice girl?'"

"I'm sorry," he said.

"Sorry doesn't cut it." She snorted in disgust. "It doesn't even come close."

"I was only trying to do what I thought was best for you. We all did."

"Well, now you know that you don't always know what's best for me. And neither do the other guys."

"Jeez Louise, Gracie," Dillon grumbled, hunching his shoulders as if he expected her to hit him.

The idea was tempting, but she was afraid that if she started releasing her anger that way, she might not be able to stop. "Face reality. If I *had* contracted an STD and passed it on to the boys, I wouldn't have known we needed medical treatment for five years."

He looked down for a moment, as if he couldn't stand to meet her gaze any longer. Then he shoved his hands into his front pockets and looked at her again. "Are you ever gonna forgive me?" His voice sounded raw and full of regret.

"Probably, but I'm not ready just yet." She sighed, then shook her head. "There's one thing that might help."

"What's that?"

"Call me Grace. For God's sake, I have two half-grown sons. Don't you think I've earned the right to a grown-up name?"

"Yeah, I guess," he said, though his tone indicated

he had his doubts. "It's gonna take a while to break the habit, though."

Grace allowed herself a slight smile. "I know. I'll probably have to whack you upside the head at least fifty times before it'll start to sink in."

"Yeah, and you'll love every whack." He paused for a moment, then asked. "What about the other guys? Are you ready to forgive them yet?"

She almost laughed. Poor Dillon. The "other guys" in the family undoubtedly had been blaming him for breaking the sacred male code of silence and getting them into hot water with her.

"They knew more about Johnny than you did, but they didn't have the decency to tell me, either. Why should I forgive them?"

"Because you need to for your own sake. If you don't watch yourself, this thing'll eat you alive."

"I'll risk it. But you can always pass along the word about calling me Grace."

"All right. I'll do that." He glanced at his watch. "I'd better get on down to the guest house and see how Travis is doing. He'll want a tour first thing."

She turned away for fear of giving away her suspicions about why Travis was at the Flying M. When she heard the back door bang shut behind him, however, she thought about what Dillon had said. She didn't like being angry at her brothers. She didn't want her anger to eat her alive, either. Sometimes she wasn't even sure if she was angry because none of them had told her about Johnny five years ago, or because Dillon finally had, forcing her to face the truth about her "perfect" marriage.

No matter how hard she tried, she couldn't stop agonizing over it. What had she done wrong to make

Johnny unhappy enough to stray? Or was it simply that she hadn't been woman enough for him? And, if she hadn't, would she ever be woman enough for any other man? Why hadn't she known he was cheating on her? How could she have been so blasted blind? And worst of all, why couldn't she find any answers to all of these dang questions?

Travis bounced along beside Dillon in the pickup, wondering if this old rig had ever had a new set of shocks. Nah. They wouldn't last long on these dirt roads anyway. He could handle the jolts and bumps. Dillon's brooding was a different breed of horse.

"Is this what happens to a guy when he's been off the circuit for as long as you?" Travis asked.

Dillon shot him a scowl. "I'm givin' you a tour of the ranch. It doesn't come with an entertainment package."

"I'd settle for a little conversation. Correct me if I'm wrong, but I thought you were gonna tell me what you wanted me to do, not drive me around and show me every pothole on this ranch."

"I will," Dillon grumbled. "Soon as we get someplace you need to know about."

"Are you always this agreeable, or did you swallow a grumpy pill at breakfast?"

Dillon let out a strangled laugh. "Sorry, Travis. I just let my little sister get under my hide."

"Grace?" Travis asked.

"Yeah. Grace. I'm tellin' you, that woman is so stubborn, she could drive any sane man to drink."

"No way," Travis protested, thinking Dillon himself was no slouch in the stubborn department. "I danced with her up in Billings last Saturday. Spent the whole evening with her. Seemed like a real special gal to me.''

Dillon snorted. ''Well, don't be too impressed. You just saw her good side.''

''Not really.'' Travis grinned at the memory of Grace telling Alex a thing or ten. ''She pinned Alex's ears back but good, right there in the bar. It was great.''

''Yeah, I'll bet,'' Dillon said, ''especially if you like a woman with a hot temper and a sharp tongue.''

''Beats a mealymouthed gal who'll never speak up and tell you what she wants. Then some fine day when you think things are going along just fine, she blows up and dumps every sin you've committed in the past year on your head all at once or shoves a knife in your gut. That's what the shrinks call being passive-aggressive, and believe me, pard, I'll take an up-front, in-your-face woman like Grace any day.''

''If you've got half a brain, don't even think about getting interested in her. Take my word for it, she's not in good shape to handle any kind of a romance.''

''I don't suppose you'll tell me why.''

Dillon shook his head. ''It's not my place to say.''

Travis thought about that for a quarter of a mile, then shook his own head. ''I'm sorry if she's had a bad time of it lately, but I won't lie to you. I'm already interested in her.''

''Oh, yeah? Just how interested?''

''Relax, will ya? I'm real interested, but I know better than to play fast and loose with a buddy's sister. Especially when he's as big, mean and ugly as you are, McBride.''

Dillon tipped back his head and roared with laughter. Travis joined in, glad to see that his friend hadn't lost his sense of humor. Dillon had always been one of the best-looking cowboys on the rodeo circuit, and it made Travis sad to see the damage done to the left side of his face. All the more reason to acknowledge his loss without the taint of pity fouling the air.

"Thanks." Still chuckling, Dillon swiped at the corners of his eyes. "I'd forgotten just how blunt you are sometimes. You'll never know how much I've missed that."

"Hear anything about when you'll be leaving for California?"

"Not yet," Dillon said. "Should be any day, though. God only knows what they're doing to that film now."

"I can hardly picture you all settled down and married."

"I'm not, yet. Tell you the truth, I can still hardly believe Blair would want an old, broken down ex-bronc rider for a husband. But every night I pray she won't change her mind when she sees me again."

"Yeah, you're older than dirt. It's a wonder you can get around without a cane."

"Stuff it, Sullivan. You know what I mean. She's so…"

"Beautiful? Gorgeous?" Travis said, calling up a mental image of the woman Dillon wanted to marry. Blair DuMaine was an actress from an illustrious acting family, the kind of woman a lot of men lusted after in their dreams, but never really hoped or expected to meet in person.

"She's all of that, but I love her heart the best."

"Whoa, you really are in love," Travis said.

Dillon shot him a wry smile. "Yeah. It's not really all that bad, either. Someday you ought to give it a shot."

The idea of seriously losing his heart to another

woman gave Travis gooseflesh. And yet, if that woman should turn out to be Grace... Nah. He was attracted to her and all, but he trusted Dillon's judgement about his own sister.

Besides, she hadn't acted all that thrilled to see him again. That pinch he felt in the region of his solar plexus was just a little dent in his ego. From now on, he'd better work hard at pretending Grace was his sister, too.

He spent the rest of the day with Dillon, checking out every part of the Flying M. He gave the McBrides full credit for running a first-class operation. If he ever had a ranch of his own, he'd want it to be just like this one. But did he really want to be a rancher? Even if he was the owner, free to run things however he wanted?

This temporary job with the McBrides would be fun, but did he want to do this for the rest of his life? Not hardly. Staying in one place and contending with the endless routine of ranch chores would bore him silly in a few months.

After so many years on the rodeo circuit, he needed more action and excitement, more people, more stimulation than he'd ever find on a ranch. He'd mourned his rodeo career enough. It was time to figure out what came next. By the time he left the Flying M, he hoped he would.

The early winter darkness ended Dillon's tour around five o'clock. When they pulled back into the ranch yard half an hour later, the parking area beside the main house looked like a four-wheel-drive dealership. Cursing under his breath, Dillon smacked the side of his fist on the steering wheel. "I can't believe I forgot."

"Forgot what?" Travis asked.

"It's Riley's birthday." Dillon flicked a finger toward the herd of pickups and sport utility vehicles.

"The whole family's here for supper and I left the kid's present back at my place. I'll have to go get it. Why don't you go on in and have a beer with the guys?"

"Hey, if this a family deal, I'll just grab a bite in town and turn in early."

"No way. You'll be part of the family inside of a week, and you know most of 'em anyway. Go on in and get acquainted with the rest."

Travis stepped out of the pickup and headed for the house. Other than its generous size stretching three full stories, there wasn't anything particularly ostentatious about it, but in the way of the best old ranch houses, it looked incredibly warm and welcoming. He'd used the front door this morning, but the freshly shoveled path made it obvious that the back door served as the primary entrance.

After kicking the snow off his boots, he entered the mudroom, wiped his feet on a thick mat and appropriated a free hook for his coat and hat. The muted sounds of voices and laughter came through the closed kitchen door. He slicked back his hair with his hands, wiped them on the seat of his jeans, then gave the door a perfunctory knock and let himself into the kitchen.

His mouth instantly watered from the tantalizing aromas of beef roasting in the oven and freshly baked dinner rolls cooling on a rack beside the stove. The women gathered around the work peninsula suddenly fell silent and turned toward him as a unit. Ah, the Billings gang. Three out of the four smiled at him. Grace's expression wasn't exactly a frown, but it sure wasn't a smile, either. Not even a polite one.

It was more deadpan than anything else, the kind of expression he might use when he didn't want anyone to have a clue about his feelings. And wasn't that an interesting idea? *Was* she feeling some emotion toward him she didn't want him to see? He doubted that she actively disliked him. She didn't know him well enough for that yet. So maybe she liked him a lot. And maybe his ego was coloring his vision.

Whether or not it was, he knew right then and there that he would never be able to look at Grace as a sister. His immediate reaction to her was purely visceral. Without even getting close enough to smell her perfume, he wanted her like hell on fire. He didn't know why. He just did.

She'd exchanged her flannel shirt for a red sweater that, while it didn't cling, sure let a man know that this woman had curves. Her hair was down around her shoulders, and she wore dangling silver feathers in her ears that made him want to nibble on her lobes and her neck and... Well enough of that, or he'd get himself into more trouble than he wanted.

Ambling across the room, he gave them his best aw-shucks-ma'am grin, the one that had melted more than one woman's heart. "Hi, ladies. Sure smells good in here."

"That's nothing," Alex said. "Wait'll you taste Gracie's cooking and you'll think you went straight to heaven."

"Shut up, Alex," Grace said in a pleasant tone so at odds with her words, Travis wanted to laugh. "Would you like a beer, Travis?"

"Sure would. Just point me—"

Before he could finish his sentence, she turned away, took a brown bottle out of the refrigerator, pulled a frosted mug out of the freezer compartment and set them on the counter. Then she twisted the cap off the bottle and poured the contents into the mug with the quick, efficient movements of a bartender and slid the mug toward him. He caught it before it was in any danger of landing on the floor and took a drink, smiling his appreciation.

Lori chuckled at him. "Nectar of the gods, right?"

"Close," he admitted.

Grace lifted a lid off a pot sitting on a back burner and said, "Dinner will be ready in fifteen minutes. The other guys are in the living room, if you want to join them."

He'd much rather stay right where he was and see if he couldn't provoke a more personal reaction from her, but decided against it. He nodded as if he'd planned to leave the hen party anyway. When he stepped into the back hallway that led to the living room, he heard one of the women say, "I told you before and I'll say it again, that man is *prime,* Grace. Grab him."

Travis paused to hear Grace's reply, but the dang woman spoke so softly, he couldn't make out her words. The men gave him a hearty welcome. A bunch of kids came in later, followed by Dillon, his neck, ears and the tip of his nose red from the cold.

A black-haired boy about five-foot-six turned to face Dillon and walked backward to keep from getting run over. "Come on, Uncle Dillon, give me a hint. Just one."

Dillon shook his head and gave the kid a smug grin. "No way, Riley. You'll just have to wait until we're done with the cake and ice cream."

So this was one of Grace's boys, Travis thought, enjoying Riley's flair for the dramatic. Riley clutched both hands to his chest. "But I'll die of curiosity by then,"

"Doubt it, kid," Jake called to him. "Happy Birthday."

"Thanks, Uncle Jake."

Dillon spotted Travis and herded the kids over to meet him. In addition to Riley and his younger brother, Steven, he met Alex's daughter Tasha and her stepson, Rick, and Zack's stepson, Brandon. Tasha and Rick were teenagers, and they slid out of the group after a quick hello. Riley, Steven and Brandon wanted to know all about his rodeo career and asked if they could see Travis's championship belt buckle and if he would give them all an autograph.

The attention—well, hero worship was more like it—flattered him, but he would have liked these boys without it. Bright, good-humored and radiating restless energy, they reminded him of a trio of overgrown pups. He didn't blame Grace a bit for being so proud of her two.

Alex called them all to the dining room, and a moment later, Travis found himself wedged between Dillon and Cal at a long, beautifully set table, complete with china, crystal, white linen napkins to match the tablecloth and more silverware than he'd ever seen outside of a five-star restaurant. Nobody else seemed surprised by such finery, and Travis wondered if the McBrides ate this way every day.

Jake said a brief blessing, and then bowls and platters of food passed from one person to the next. While her family appeared to take it all for granted, Travis noticed lots of little touches that made the dinner more special. From fresh lemon slices in the water glasses to the horse radish sauce that went with the meat, to the clever centerpiece made of pine cones, holly berries and a shiny new pair of spurs, everything showed a loving attention to detail. Laughter, teasing and lively stories kept the atmosphere festive.

When Grace carried in the cake everybody cheered. Cal told him it was a dirt cake, which was about what it looked like. Black crumbs of some kind covered the top, and there were plastic bugs and fat candy worms coming up out of the "dirt." There were even twigs of sagebrush and a couple of tiny pine trees on the thing. The boys argued over who was gonna get what while Grace ladled hefty servings into bowls.

Travis picked off all the plants and plastic bugs, then warily spooned up his first bite. After several more bites, he figured out it was a layer of crumbled up chocolate cake on the bottom, a layer of chocolate pudding in the middle and a layer of crushed chocolate wafers on top. The best part of it all was seeing how much the boys loved eating something designed just for them.

At last it was time for Riley to open his presents, and the kid was practically vibrating with anticipation. As Riley opened one carefully selected gift after another, it became clear that the family had intended this birthday celebration to be his rite of passage into manhood.

A new pair of boots, a Stetson hat, good leather work gloves, a rope and a slicker appeared one at a time, all tools for a working ranch hand. When he'd finished with those, Dillon blindfolded Riley, everybody grabbed a coat and they all tromped out to the barn. Dillon led Riley to a stall near the front of the barn, then took off the blindfold.

The boy opened his eyes and when he found himself face-to-face with a two-year-old black gelding, his expression of shocked joy was priceless. When Dillon brought a brand-new saddle out of the tack room and told him it went with his new horse, tears welled up in Riley's eyes.

"Wow!" He swiped at his cheeks with the back of one hand. "This is so cool, I don't know what to say."

"You don't have to say anything," Zack said. "You're gettin' to be a man now, and you're starting to do a man's work."

"That's right," Jake said. "And if you're going to do a man's work, you need to have a man's tools."

Riley gulped, then swiped at his eyes again and squared his shoulders, giving everyone present a glimpse of the man he would one day become. "Thanks, everyone. I'll remember this birthday as the best one ever."

The family converged on the kid, ruffling his hair, slapping his back, hugging him, razzing him. Travis's chest suddenly felt tight, and his throat clogged up on him. Jeez, if he'd had half as much support when he'd been growing up, he'd probably be a brain surgeon or an astronaut or maybe a U.S. Senator by now. He wasn't going to feel sorry for himself, but he'd had just about all the family togetherness he could stand for one night.

He took one last look at Riley. His mother and little brother stood on each side of him now, their arms slung over his shoulders. The tenderness and approval in Grace's smile as she listened to her son gave Travis's heartstrings a painful yank. He slipped out of the barn and took off for the guest house.

Once inside, he restlessly wandered the small rooms like a cougar locked up in a cage. The guest house was a nice, homey cage, though. The walls were liberally decorated with framed artwork and shelves of knick-knacks. There were handmade pillows on the sofa and a soft, colorful afghan draped over the back. He thought he recognized the same hand at work here as he'd seen in the main house. Grace's hand.

The woman fascinated him. If he was looking to settle down, she'd come mighty close to his image of an ideal wife. And, if he could have a family like hers, he might not even mind settling down all that much.

"Yeah, right," he muttered, wishing the sound of his voice would snap him out of this weird mood. Dammit, he *wasn't* looking to settle down, and he *wasn't* going to start thinking of Grace as a wife, ideal or not. He really wasn't that drawn to *her*. He was just falling in love with her cooking. "Yeah, right."

Chapter Four

A week later Grace moved around the kitchen, cooking breakfast for the men and chuckling to herself at the memory of a joke her son Steven had told her before he'd left for school. During the winter months, the men usually waited to start the chores until the sun was up and the temperature had had a chance to climb a few degrees. Not that it would climb much today with the wind blowing in a new storm straight out of Canada, if the weatherman at the radio station turned out to be right.

Dillon hauled his winter gear in from the mudroom to warm it while he ate. Grace frowned, hating to think of anyone having to go out in the cold. She poured Dillon a cup of coffee and went back to work, turning the bacon, cracking a dozen eggs for scrambling, pouring the sourdough batter onto the griddle for the first batch of pancakes.

Humming softly, Grace started browning meat for the stew she planned to serve for supper. The storm door on the back porch banged open, then shut. That would be Travis.

He brought in a blast of cold air with him, along with his gear and his usual smile. Compared to most Mc-Brides, Travis was uncommonly cheerful early in the morning; he was even capable of carrying on a conversation before he had coffee. Other than that and what little he'd told her about himself that night in Billings, she didn't know much about him.

When he'd first come to the Flying M, she had feared that he might hang around all the time and make a pest of himself. But ever since Riley's birthday party, Travis had distanced himself from everyone, coming into the main house only for his meals and coffee breaks.

He was polite while he was eating, but the minute he finished, he left. So maybe he wasn't as interested in her as she'd thought. Well, go figure. She wasn't interested in him, either, not really. And her ego wasn't smarting. No, not a bit.

She filled a mug for him. He thanked her, wrapped both hands around it and sniffed the fragrant steam. Taking a sip, he shut his eyes, held the liquid in his mouth for a moment before swallowing. Eyes still closed, he murmured, "Man, that's good coffee," in a tone that suggested he might be in the throes of a religious experience.

He did the same thing every morning, but Grace still found his coffee ritual fascinating. There was something really sensual about a man closing his eyes and focusing all his attention on his taste buds. Especially when he was standing so close she could see his eyelashes.

Then he opened his eyes and gave her one of his patented sexy grins. "'Morning, Grace," he said.

"'Morning, Travis," she replied. She might have asked him how bad the wind was, but he abruptly turned away and carried his coffee to the table.

Jake walked into the kitchen next, hauling his winter gear as the others had done. Grace handed him a mug of coffee, then brought the first load of steaming food to the table. The three men dug in, heaping their plates to give themselves adequate fuel to fight the elements outside.

When Grace returned with the last batch of pancakes from the griddle, she found Dillon and Jake studying her. "What?" she said, more than a little unnerved by their sudden attention. "Do I have dirt on my nose?"

Dillon shook his head. "No, I was just wondering when you got so darned pretty."

She shot a pointed glance toward Travis, who, thank heaven had his nose buried in yesterday's sports page. Today's paper wouldn't arrive until somebody drove into town and got the mail from their box at the post office. She turned back to Dillon with a scowl. "Knock it off."

"Can't a man even compliment his own sister anymore?" Jake asked with a wicked grin.

"You two hardly ever do more than grunt at me over breakfast. What's gotten into you this morning?"

Dillon shrugged. "Nothin'. You just seem happier lately. I'm real glad to see it."

"Me, too," Jake drawled with a grin. "I liked hearing you humming this morning. Can't say as I knew you could carry a tune so well, Gracie."

"Grace, Jake. My name is *Grace*," she insisted, sitting at the table.

"Sorry." He winked at her. "I'll get it right. You wait and see."

"At the rate you're going, it'll be about the time I start cashing my Social Security checks. Did you have some point you wanted to make?"

"Not really," Dillon said. "Just wondered what caused the change. That's all."

She got up again and brought the coffeepot back to the table. After returning the pot to the warming plate, she sat down and gave the men her blandest smile. "It's probably just the Christmas spirit. You should try it sometime."

Jake clasped his fingers around his mug and braced his elbows on the table. "Yeah, that must be it. And, seeing as how you're into the spirit of the season…"

Grace rolled her eyes, then noticed that Travis now was openly listening to the conversation. Not that she could blame him for it. She wouldn't have been able to ignore this one, either. "I knew you two wanted something. What is it?"

"Well," Dillion began, "we just thought that since it was the season of peace and goodwill, maybe you were ready to forgive all of us."

"Right," Jake said. "You know we never meant to hurt you, and it's not like you to hold a stupid grudge this long."

That tore it. If her brothers thought having an audience would force her to be "nice," they were wrong. She rose to her feet and leaned across the table, bringing her face close to Jake's. "That's all you think this is? A stupid grudge?"

Jake slid into his most annoyingly patronizing tone of voice. "Now, Gracie, don't get your drawers all knotted up."

Grace sucked in a deep breath, holding on to her temper by the thinnest of threads. Before she could unleash her anger, the phone rang. Since he was the closest, Dillon got up and answered it. Grace and Jake continued scowling at each other until Dillon began talking into the receiver.

"Marsh? What's up, bro?" Dillon was silent for a moment, then all of a sudden his whole body went rigid. "By Friday? Are you nuts? It's so close to Christmas, I'll never get a flight."

Grace and Jake exchanged startled glances, then looked back at Dillon. He raked his left hand through his hair as if he might pull out a handful any second.

"Dammit, Marsh. Couldn't you have called a little earlier? Yeah. Yeah. All right, little brother. I'll be there if I have to hijack a plane. No, I won't make any jokes like that at the airport. See you Friday." He banged down the receiver and curled his big hands into fists.

"Is Marsh all right?" Grace asked. Marsh was the renegade McBride, the only one who had left Sunshine Gap and showed no inclination of ever coming back to stay. And why would he when he'd worked so hard to carve out a career as a screenwriter and success finally was coming his way?

Dillon whirled around. His hair had deep finger tracks through it; his eyes looked wild. "Marsh is fine. He was calling about Blair."

Grace smiled at the thought of Dillon calling Blair DuMaine by her first name. Dillon had coached the famous actress on doing ranch chores for her part in the movie that had been filmed on the Flying M last summer. They had fallen in love, but put off making plans for the future until this movie was finished, and now suddenly, Dillon's moment of truth was fast approaching.

"What about her?" Jake asked.

"She's almost done editing the movie," Dillon said. "They're gonna have their first big screening on Friday. How am I gonna get a flight to L.A. now?"

"We'll find a way." The argument shelved for the moment, Grace hurried to the phone, giving Dillon a none-too-gentle nudge on the way. "Go home and pack. I'll make the calls."

"Thanks." Dillon raced out the back door without his coat, jumped into his pickup and roared off in the direction of his own house on the other side of the ranch.

Jake started yanking on his winter gear. "I'll put the chains on my pickup and drive him to the airport." Turning to Travis, he added, "Gracie can help you feed. She handles the team like a pro."

Travis told Grace he was going out to bring the team in from the corral. She nodded her understanding, grabbed the phone book and flipped through the yellow pages. The Cody airport was closed due to poor visibility. By the time Dillon stomped back into the kitchen, she'd managed to book him on a roundabout route starting late that afternoon in Jackson Hole, which would get him as far as San Diego by Thursday night. From there he was on his own to find a way to Blair's studio.

Dillon gave her a one-armed hug. "Thanks, sis. You always come through for us whether we deserve it or not."

Grace smiled at him. "You really love her, don't you?"

"Yeah, and I'm scared spitless she won't feel the same way."

"Oh, *right*. Like Blair DuMaine isn't completely and totally nuts about you. You get your butt down there and bring her back with an engagement ring on her finger or you'll answer to me."

His crooked smile pulled the scar tissue on the left side of his face taut. "Thanks, Grace. For everything."

Suddenly needing to clear the air between them before he stepped into one of those crowded, fragile airplanes, she hugged him hard. "You're my brother and I'll always love you, no matter what. I still don't agree with what you did, but I know your intentions were good. No more hard feelings, okay? I forgive you."

Crushing her against him, he rested his chin against the side of her head. "That's the best Christmas present you could've given me."

"What about the rest of us?" Jake asked from the doorway.

Grace shook her head at him. "You guys knew what Johnny was doing a long time before Dillon did, and you let me go on making a fool out of myself in front of God and everybody. When I'm ready to forgive you, you'll be the first to know."

Jake let out a snort of disgust. "Well, come on then, Dillon. It's a long way to Jackson."

Grace stood there while the sounds of the pickup's engine faded away, feeling the oddest combination of closure on one hand and abandonment on the other. Since he'd walked out of the hospital following the accident that had killed Johnny, Dillon truly had been there for her. He'd given up a promising rodeo career, taken over the lion's share of the hard, physical labor of running the ranch and played a father's role for her boys.

In fact, he'd become as much a prisoner of his decision to withhold the truth about Johnny from her as she had been. Dillon paid a huge price for attempting to stop her drunk husband from driving. Though she'd often complained about his interference in her life, she now realized she would miss having him right beside her.

"Lord, you really are perverse," she muttered, shaking her head at her own convoluted thought processes. "Time to grow up, Grace."

Travis whistled softly while he brushed the snow off Pete and Repete, the huge dappled-gray Percherons Dillon used to haul hay to the stock when the snow got too deep for a tractor. Travis hadn't worked much with draught horses, but these two were beauties, and he liked their playful disposition. Pete kept trying to yank the wool Scotchman's hat off Travis's head with his teeth, and Repete liked to blow hot breath down the back of Travis's neck.

"Knock it off," he said, laughing when Pete snagged the cap, pulling a hunk of Travis's hair in the process. He reached up to take it back, and the horse raised his neck and turned his head away, holding the hat out of reach like a big kid taunting a smaller one. Repete moved in for another blast of breath down Travis's neck. Travis laughed again and shoved the animal's muzzle away. "Cut it out, hay breath."

"Having a problem?" Grace asked.

"No, they're just a little frisky."

Travis watched her stride down the barn's center aisle, and thought she looked adorably chubby with all those layers of clothing on. Come to think of it, with a pair of long johns under his jeans, insulated bib overalls, a flannel shirt, a hooded sweatshirt and a heavy-duty work coat, he probably looked chubby, too.

"Yeah, they're frisky when you let 'em get away with it." She walked up to Pete, patted his neck and held her palm out under his mouth. Speaking in a low, firm voice, she said, "Pete, give it back."

Pete blew a loud snort out of his nostrils and shook his head. Grace waited for him to settle down and showed him her palm again. "Pete, drop it. *Now*."

Travis looked from Pete to Grace and back to Pete, never doubting that, while the horse easily weighed a ton, the woman would win this battle of wills. Sure enough, Pete slowly lowered his head and dropped the cap into Grace's hand. She scratched his forehead and crooned, "Good boy, Pete. Good boy."

Repete butted Grace's arm with his nose, demanding his share of attention. She patted his neck and scratched around his ears. Tossing Travis his hat, she suddenly was all business, helping him slide the big collars over the horses' heads and adjusting the harnesses. Before leading them outside again, Travis and Grace pulled up their sweatshirt hoods, donned an extra hat and raised their coat collars for good measure. With insulated rubber packs on their feet and two sets of gloves for their hands, they were ready to brave the storm.

Pete and Repete stood quietly while Travis hitched them to a flatbed hay wagon whose wheels had been replaced with sled runners. When he'd climbed aboard, Grace popped the reins over the horses' backs. The team took off at a slow clip, gradually picking up a little speed as the sled started moving.

A pair of cow dogs ran after them, jumped onto the wagon and stood at attention, scanning the countryside. Grace ordered them back to the barn, and they looked so heartbroken before they jumped off and slunk away, Travis had to chuckle. If she heard him, Grace ignored him. He didn't like that much.

The sled runners crunched through the top crust of snow. Carefully making his way to the front, Travis stood beside Grace. She glanced in his direction, then turned back to the team. Steam wafted from the horses' nostrils and their big hooves kicked up loose snow for the wind to toss around. The sky was one giant snow cloud waiting for some magic signal to bust wide-open and drop another fat load of flakes.

"You want to tell me what that was all about with Dillon and Jake?" he asked.

"Not particularly," she said without looking at him. "I'm sorry you had to hear us arguing, though."

"That was an argument?" He laughed. "Shoot, that was just a little spat. In my family, it wouldn't even come close to passing for an argument."

Grace's lips twitched. "Oh, we've been known to get a lot louder. If Zack, Cal and Alex had been involved, your ears would be smoking."

"I doubt it. You McBrides are a pretty tight bunch. I envy you that." He hadn't meant to add that last part, and when she shot him a surprised glance, he wished he'd shut up sooner. He was trying to find out more about her, not blab about his own problems. "I couldn't help noticing there's been some tension between you and your brothers, though. They seem to care a lot about you."

"They do," she admitted. "They just don't know the difference between caring and smothering. It's hell being the youngest in a family this size. Everybody knows what's best for me better than 'little Gracie' does."

"I hear you. But it doesn't have anything to do with

the size of your family. You just have to be the youngest."

"You're one, too?"

"Yup. I only have one brother, but he's five years older than me. Whole time I was growin' up, I couldn't do anything as well as Luke."

She gave him a sympathetic smile that warmed him in spite of the wind. "Boy, do I ever know what you mean. And the older they are, the worse they are. Marsh is only a year older than me, and he's never given me half the trouble Dillon, Jake and Zack have. Those guys are more protective than my parents."

"That doesn't sound like such an awful sin to me," Travis said. "If I had a sister, I'd be watching out for her."

"Watching out for her? Or making all her decisions for her? There's a difference."

"Well, yeah, I suppose, but—"

"But nothing. I didn't learn to walk until I was two because those big lugs always carried me around like I was a doll, and they never let me stay on the floor long enough to try. I hardly ever talked until I was three, because they always figured out what I wanted and gave it to me without making me ask for it. They helped me so darn much, I didn't learn a lot of things I should have."

"Like what?"

"The list is endless." She chuckled, then shook her head.

Though he wanted to know more, Travis decided to leave well enough alone for now. Grace was cutting paths between the pasture haystacks and the cows, and when she finished with that, it would be time for him to get to work. Jake was right about one thing. She handled the team like a pro.

Back at the haystack again, she loaded the seventy-five-pound bales he tossed to her with practiced ease. In minutes they were headed back toward the cows, mostly heifers carrying their first calves in this pasture. When they saw the sled coming back, the heifers came out to meet them.

While Grace slowly drove the team in a sweeping arc, Travis cut the baling twine and sliced off eight-inch flakes of hay and tossed them to the ground, keeping an eye out for any animals that looked sick, injured or what they called "heavy," which simply meant they were almost ready to give birth. In this weather any heavies would have to be brought closer to the barn to give their newborn calves a better chance of survival. Grace shouted and pointed at a heifer with a case of the scours.

Travis gave her a thumbs-up, and when he ran out of hay, he jumped off the sled to have a look at the animal. Great. Not only did she have the scours, she was heavy, too. He climbed back on the sled and reported the news to Grace. She nodded and drove to a different haystack and started the loading process all over again. They'd come back on horseback to get that heifer.

The Flying M was a big enough operation to divide the herd into separate pastures. The next pasture held all the bulls, another the yearlings, another the unbred heifers, another the cows. By the time they'd fed all of the groups, chopped holes in the ice forming over the creek and the water tanks and made their way back to the barn, Travis's face felt half-frozen and his fingers were tingling something fierce. He knew Grace must be miserable, too, but she never uttered a word of complaint.

What a woman. Whether she was working in the kitchen or doing a man's chores, she performed every task with a calm, efficient strength and confidence he admired. He suspected that since she wasn't as vocal or flamboyant as some of her siblings, the others tended to overlook how competent she really was.

If a guy wasn't paying any attention to her, she sort of blended into the background, and it was a shame she didn't get the credit she deserved for all the things she did so well. Maybe he should start pointing them out for her.

They unhitched the team beside the barn and led the Percherons inside. While he unharnessed the Percherons and rubbed them down, Grace went out to feed the saddle horses, brought in a pair of bay geldings and started drying them off.

"You don't have to go back out there," he said. "I can handle one heifer by myself."

Lips pursed, she eyed him for a moment, as if trying to judge just how much of a jerk he was going to be about this. "If I were one of the guys, you'd expect me to come along."

"Well, yeah, maybe but—"

Frowning, she interrupted him. "Let's just pretend I'm one of the guys and get on with it. I don't like the look of that sky out there, and I've been wondering if we should call Zack and Cal to come help us move the whole herd closer to the barn."

Travis nodded. "I thought about that, too, but Dillon has them so well situated, I doubt it's necessary. They're not that far and they've all got some trees for shelter."

''You're right. I'd just hate to have Jake come back tonight and start yelling that we should've done it.''

''If he does, just send him to me.'' Travis winked at her and gave her his best John Wayne imitation. ''I'll take care of him for ya, little lady.''

''No!'' Laughing, she grabbed a handful of soggy snow from her coat and threw it at him. ''Please, God, not another protector! I'll take care of Jake all by myself.''

''How do you plan to do that?'' He tossed the snow back at her and took one of the geldings off her hands. Independent as she was, she'd probably saddle a horse for him if he'd let her.

She smiled at him, her eyes glinting with mischief and maybe a secret or two. ''I have a few ideas.''

''Such as?''

''You won't tell him?''

Travis held both hands up beside his head. ''No way. Do I look dumb enough to get in the middle of something like this?''

''Sure you want me to answer that one?''

Her wicked grin took him straight back to that bar in Billings when he'd had so much fun with her. Nuts. For a whole week he'd been careful to keep his mind on business and off Grace, and now, in the space of one morning, all that effort was shot to hell. His attraction to her was growing stronger every day, and he might as well admit it, if only to himself.

''No, that's all right,'' he said. ''Just tell me what you're planning to do to Jake.''

She swung her saddle onto her horse's back. ''Nothing much. But if he doesn't back off, I'm going to find him a woman.''

''A what?''

"A woman. Since Zack and Cal got married, they haven't bugged me half as much, and now Dillon will have Blair to distract him. If falling in love keeps them out of my hair, I figure it oughta work for Jake, too."

"Got any likely candidates?"

"Uh-huh. I don't know if he'll fall in love with her, but I can guarantee she'll distract him."

Grace's low, throaty chuckle brushed over his nerve endings, making him wonder if she would laugh like that in bed. "Does she have a name?"

"Yup. But I'm not going to tell you," she said.

"Why do I have the impression I should feel sorry for Jake?"

"Beats the heck out of me." She yanked on the saddle horn, tightened the cinch and lowered the stirrup. "Jake's the worst. He's had more than a fair warning, and if he doesn't quit treating me like a little kid, he deserves whatever he gets."

With that, she led her horse outside. Travis followed, wishing he didn't find Grace so blasted appealing. But he did, and there was no using trying to deny it any longer.

The sick heifer didn't want to go anywhere, and she put up such a fuss when Travis finally roped her, Grace was threatening her with a trip to the meat packing plant. While he got the first-calf heifer doctored and settled, Grace saw to the horses. Then they both ran for the house. Stripping off gloves, heavy coats, bib overalls and packs in the mudroom, they hustled into the kitchen.

She checked her fingers and toes for signs of frostbite and bullied Travis into letting her check his while she was at it. Men were too quick to say they were fine, when a little extra care would head off a serious problem before it got started. He sighed heavily and shifted his weight on the chair, as if it embarrassed him for her to see his toes, for Heaven's sake.

"Looks okay to me," she said.

He grumbled, "Told you so," and reached for his socks.

"Don't you dare put those cold things back on." She went into the laundry room and grabbed a clean pair from a basket she hadn't hauled upstairs yet and tossed them to him. "Jake's got so many socks he'll never miss these. Put 'em on."

"Will you listen to yourself, lady?" He gave her a taunting grin. "You think you have any room to talk about Jake treating you like a little kid?"

Grace gave him a long, deadpan stare. "When it comes to taking care of themselves, little kids have more sense than most grown men I know. Children would never put on cold, clammy socks when they're trying to warm up their feet."

Travis let out a big, booming laugh. "All right, you got me there." His gaze moved over her the way it had that night in Billings, and his subtle smile goosed her pulse a good one. "You could always rub 'em for me. As I recall, you owe me a foot rub."

She ought to do it, Grace thought, if only to make him eat that sexy smile. And what kind of a game was he playing, anyway? Blowing cool one minute and hot the next. Did he think she was so dumb, she couldn't see what he was up to?

She peeled off her sweatshirt, nearly taking her flannel shirt off with it. She took her sweet time pulling the hem of the flannel shirt back down to cover her bare midriff and let it settle over her hips. Tossing the sweatshirt onto the counter behind her, she pulled the elastic band out of her ponytail, fluffed up her hair, then shook it down around her shoulders in a wild tangle of curls. She returned his smile, noting with satisfaction that his pupils had dilated.

"Well, you've got two choices, Sullivan." She lowered the pitch of her voice enough to put a husky little purr in. "I can fix us a hot meal, or I can rub your feet. But I can't do both. Which do you want the most?"

Licking his lower lip, he glanced away and shook his head as if to clear it. When he looked back at her again, his face was flushed and he appeared to be distinctly uncomfortable. She'd never batted her eyelashes in her life, but she couldn't resist batting them at him now.

"You're not...ticklish, are you, Travis?"

He cracked a sheepish grin, then rose to his feet and ambled across the room. Standing directly in front of her, he laid his palms on the counter, one on either side of her hips. Uh-oh. She felt as vulnerable as a kid who's just pulled a bull's tail and realized the fence is farther away than she'd thought it was.

Travis lowered his voice the way she had, and the resulting rasp slid a sweet little shiver the length of her spine. When he focused his gorgeous green eyes directly on hers and then on her lips, she thought she might melt into a puddle, right there in the middle of her kitchen floor.

"Good move, Grace. You got me," he said. "But what are you gonna do if I call your bluff?"

Her stupid lips were tingling. Shoot, her whole body was tingling. Well, she'd just have to brazen this one out or she'd never hear the end of it. Working up what she hoped was a bored expression, she straightened her shoulders. "What bluff?"

He raised his right hand and combed his fingers

through the springy curls falling over her shoulder. She felt his breath striking her cheeks in warm, gentle puffs and serious heat radiating from his arms and torso. She wanted to lean into him, put her arms around him and hold on tight. It would be utterly sweet if he held her in return. Just for a minute or two.

Now, here was a man who could keep her bed warm during the long, cold winter nights.

The thought had no more crossed her mind than her face burned and she knew he could probably guess what had caused her to blush like a teenager. She was out of her depth with this guy. If he made fun of her, she'd die of mortification.

He tucked a fingertip under her chin, silently urging her to look at him. Gathering her courage, she swallowed, then slowly raised her gaze to meet his. Instead of mockery, she found tenderness. The expression in his eyes, the slant of his smile, even his posture had softened.

"Don't be embarrassed, darlin'." He stroked his fingertips along the ridge of her jaw, as if he relished the slightest contact with her skin. "I feel it, too."

"You do?" she whispered.

"You know I do," he said.

Oh, mercy. If he didn't back up one step, her knees were going to give out, but she really didn't want him to move. If he felt it, too, why didn't he put them both out of their misery and just go ahead and kiss her?

Chapter Five

He *had* to kiss her. It didn't have to be heavy, just a nice, friendly little kiss they could laugh off later if they wanted to. But he *had* to kiss her. Lowering his head, he gently brushed his mouth over hers, giving her an opportunity to object.

She froze for a moment, then emitted a soft moan, raised her hands to his shoulders and kissed him back as if she'd been wanting to do this every bit as much as he had. He wrapped his arms around her waist and pulled her closer, then moaned himself when she went up on her tiptoes, slid her arms around his neck and parted her lips for him.

Feeling her lush curves pressing into him stole his ability to think. Forget nice and friendly. In less than thirty seconds the kiss had already gone beyond that. He delved into her mouth with his tongue, tasting a sweetness he couldn't name. Her tongue ventured out to meet his, touching some deep, inner part of him that made his head spin with a rush of pleasure.

She ran her fingers through his hair, her every touch on his scalp, his ears, the back of his neck a caress. Damn. After she'd refused to kiss him in Billings, he hadn't expected such an enthusiastic response. Not that he minded. Women always acted this way in his fantasies, but finding a real woman with a hunger to match his own put him in danger of losing control.

That never happened to him. Even as a kid he'd known that if he wanted to chase his rodeo dreams, he had to steer clear of long-lasting entanglements with the girls he dated. That had meant keeping his wits about him, even when he was necking with Terry or Kathie or Patsy in the back seat of his dad's old car.

The practice had served him equally well on the circuit. His one detour into matrimony had been such a disaster, he'd never even been tempted to maintain another relationship past the length of time the rodeo stayed in town.

So what the hell did he think he was doing, playing tonsil hockey with Grace? She was one of those women marriage had been invented for. Instead of holding on to her as if he never wanted to let her go, he should be running for his life. He would if he had a clue which way to run; but he'd lost his old life, and he didn't have a new one yet.

Still that didn't justify taking advantage of Grace because she was available. She deserved better than he could give her, and kissing her like this would give her all kinds of ideas, none of which would be fair or realistic. But damn, if she wasn't the most delicious woman he'd ever kissed....

Scraping together every ounce of common sense he

had left, Travis pulled his mouth away from Grace's, rested his forehead against hers and stroked her hair with an unsteady hand. He drew in a ragged breath, then blew it out and released her. Her cheeks were flushed, her eyes shining, her lips moist and plump. Her tentative smile made him groan in frustration.

"Aw, Grace. Don't look at me like that. You're scaring me to death."

She blinked in surprise. "Scaring you?"

Travis inhaled a deep breath and felt his heart banging hard enough to rattle his rib cage. He'd thought he was the one who had *her* caged, but here he was, as trapped as she was, with no desire to escape. He could look into her dark eyes for hours—days, even—and never learn everything he wanted to know about her. She gulped, cleared her throat, licked her lips, radiating an edgy excitement that might as well have been a written invitation to kiss her all over again.

"Oh, yeah." Needing to touch her, he tucked a wayward curl behind her ear. "You're exactly the kind of woman who scares the hell out of guys like me."

"What kind of a woman do you think I am?" she asked, her voice soft and still a little breathless.

"You're a nester." He smiled to show her he meant no insult. "The kind of woman who can make a shack into a home with nothing but her hands and her smarts. The kind who makes a man feel so at ease, he never wants to leave."

"And you're a rodeo man, terrified of a nester 'cause she might tie you down?" Her lips curved into a wry smile. "And here I thought you crazy bulldoggers were so brave."

He shrugged, but didn't smile back at her. "Everybody's afraid of something."

She held his gaze for a long moment, her smile slowly fading. Then she raised her chin. The warm, amused lights in her eyes cooled. She put her palms on his chest and firmly pushed him back. When his arms dropped to his sides, she sidestepped him and walked behind the work peninsula.

"You're right," she said, her tone brisk. "You want mustard or mayo on your sandwich?"

Travis felt stunned by the abruptness of her withdrawal and change of subject. Stunned and saddened. "I didn't mean to offend you."

"I'm not offended." She turned away, opened the refrigerator and set a jar of pickles on the counter, then a chunk of leftover meat loaf and a head of lettuce. "In fact, I appreciate your honesty. Tell you the truth, I almost forgot how soon you'll be leaving."

"Well, I'm not gone yet," he protested.

She set a cutting board on the counter, slapped a homemade loaf of bread on top and cut thick slices with a wicked-looking knife. "Let's see if I've got this right. You just gave me a fair warning that you'll be moving on. And now that you've got a clear conscience, you want to have an affair with me before you hit the road again. Isn't that how it usually works? Thanks, but I'll pass."

The dang woman was twisting everything he said. "Now, wait a second," he said. "I only kissed you once, and I never said anything about having an affair."

"You didn't have to. Your kiss said it for you." She huffed out a soft laugh. "This is such a cliché, it ought to be funny. I'm a nester, all right, and darn glad to be one. You need your freedom and I sincerely want you to have it. Far be it from me to clip a man's precious wings."

He frowned at her. She wasn't supposed to agree with him about that. Not yet, anyway. "Aw, Grace—"

She cut him off with a shake of her head. "Please, Travis, we can be friends, but no more. I really don't want you to kiss me again."

"Liar." He shouldn't have said that, but the word was out of his mouth before he realized how tactless it would sound.

Her eyes narrowed, but her voice remained perfectly calm. "All right, let me phrase it another way. I would rather you didn't kiss me again, because it will be a whole lot easier on both of us when you leave. Is that too much to ask?"

It wasn't, of course. In fact, he owed her that much and more for all the kindness she'd shown him.

He watched her assemble the sandwiches with the efficiency of a robot. The closed expression on her face, the brittle silence between them grated on his nerves. This was a cynical, disillusioned Grace he didn't know. He wanted to see the other one again—the breathless, excited Grace who had kissed him. She'd made him feel more alive than he had since he'd woken up after surgery and found out his rodeo career was over. He needed to feel alive again, dammit. That was why he not only wouldn't, but couldn't leave her alone.

The storm door to the mudroom banged open and shut. He heard feet stomping, then Riley's and Steven's voices spitting out indistinguishable words. Grace glanced at the wall clock and raised her eyebrows in surprise. An instant later, the boys burst into the kitchen, energy gushing out of them like a geyser erupting in Yellowstone Park.

"What are you guys doing home so soon?" Grace asked.

"They let the bus kids go home early 'cause the weather's gettin' so bad," Steven said. "Isn't that great?"

Riley checked out the sandwiches Grace had made and gave her a hopeful smile. "Are those for us?"

"No. Didn't you eat lunch at school?"

"That was at least an hour ago. I'm starving."

"Me, too," Steven said.

Grace grabbed a plate from a nearby cupboard, set two fat sandwiches on it and added a dill pickle. Shoving it in Travis's direction, she said, "Eat these quick before these vultures get them. Help yourself to the milk or whatever you want to drink."

"Aw, we're not *that* bad," Riley said.

"No, but you're getting there." She ruffled his hair and smoothed it back down in a maternal gesture that made Travis smile in spite of the tension between him and Grace.

Riley shot Travis a glance, then ducked out of his mother's reach. "Knock it off, Mom. I'm not a little kid anymore."

"All right, son. I hear you."

Her wistful smile said he would always be her little boy, but she wisely refrained from saying so. A moment later she ordered the boys to go wash their hands, reached for the bread and made two more sandwiches before they returned. The kids joined Travis at the table and Steven proceeded to give him a moment by moment account of everything he'd done and seen since leaving the house that morning. Travis got a kick out of the boy's keen observations and witty impersonations.

Jake called from Jackson Hole and reported that Dillon's plane had been delayed two hours, but finally had managed to take off. Unfortunately, whilc Jake had been waiting at the airport with Dillon, the state patrol closed the highway. He wouldn't be home before noon the next day.

After hanging up the phone, Grace joined Travis and the boys at the table. The four of them sat around munching and talking, and Travis began to feel an undemanding sort of connection to Grace and the boys. They hadn't talked directly to him much before today, but he realized now that he mostly talked to Dillon and Jake during meals. And these kids usually were too polite to interrupt an adult conversation.

When the boys went out to do their afternoon chores, Travis went with them, planning to check on the sick heifer. The wind assaulted them, driving the snowflakes at their faces with stinging force. Travis wondered if he shouldn't hang on to Steven in case it knocked him off his feet and blew him to Nebraska, but he figured the boy would be insulted.

Ranch kids were tough, resourceful and independent, especially boys headed for puberty. Nevertheless, Travis decided to stay with these two. The wind was so loud, he'd never hear them if they got into trouble and called for help.

Riley was all business, feeding the chickens, giving them warm water and adjusting the heat lamps. Steven tended to stop and play along the way. The kid was an animal magnet, and he visited with each critter he encountered, from a battle-scarred tomcat to a fat spider sitting on its web.

"Knock it off, runt," Riley said to his little brother. "It's your turn to feed the dogs and cats. Now get movin'."

His face mutinous, Steven trudged toward the storeroom at the back of the barn. Riley headed for the stalls.

Needing to get the heifer's medicine, Travis followed Steven, grinning to himself when he heard the boy muttering curses that would have earned Travis a soapy mouth if his mother had heard him.

Grace wouldn't do that, though. She was too affectionate with her boys to do that. She might scold the ears off of them, but he couldn't see her using physical punishment. When he entered the storeroom, Steven gave him a wide, oh-so-innocent smile. Travis smiled back, wondering how many adults the little devil had fooled with that particular act.

Steven went back to scooping dog kibble from the bin into a plastic dishpan. Travis opened the medicine chest and found the medicine he wanted. He picked up the piller, a long, tubelike contraption used for poking a pill down a farm animal's throat, but before he could leave, the boy straightened up and looked him in the eye.

"Do you like my mom?"

"Sure," Travis answered, hoping Steven couldn't see how uncomfortable the question had made him. "What's not to like about her?"

Scowling, Steven gave his head an impatient shake. "No, I mean do you *like* her. You know, like a boyfriend?"

Damn, the little guy really was a keen observer. Travis shifted his weight to the opposite foot and searched for an honest enough answer to satisfy the boy without getting himself in hot water if Steven talked about it—which he undoubtedly would do. This kid wouldn't know discretion if it kicked him in the head.

"How would you feel about it if I did?" Travis asked.

Steven scrunched up one side of his nose and mouth

for a minute. "Might be all right. You seem like an okay guy."

"Gee, thanks for the vote of confidence, Steven. Pardon me if I'm a little underwhelmed by it."

"What does that mean?"

Travis chuckled. "Don't worry about it. I just hoped I'd made a better impression on you than that."

"Oh, I get it," Steven said with a grin. "You wanted me to say you were a great guy. Right?"

"That about covers it," Travis agreed.

"Well, you *might* be a great guy," Steven assured him. "I just don't know you well enough to say that yet. I mean, if you wanted to be Mom's boyfriend, me and Riley'd have to keep a real close eye on you to make sure you were treatin' her right."

Travis gave him a nod. "Yeah, I suppose you would. But you know, I've never been mean to a woman in my life. I'd never intentionally hurt your mom, you can count on that."

Steven's eyes brightened. "Does that mean you like her?"

"It's not that simple, Steven."

"Why not?"

"It just isn't. Maybe your mom doesn't like me that way."

The kid rolled his eyes, then dropped the scoop back into the bin and propped his hands on his hips. "She does, Travis. I know she does."

"She told you that, did she?"

"No, but she likes you plenty."

"How do you know?"

"I just do," Steven said earnestly. "You gotta trust me on this one."

"Uh-huh. Well, I'll think about it." Dying to laugh,

but unwilling to offend Steven, Travis bit his lower lip and carried the piller and medicine bottle back to the stalls. He had a sick heifer to tend to, and from the look on Riley's face, he'd bet he had another grilling in store. Grace had so darn many self-appointed protectors, a man would have to be extremely brave or stupid to pursue her.

Sighing inwardly, Travis wondered which word applied to him, then decided it didn't matter. Contrary to her belief, they didn't *have* to be a cliché, and she didn't have to be so damn quick to push him away. Shoot, if even Steven could see the attraction between them, Travis figured it was time to give in and find out if they could have something special together.

Brave or stupid, he *was* going to pursue her.

While Travis and the boys were out doing chores, Grace haunted the kitchen windows, wishing they'd hurry up and come back one moment, praying they'd stay away longer the next. It had nothing to do with the boys, of course, and everything to do with Travis. He wasn't the only one who was scared of the attraction between them.

Every time she remembered how he'd kissed her, her insides trembled. Darn his hide. She'd thought Johnny had been a great kisser. Hah!

After that one, soul-destroying kiss from Travis, keeping her hands and her lips off him would be sheer hell. But she had to do it, or she'd find herself mixed up with another man who probably wasn't all that different from Johnny under the skin. When you got right down to it, maybe none of them were. No, that wasn't true and it wasn't fair. There were good, faithful, safe men out there, all right; she just didn't happen to be attracted to them.

No, she always went for the bad boys, the guys who were a little dangerous and mysterious, the men her family never wanted her to have. Oh, phooey. Denial be damned, her life had been a whole lot simpler when she'd clung to Johnny's memory. She hadn't felt such wild and crazy emotions then, but there was a lot to be said for maintaining a certain level of serenity.

It sure beat the heck out of feeling all nervous and twitchy every time she even thought about Travis. When he put his big feet under her table or complimented her cooking, she got so flustered and silly you'd think she'd never cooked for a man before. She hated for anyone to have that kind of power over her, hated feeling so confused, and she wanted it to stop.

She really wished he'd never kissed her.

For pity's sake, what was taking those guys so long? She and Travis should check the herd again for heavy cows before nightfall. They weren't supposed to start calving until January, but nobody ever told the cows or the calves that. From the middle of December on, anything could happen, especially when a big storm like this one rolled in.

Oh, Lord, there would be no escaping the man. Or controlling her unruly, lustful thoughts about him. Muttering furiously, she yanked the lid off the slow-cooker and stirred the stew she'd put together that morning.

She needed a distraction, something to occupy her mind and her hands. The best idea she could come up with was baking Christmas cookies. She already had most of her holiday baking neatly packaged and labeled in the freezer, but no matter how many cookies she made every year, her family always managed to eat every crumb. The boys could decorate these while she and Travis were out with the stock.

She'd just taken the first batch out of the oven when Zack arrived. He came into the kitchen with a blast of frigid air and gave her a cheek a cold peck. "Hey, there, Gracie. How's it goin'?" Without waiting for an answer, he sniffed the air appreciatively, then filled a mug with coffee and brought it back to her work area.

Grace slid another cookie sheet into the oven, then rolled out another ball of dough and pretended she didn't see her cousin filch one of the hot cookies. He'd probably finish the whole batch with his cup of coffee, but she didn't mind. Cookies were made to be eaten. Munching away, he studied her intently until she thought she'd hit him if he didn't say something.

She cut out a dozen angels and transferred them to a cookie sheet. "Did you need something besides coffee and cookies?"

He shook his head and took another cookie. "The weather's gettin' so bad, I just came over to see if Dillon needed more help. Did the boys get home from school all right?"

"You bet. They're out chorin' with Travis, but they should be in soon."

"Where are Jake and Dillon?"

She told him about Marsh's call. He grinned at her description of Dillon's reaction, but when she mentioned that Jake wouldn't be back before morning, Zack's eyebrows came together in a scowl. "That means you'll be in the house alone tonight."

"It's okay." She used a tone more appropriate for a five-year-old than a grown man, but after a dumb remark like that, she couldn't resist. She'd always known her big brothers could be dense at times, but lately it seemed as if they'd all gone loco. "I'm a big girl now. Honest."

Grinning, he ruffled her hair. "I know that, Gracie."

She reached up and tweaked his bushy beard. "If you did, you wouldn't call me that, Zackie."

"It's just a nickname."

"Fine, Zackie. Whatever you say."

He heaved a long-suffering sigh and grumbled, "There's no talkin' to you anymore."

"Not the way you've always done it," she agreed. "It's insulting."

"Come on, you know it's not meant that way."

She propped her fists on her hips and looked him straight in the eye. "Doesn't matter. I still find it insulting, and all of you guys need to change how you talk to me."

"You're really serious about this."

Closing her eyes, she counted to fifteen. Why was this concept so difficult for him and her brothers to grasp? They were all reasonably intelligent men, except for when their protective instincts toward her were aroused. "Wouldn't you be, Zackie?"

He banged his mug down on the counter. "I'm going out to help Travis."

"Fine." Grace waited until she heard the back door slam before muttering, "Come back when you can't stay so long."

She didn't really mean that. A lump formed in her throat and her eyes stung with tears she wasn't about to shed. Dammit, she loved her family and she missed being able to enjoy their company, but this was one battle she had to win.

She needed to learn how to stand on her own two feet, to make her own decisions and her own mistakes.

That would never happen if her family didn't stop treating her like a child. Since her efforts to get them to call her Grace had failed, she would have to find a way to send the guys and Alex a stronger message. Would a taste of their own medicine do the trick?

It was fully dark by the time Travis and Zack drove the heavy cows to the barn and settled them into clean stalls. Zack immediately left to go back to his own house. Waving him off, Travis stood outside the barn for a moment, looking at the ranch house and the blinking Christmas lights outlining the kitchen window. He felt hungry and chilled clear through to his bones again, but he hesitated, debating whether or not he should go inside.

From Zack's foul mood and a couple of comments he'd made, Travis had guessed that Grace had pinned Zack's ears back but good. Travis doubted her attitude toward him would be any better, and he'd had enough of cranky McBrides for one day. Maybe he'd head on back to the guest house, heat a can of soup and sleep until he had to check the cows again in three hours.

His stomach rumbled, as if telling him his idea reeked. The sleeping part was okay, but Grace's cooking was so much better than anything he might concoct, his stomach won out. He hurried into the mudroom, peeled off his gloves and heavy coat, then sat on the wooden bench to take off his packs.

The laces were coated with ice, his cold fingers clumsy. In seconds he'd created a knotted mess. Cursing, he sat up and leaned against the wall to catch his breath and rest his aching shoulder. Though it was supposedly healed from his surgery, the frigid, damp weather sometimes made it ache.

The kitchen door opened and Steven stuck his head through the gap, releasing a cloud of tantalizing aromas into the mudroom. Travis's stomach let out a ferocious growl. Steven laughed. After studying Travis's face for a moment, the boy's expression abruptly turned sober.

"You okay, Travis?"

Travis nodded and tried to smile. "Think so. I'm just cold and tired, and I can't get my dang packs off."

"Well, why didn't you yell for help?" Steven charged across the room and knelt at Travis's feet. His nimble fingers jerked and tugged at the knots, and the laces surrendered in less than a minute. Steven loosened them, then pulled the insulated rubber boots off Travis's feet and shot him a wide grin.

Travis never had seen anything sweeter than Steven's obvious pleasure at helping him. "Thanks, Steven."

"It's nothin'." Steven clambered to his feet and stuck his hands in his back pockets. "I do it for Uncle Dillon all the time. He's missin' one of his thumbs, so he really has a bad time if his laces get fouled up like that."

"I'll bet he appreciates your help as much as I do."

"Well, hurry up," Steven said. "Mom's made biscuits and stew, and Riley and I decorated a zillion cookies while you were out with Uncle Zack. Mom said we can have them for dessert."

His mouth already watering, Travis stripped off his padded bib overalls and followed Steven into the kitchen in his stocking feet. Grace didn't greet him with a friendly smile, but she handed him a steaming mug of coffee, sent Steven to the laundry room to find him another pair of dry socks and fussed over him until she'd convinced herself that he was warm, dry and well-fed.

Travis reveled in her attention. He hated it when his mother fussed over him, but then his mother always yapped at him, demanding to know if he wanted this or that, and then how did he want it, and giving him so many decisions to make, what he wanted was to get away from her. She cooked, cleaned and took care of her family because that was her job. It had been assigned to her on the basis of her gender, not because she liked or was suited to the work.

On the other hand, Grace gave every impression that she really enjoyed her work, and she was a more restful, serene sort of person than his mother—when she wasn't arguing with her brothers, of course. She also had some kind of instinct or intuition that told her what a man needed without having to ask him. Maybe growing up with so many guys around had given her a special insight into the male psyche.

Whatever forces had made Grace into the woman she was, Travis didn't question his good fortune; he simply soaked up her quiet nurturing and enjoyed her small acts of kindness. Over the course of the meal, he relaxed, listened to the boys' chatter and pretended his little spat with Grace hadn't happened. The oddest sensation gradually came over him.

It felt as if he almost belonged here. If he wanted to bad enough, he could be a part of this small family unit. But did he? Well, he sure wanted Grace, and he really liked her boys.

Did he want everything else that came along with them—the extended family, the huge herd of cows and the headaches of calving, feeding, branding and whatnot? No, he didn't want those headaches, and he didn't want to wind up working for her brothers. But Grace and the kids were ranch people, and they obviously liked all that stuff.

So the question he needed to answer next was, could he be a part of their family and still do what he wanted to earn a living? And just what might that be? All right, so he'd had a dream once that Grace and the boys might like to share. He'd even drafted some crude plans, but he'd shelved them long ago. He couldn't pull off something that big. Could he?

Biting back a few choice words, he excused himself and headed back out to the barn. He'd check all the heavy cows and if everything looked good, he'd go to the guest house for a couple hours of sleep before he had to check them again. The only thing he knew for certain right now is that Grace was right. He shouldn't kiss her again, and he shouldn't let Riley and Steven get too attached to him.

If he decided to move on, he didn't want to leave any broken hearts behind.

Chapter Six

Grace spent half the night in the barn, helping Travis pull two calves and doctoring the heifer with the scours. She spent the other half of the night struggling to purge all thoughts of kissing Travis from her memory. Her efforts were doomed to failure, of course. As long as she had to work alongside Travis, she honestly hadn't expected to forget anything about him. She'd simply felt obligated to try.

The funny thing was, when she'd brought him a thermos of coffee at 2:00 a.m., he'd eyed her warily and answered her questions with grunts or one-syllable words, clearly wanting to keep as much distance between them as she did. Realizing that bothered her more than she wanted to admit.

It bothered her even more to realize her thoughts didn't make a lick of sense. She *knew* she shouldn't be entertaining hopes for a relationship with Travis. Instead of feeling hurt because he was helping her to do what was best for her and the boys, she should have been grateful. But she wasn't.

How could she be grateful when every time she saw Travis, she wanted to kiss him again? It was actually a little insulting that he could kiss her senseless and then turn off his feelings like a dang lightbulb. Shaking her head in dismay, she sighed.

Well, there was no need to beat herself up over it. It was just sex, after all, a perfectly natural reaction to the first handsome man who had showed an interest in her since she'd learned the truth about Johnny. Now that she thought about it, her attraction to Travis might not have anything to do with him personally. After five years of celibacy her hormones were working in overdrive. A lot of guys would look pretty darn good to her. She just hadn't been paying enough attention.

Pleased to have it all straightened out in her head, she hurried downstairs the next morning, tired but confident she could handle Travis Sullivan. She hauled her winter gear in from the mudroom and looked out the kitchen window facing the barn. The storm had left some awesome snowdrifts before moving on during the night.

She switched on the radio in time to hear that school had been canceled in Sunshine Gap. Highways all over the area would be closed until the snowploughs could clean them off. The boys would be ecstatic, but if the wind picked up again, poor Jake might be stuck in Jackson Hole for another day. And she'd been hoping to make one final trip to Cody for last-minute Christmas items and fresh produce for the family dinner.

Well, it wouldn't be any great tragedy if she didn't get there, and today was only the twenty-second. Maybe she could go tomorrow. She started a pot of coffee, drained and rinsed the beans she'd left soaking overnight and got out the iron kettle her mother always used to make chili. In weather like this, it never hurt to have a hot meal simmering on the stove.

Riley and Steven straggled down for breakfast an hour later. More bleary-eyed than usual, Travis came in from the guest house and accepted a mug of coffee with a grateful smile. He sniffed the steam and went through his tasting ritual, much to the boys' amusement. After breakfast, they all went out to feed the stock.

When the outside work was done Travis played board games with the boys while Grace watered the huge Christmas tree in the living room and finished wrapping the gifts she'd made. Jake finally made it home while Travis and the boys were out making a second check on the stock. He'd stopped at the post office and brought home a couple of big boxes from both sets of McBride parents who were traveling through Italy. Grace helped him haul the boxes into the living room and refused to unpack them. If they remained undisturbed until Christmas Day, the gifts inside couldn't be poked, shaken or damaged.

Travis and Jake carried most of the conversation at supper. Grace noted, however, that Travis made an effort to include the boys whenever he could. Riley was sitting taller than he usually did, and he watched Travis's gestures as if he were committing them to memory.

When she got up to clear the table, Travis also got up and helped her. Knowing the reaction he was going to get, Grace bit the inside of her lower lip, struggling to hold in a laugh that desperately wanted to come out. Travis set his load beside the sink, then turned around and found Jake, Riley and Steven staring at him as if he'd violated a cardinal rule of manhood. Which, of course, he had.

Travis put his hands on his hips and stared back at them. "What's the matter?"

Laughing, Steven shook his head. "Don't you know you're not supposed to do that?"

"Do what?" Travis asked.

"The dishes," Riley said, his voice dripping with disgust.

Jake echoed Riley's tone. "Yeah. That's women's work."

Both eyebrows raised in apparent disbelief, Travis turned to Grace. "They're not serious?"

Grace shrugged one shoulder. "Didn't you hear the oinking?"

"Mo-om," Steven protested. "Don't call us that weird kind of pigs again."

"You mean the male chauvinist ones?" Grace asked.

Steven nodded. "That's it. But you shouldn't call us that."

"Hey, if the oink fits, you've gotta wear it," Travis said with a laugh. "Do you guys really think that attitude's fair?"

"Course it is," Jake said. "Why wouldn't it be?"

"Grace doesn't hesitate to take on a man's job around here when you need her. She lost as much sleep as I did last night, helped pull calves, drove the team and then cooked and cleaned up after every meal we've all eaten. Then she made sure our gear dried out and did a bunch of laundry for everybody besides, even me. She's got to be tired, and I think it's only fair that we give her a hand, don't you?"

"Gol, Travis," Riley said with a fierce scowl.

"Knock it off or she'll have us doin' the damn dishes every night."

"Riley, watch your language," Grace said.

Riley scowled at her, but said, "Okay, Mom."

Steven jumped into the conversation. "Yeah, and if we do the dishes every night, the other guys'll call us sissies."

Travis walked over to the table and loomed over Steven. "You callin' me a sissy, kid?"

His eyes big as half dollars, Steven shook his head, then spoiled the effect by cracking up. He slid off his chair, took two steps back and said, "Hey, if the apron fits, you've gotta wear it, Travis." Then he turned and sprinted for the back stairs, his laughter trailing after him.

"Come back here, you little varmint," Travis called, but his eye twinkled and his voice carried no real heat.

"What do you think, Uncle Jake?" Riley asked.

Jake squirmed on his chair. "Well, Riley, Travis may have a point, but he's forgetting that your mom gets paid to do the housekeeping chores. That's her job."

"But does she get paid extra when she helps with the stock?" Riley asked.

"No, but she's one of the owners of this ranch. We're all supposed to pitch in when we can."

Riley still looked troubled. Grace came to the table and affectionately ruffled his hair. "It's all right, honey. I love my job here at the ranch, and I don't mind helping outside. It all comes with the territory." She smiled at Travis then, and added, "But I have to say, it's been real nice to have somebody notice when I do a little extra."

"A little?" Travis rolled his eyes. "You've got these

guys so spoiled, they don't notice half the things you do for them.''

"And I suppose you do?" Jake scoffed.

"Darn right." Travis picked up the empty cornbread pan and the shaker of chili powder. "That's why I'm helpin' her tonight. You two can go ahead and call me a sissy, but if you ever want a modern woman in your life, you'd better get with it and learn how to pitch in around the house."

Jake climbed to his feet and pushed his chair under the table. "That's why I'll die a bachelor."

"Me, too," Riley said, following Jake's example.

Travis waited until they left the room, then turned to Grace. "You're gonna let 'em get away with that?"

She smiled at his indignant tone. "For now."

"Why? Don't you want Riley and Steven to be able to take care of themselves?

"Of course I do." The dishwasher was nearly full, darn it. She squirted dishwashing soap into the sink and ran hot water on top of it. "They'll be able to cook, clean and do their own laundry before they leave home.

"Why wait?" He found a dish towel and waited for the first dishes to reach the drying rack.

"The boys already do a lot of chores outside and I want them to have some time to be kids. They have a lot of 'man' things they need to learn, too, and it's not always easy for them when they have to wait around for an uncle to be available to teach them. Right now, I think it's more important for them to be identifying with the men in the family."

"Even if the guys teach them to be chauvinists?"

Grace chuckled. "Afraid so. Fathers are the ones who teach boys how to take risks, defend themselves and a lot of other things mothers usually don't like, but that's how boys learn to be men. That's why Riley and Steven need to hang around with their uncles more than their mother.''

Travis gazed at her in pure admiration. ''Jeez, Grace, you're amazing.''

She wrinkled her nose at him. ''Oh, please, not that. I've heard every one of those jokes a million times.''

''What jokes?''

'''Amazing Grace.' You know, the old hymn?''

''I wasn't talking about that,'' Travis said with a laugh. ''I really think you're an amazing mother.''

She dipped a big ladle into the rinse water and set it in the dry rack. ''I'm doing the best I can, but most mothers do. Besides, I've made my share of mistakes with the boys. Just ask them and they'll tell you.''

''That's because they're normal, healthy kids who aren't afraid to say what they think.''

''Is that so unusual?''

''I don't know how it is in other people's families, but in my family it sure was. I learned to keep my contrary opinions to myself by the time I was five or six.''

Grace frowned. ''What happened if you didn't?''

''No big deal, really,'' Travis said. Damn, he was doing it again—telling her more than he'd intended. ''I'd either get a blank stare or a mocking smile. Either way, I'd feel really stupid for disagreeing.''

''That's sad, Travis. I don't want my boys to be disrespectful, but they need to know how to think for themselves. How would we ever make any progress if everybody thought the same way about everything?''

He grabbed a handful of dry utensils and turned away, more because he didn't want her to see his face than from any burning desire to put things where they belonged. He opened a drawer, gaped, then opened another and another. Sputtering with laughter, he glanced over his shoulder and saw Grace looking back at him, her eyebrows raised.

He pointed at the closest drawer. "Did you do this?"

"Do what?"

"Put in all these little partitions and organizer things. And the outlines you've drawn."

"Now, who's oinking? Guys do that stuff all the time with their workbenches and nobody says a word. Why can't I?"

He laughed again. She was so serious, he couldn't help himself. "You can, but these are so perfect, they're—"

"Ridiculous? Scary? Obsessive?" she offered in a dry tone. "I've heard it all before."

He walked back to the sink, picked up a plate that was nearly dry and wiped the dish towel over it. "I take it that doesn't bother you."

She shook her head. "A lot of people use this kitchen, and the outlines help them put things away where they belong. When you're busy cooking, all the gadgets in the world aren't worth a darn if you can't find the one you need."

"That makes sense." He waited a couple of seconds, then added, "I guess."

"You only guess?" Grinning, she scooped up soap-suds with her finger and flicked them at him, catching him across his jaw. "That's a lousy attitude."

He wiped them off with his shirtsleeve, then snapped the dish towel at her without coming close to hitting her. "You wanna play rough?"

"No." She held up one hand like a traffic cop. "Stop. I don't want to play at all."

"That's no fun."

"Too bad. I've got to make one last thing for Christmas tonight."

"More cookies?"

She chuckled at his hopeful, boyish grin. "No. A centerpiece for Christmas dinner."

"How do you do that?"

"It's not hard. I just get out my wand and wave it around, and—"

He cut her off with a snort. "Anybody ever tell you you're a real smart aleck?"

"Around here, it's a survival skill."

"That I can believe," he said.

They finished the dishes in a companionable silence. Grace snuck a few glances at Travis, then decided there was no use trying to figure him out. On the surface, he was a lot like the men in her family, but somewhere underneath the skin, he was different in some mighty intriguing ways.

To her surprise, instead of going to the living room to watch TV with Jake and the boys, he stayed in the kitchen, watching her lay out her glue gun, the evergreen branches she'd had standing in a pail of water in the laundry room and the big box of stuff she kept on hand from the craft store. At first his scrutiny bothered her, but then she found a wire form with two concentric circles, and after studying it for a moment, the joy of creating took over, blocking out distractions.

She'd never had formal training, just an instinct for putting the right pieces together to make something pretty and useful. After weaving the branches around and through the wires with red, green and gold ribbon, she glued down the ends and dug through the box for doodads she could use for ornaments. Tiny wrapped packages, fake pine cones, sprigs of holly and mistletoe, shiny bows and miniature wooden toys piled up on the table.

She tried various combinations on the branches until she found the one she liked best. It only took a moment to glue them in place. She glanced at Travis and caught a mystified smile on his face. "What's the matter?" she asked.

"Nothing, I guess. Is that it?"

"Not quite." She dove back into the box, brought out a fat red candle and carefully settled the circle of branches and ornaments over the top. She glanced at Travis again. He was studying her creation through narrowed eyes; his eyebrows were beetled in concentration.

"Now what's wrong?" she asked.

"Got any way to put some snow on it? Or maybe a little tinsel?"

"Snow," she agreed. Out came the can of fake snow. She gave the wreath a couple of light sprays, then stood back for another look. "Done."

"Yeah." A slow smile stretched across his face. "Now it's perfect."

"Thanks." She felt ridiculously pleased with his approval.

"I'll pay you fifty bucks to make another one of those for my mom."

"Don't be silly," she said, waving his offer of money aside. "I've got plenty of supplies and I'll be glad to make your mom one, but I won't take money for it." She reached for the box, but he grabbed her arm and held it until she met his gaze.

"Are you nuts? You've got a talent here, Grace. You could make some real money—"

Pulling her arm free, she frowned at him. "If I did it

for money, it'd be a job. And then it wouldn't be fun anymore.''

"Why does it have to be that way?" he asked. "What's wrong with having a job that's fun?"

She held one hand up to her ear. "What's that I'm hearing? An ex-rodeo cowboy's lament?" He rolled his eyes at her and she laughed. "Sorry, Travis. I've just heard that from Dillon too many times."

"All right, all right," he admitted with a grin.

Grace pulled another wire frame out of the box, took some more branches and went to work. "How many people will you have at Christmas dinner?"

"Seven."

"Any children?"

He nodded. "My nieces. They're six and eight now."

She went to her baking cupboard, pulled out a bag of cinnamon bears and brought it to the table. In ten minutes she'd finished a second candle ring for Travis's mom, and it was pretty darn cute if she did say so herself. Not that she had to with him around. The way the man carried on, a person might think she'd spun gold out of straw. Still, it was awfully nice to be appreciated for a change, and she couldn't help smiling at him.

The smile he returned had a lusty quality to it that flustered her "I, um, don't have another candle that size," she said, "but if the roads are open I'm going to Cody tomorrow afternoon. I'll pick one up then."

He pushed back his chair and stood, then ambled around the table to join her on the other side. "Hey, if Jake doesn't need me, could I tag along?" he asked. "I need to find a gift for my sister-in-law and I don't have any idea what she wants. Maybe you could give me some suggestions."

The urge to back away from him was nearly irresistible, but somehow she managed. It wouldn't do to let him think he could intimidate her that easily. "I could try. Of course, since I don't know her, I might choose something she'll hate."

"No, you wouldn't." He sidled right up to her, stopping so close, she could feel his body heat through her clothes. "You have good taste. Sure you won't let me pay for that centerpiece?"

She shook her head, and he went right on talking. "Well, shoot, darlin', since you won't let me give you any money, I'll just have to find another way to pay you."

He reached for her, and before she had a fair chance to react, he wrapped his big arms around her and put one hand at the small of her back. She shrieked when he arched her over one forearm and dipped her until her hair brushed the tile floor. Blood rushed into her head and all she could see was his grinning face and the ceiling light shining far above his head.

Clutching at his shoulders, she opened her mouth to yell at him, and he pounced, laying such a hard, driving kiss on her lips, she nearly fainted from the pleasure of it. He pulled her closer, supporting her weight as easily as if she were a fragile child, which she certainly was not. She'd never fainted in her life, either. But, oh, merciful heaven...

She lost track of everything but the stunning sensations he created for her with only his lips and his tongue and the rough, guttural noises coming from his throat. Her toes curled so hard they ached and her heart slammed against her breastbone. It was glorious. She'd never felt so feminine, so desirable, so totally wanted in her life.

Then he took his clever mouth away and pulled her

upright, making the blood rush out of her head this time. She had no idea how long she stood there and stared at him like a doofus, but he stood there and grinned back at her the whole time. Just about the time she found her voice again, he gave her another hard, fast smooch, patted her cheek and said, ''Thanks, sweetheart. My mom's gonna love that thing.''

With that he sauntered out the door to the mudroom, where she heard him rummaging around for his jacket. Then the back door opened and shut, and she finally allowed a soft, slightly hysterical giggle to escape her lips.

''Oh, brother. Now I've seen everything.''

At the sound of Jake's voice, practically dripping disgust, she whirled around. He stood in the doorway that led to the back hall, his shoulders nearly touching wood on either side. His scowl could have sucked all the sunshine out of a bright summer day. She wondered how long he'd been standing there.

''Dammit, Gracie—''

''Don't start. Whatever you want to say, I don't want to hear it.''

His scowl deepened into a full-fledged frown. ''That's what you always said about Johnny.''

''Shut up, Jake.''

As usual, he paid no attention to what she said and stepped farther into the room. ''He's charming and witty, and he has no real ties and no real responsibilities. And he's what? Thirty-five? Thirty-six? He's another Peter Pan. And you need to watch out for that, Gracie. Know what I mean?''

Grace stared Jake down for a moment. ''Fine. You've had your say. Now go somewhere else and mind your own business for a change, will you?''

She pushed past him, rounded up the boys and sent them off to bed in case the schools reopened the next day. Once they were tucked in, she got herself ready for bed and turned in. Usually, after such a long, busy day, she went right to sleep and barely moved until morning. But Jake's words haunted her long into the night.

He was wrong about Travis; she knew he was. But what if he wasn't? What if Jake was right and Travis turned out to be as big a louse as Johnny had been? What made her think she would even know a good man if she ever met one?

Chapter Seven

When Travis walked into the kitchen for breakfast the next morning, everything looked fairly normal. Jake sat at the table drinking a mug of coffee and studying a stack of paperwork; Grace stood at the stove turning sausages in a cast-iron skillet. Neither of them spoke to him, however, and Grace didn't even grin when he pronounced the coffee better than ever.

The tension simmered and grew during the meal, providing a grim reminder of his reasons for avoiding his own family whenever an opportunity presented itself. Travis would have ignored it if he'd thought it was a private matter between Jake and Grace, but something told him that he was involved somehow. It didn't make sense.

Well, okay, maybe he could understand that Grace might be a little miffed at him for kissing her last night. He'd only meant it in fun, but he had to admit that it had gone beyond that. Jake was shooting him dirty looks, too, though, and Travis had no idea what he'd done to tick him off. Damn, but he hated the way unspoken anger could throw manure on a man's whole day.

Appetite gone, he pushed his plate aside and went out to the barn. There was a brand-new calf nursing in one of the stalls and the other heavy cows looked okay. Pete and Repete played their stupid games with him, but he finally got them ready to pull the hay sled. By the time Jake arrived, Travis was thoroughly irritated and ready to have "it" out, whatever "it" happened to be.

Unfortunately Jake was still in his brooding mode. Travis tolerated it until they loaded the sled for the second time. "All right," he finally said, "what's goin' on?"

Jake merely raised his eyebrows at him, silently demanding an explanation. Travis shoved a bale into his midsection hard enough to drive the air from his lungs.

"You know damn well what I'm talkin' about," Travis said. "You and Grace acted pretty owly at breakfast, and you're still doing it. If you're mad at me for some reason, let's hear it and get it over with."

"All right," Jake said. "I saw you kissing Gracie last night, and I didn't like it. Keep your damn hands and your mouth off her."

Travis stared at him for a moment, then shook his head in amazement. "She's a grown woman. Seems to me that should be her decision to make."

Jake shrugged. "Maybe. But she's been through a real bad time and she's real vulnerable right now."

"That's what Alex and Dillon said, but they didn't explain it. What happened to Grace?"

"It's not our place to tell anyone her business. And if you think I'm overstepping myself here, that's just too bad. When Dillon's not here, it's my job to protect her."

"How do you figure that?"

"It's the McBride safety system."

"How does it work?"

"Real simple," Jake said, his tone dry as an overcooked steak. "When we were younger, we were all responsible for keeping the younger kids out of trouble. It didn't matter if we were siblings or cousins. If somebody younger than you got into trouble, you were in trouble, too."

"And you're the oldest," Travis said, wincing in sympathy. "Jeez, you must have been grounded all the time."

"You've got that right. I came real close to strangling Zack and Cal so many times it's a wonder they're still breathing. And Alex." Jake paused and rolled his eyes toward heaven. "Jeez, you wouldn't believe some of the stuff she pulled."

"But you're all grown-up now," Travis said. "Isn't it time to retire the system?"

"A sane person might think so, but in our family?" Jake laughed bitterly. "It'll never happen."

"I suppose those habits are so ingrained, you'd automatically protect all the younger ones without even thinking about it."

Jake nodded. "I don't want to mess in Gracie's business, but I'm not gonna stand back and watch her get hurt by you or anybody else, either."

"I don't plan to hurt her," Travis said.

"Good." Jake's expression hardened and his voice

took on an unmistakable edge of warning. "See that you don't."

With the road to Cody open again, Grace dreaded spending the afternoon with Travis, but there was no polite way to get out of it. The minute they were alone in her pickup, he would tease and flirt with her, and she would cave in and let herself be charmed. Because...she liked how she felt when she was with him.

"And the problem with that is...?" she muttered, heading out the door to clean the snow off her pickup.

Darned if she could come up with anything but the inevitable interference from her idiot brothers, who never failed to remind her of her major miscalculation in judgment where men were concerned. But that was a long time ago—fourteen years if she went clear back to her first date with Johnny.

Remembering Jake's expression when she'd spotted him in the doorway last night, she heaved a disgruntled sigh, grabbed the long-handled brush she kept in the pickup and attacked the snow covering the vehicle with so much force the flying flakes caused a miniblizzard.

"Those idiots will be reminding me of my lousy taste in men when I'm ninety," she muttered. "If they had their way, they'd just stick me in some cage where I'd be all nice and safe forever."

For heaven's sake, Travis had only kissed her twice, and the last time he'd only done it to razz her. It wasn't as if he were madly in love with her. And she wasn't planning to sleep with him or marry him. She had no desire ever to marry again, anyway, but she did want to have a little more fun in her life. So why couldn't she just enjoy the man's company for a little while without everybody in the whole family giving her their two cents' worth?

Oh, darn Jake for stirring up her old insecurities. No matter what Travis did now, she was sure to overreact and make a fool of herself. It wouldn't be the first time, either. The front door of the guest house opened and Travis stepped out, pulling on his coat as he came down the steps.

"Hubba, hubba," Grace murmured, trying not to stare. He'd obviously just showered and shaved, and he had on the same shirt and pants he'd worn that night in Billings. Well, okay, so she really liked the way he filled out a pair of jeans. Big deal. She could look, couldn't she?

She jammed the brush under the driver's seat and climbed in behind the wheel. Travis climbed in on the other side while she started the engine. She waited for him to say something, but he remained quiet all the way to Sunshine Gap. She drove through town and turned onto the Cody highway.

"You all right, Travis?" she asked.

"Huh?" He blinked and shook his head as if he'd been somewhere far away in his mind. "Oh, sure, Grace. I'm fine."

"If you keep thinking that hard, you're liable to sprain something," she said.

He rewarded her with a grin and a sheepish shrug. "Sorry. Didn't mean to be rude."

"You weren't. You just seemed troubled."

"I am, a little."

"Want to talk about it?"

"Yeah, but I doubt you will."

"It's got something to do with me?"

"Uh-huh." He shifted around on his seat until his

back rested against the door. "Well, Jake had a little talk with me today, and—"

She muttered a word that made Travis's eyebrows shoot up in surprise. "I suppose he warned you to leave me alone."

"That about covers it," Travis agreed. "Dillon did the same thing, and in a way, I guess Alex did, too."

So angry she could barely see straight, she pulled the pickup over to the side of the road. "What did they say?"

Travis held up both palms. "Not much. Just that you'd had a rough time lately and you're too vulnerable to get mixed up with a guy right now."

"Oh, for the love of Pete." Grace smacked the steering wheel with the heel of her hand. She inhaled a deep breath and wished she'd been born with patience. "So now, you're wondering what on earth happened to poor little Grace, aren't you?"

"Yeah. Wouldn't you?"

"I suppose, but honestly..." She ground her back teeth together for a moment. "Well, it's nothing you need to concern yourself with, Travis. I had a...well, I guess I'd call it a loss recently, but I'm okay. Besides, we're just friends, aren't we?"

Giving her a wicked smile, he leaned across the cab and stroked the side of her face with the backs of his fingers. "I don't know, Grace. I sure like kissing you. I like dancing with you, too. I don't know about anything more serious than that just yet, but I'd have to say the potential for more is there."

"Even after half my family's warned you to stay away from poor little me?"

"It wasn't quite like that. It was more like," he lowered his voice in a fair imitation of Jake, "Listen, cowboy, keep your horny hands and lips off my baby sister."

She burst out laughing. "Lord, you must think I'm an emotional train wreck."

"That's not how I see you," he said. "Not at all."

"Yeah? How do you see me, then?"

"You're a survivor. Sometimes there's a sadness in your eyes that tells me you really have had a tough time. But you still have your sense of humor. You're staying productive and taking good care of your kids. You're miles from folding, and you're too resilient to let much of anything take you down."

"Thanks," she said. "It's nice to know *some*body thinks I'm competent enough to handle my own life."

"Competent? Honey, you practically run that whole ranch."

She shot him a doubtful glance. "No way, Sullivan. Jake's the boss."

"Jake *thinks* he's the boss, and he's convinced the rest of you that he's in charge," Travis said. "But you control the heart and soul of the place."

"The kitchen?"

"Never underestimate the power of a kitchen. Especially yours."

Wondering where that crazy mind of his was heading, she asked, "You've got a half-baked theory to explain this?"

"It's fully baked. Just think about it." Ticking items off on his fingers, he continued. "Whatever anybody who works on the Flying M needs, you provide it. You feed them the best food in the world. You have a continual supply of good coffee. You keep the winter gear clean, dry and mended. You handle phone calls so well, you're the message center. And you keep that huge calendar updated, so it only takes a glance to figure out what work needs to be done next.''

''Anybody could do that.''

''Ha! Go on a two-week vacation and see how well they get along without you,'' he suggested. ''I'd give 'em five days to start screaming for you to come home.''

She grinned at the mental image he'd painted for her. ''Okay, I've got you figured out now. You're not an alien. You're a reincarnated cheerleader, right?''

''No, I mean it, Grace. You don't give yourself half as much credit as you deserve. If you want to change how your family sees you, first you have to change how you see yourself.''

''Wait a minute. I thought you were on my side, but it sounds like you think it's my fault they all treat me like a little kid.''

''Fault doesn't matter,'' he said. ''At this point, the only thing that matters is changing their perception of you.''

She mulled over that statement during the last five miles to Cody. Much as she hated to admit it, Travis might have a point. She probably was at least partially responsible for her problems with her siblings.

Her brief fling with teenage rebellion had consisted of dating and marrying a man her family disliked. She'd spent most of her married life defending Johnny and convincing herself that she was the only one who really understood him. When he'd died, her family had closed ranks around her, and she'd been so devastated, she'd gone right back to letting them take care of her again. *Letting?* Shoot, she'd welcomed every bit of help they offered.

She'd turned over her financial problems to Jake. He

still did her tax forms every year and handled her investments from Johnny's life insurance money. Dillon and Zack had faithfully helped with the boys and kept her vehicle running. Alex had encouraged her forays into the world of arts and crafts, and had been a best friend, a big sister, whatever Grace had needed her to be. Cal had given her occasional restaurant work when she'd needed extra cash. Marsh had called her every week or two and listened to her grief, worries and irritations.

And she'd never said, "Okay, that's enough. Thanks, but I'm okay now." She'd just gone along with it because she'd been content to play the role of Johnny's grieving widow until Dillon had forced her to face the truth about her "perfect" husband and marriage.

Damn. Why hadn't she seen this before? She'd been going about this all wrong. Her brothers had been worrying about her for so long, they didn't know any other way to relate to her anymore. And they weren't going to stop treating her the way they did until they had something else to worry about. Something more immediate. But what? Well, she'd think of something.

Changing everybody's perception of her was another proposition. She found a parking spot in downtown Cody and spotted a sign that made her smile. She gave Travis a list of places to shop for his sister-in-law and promised to meet him at the Irma Hotel for pie and coffee at three o'clock.

When he stepped inside a gift shop half a block down the street, Grace hurried into "Designer Manes: Hair With Flair." Alex had had the right idea about updating her image when she'd arranged for Grace's makeover in Billings. But maybe, she just hadn't taken the idea far enough. A stylist who appeared to be somewhere in her early twenties listened as Grace explained what she wanted, then smiled and said, "Piece of cake. Follow me."

Travis stood in front of the Irma Hotel waiting for Grace. She'd been real slick about getting rid of him, but he'd seen a reckless gleam in her eyes. He hadn't thought much about it at first, but now it worried him. He glanced at his watch. She was twenty minutes late. What the heck was she up to?

He scanned the sidewalk on the opposite side of the street. Well, finally. There she was, moving through the crowd with smooth, long-legged strides. Her arms were loaded with shopping bags and she continually turned her head this way and that, as if she was admiring the decorations along the street.

From where he stood, he could see that something about her was different, but he couldn't immediately tell what it was. He waved to attract her attention. A huge smile of recognition flashed across her face and his heart lurched at the sight of it.

Damn, but she was beautiful.

"Sorry I'm late," she said with a chuckle. "I got a little sidetracked."

"I can tell." He relieved her of the shopping bags and turned back toward the hotel. "I didn't realize you still had so much Christmas shopping to do."

"I didn't." She tucked the right side of her hair behind her ear. "These are for me."

He looked at her more closely. There definitely was something different here, but what? Besides the air of excitement about her. Was her makeup more dramatic? Yeah, that was part of it. There was a subtle, reddish sheen to her hair, too. And then he spotted the new silver stud in the upper curve of her ear. She'd been a busy lady, all right.

Before he could think of an appropriate comment, she walked into the hotel as if she owned the place. When they were seated in a booth, Grace asked him to pass her the shopping bags. She poked around until she found something, grabbed her purse and excused herself. She returned five minutes later.

A pair of fancy silver combs held the sides of her hair up and away from her face, exposing tender, kissable parts of her neck usually covered by her hair. The new ear stud stood out in bold relief, and he suddenly realized she was wearing a form-fitting purple sweater with sleeves that ended halfway between her elbows and wrists. He'd never seen that little number on her before. He would have remembered it.

"Well?" She fluffed the hair at the back of her neck. "What do you think?"

"Did it hurt to get your ear pierced up there?" he asked.

"Not too much." She let out an exasperated sigh. "Come on, Travis. Answer the question. What do you think?"

"You'll slap my face if I tell you," he said with a grin.

She sat up straighter, emphasizing the fit of that sweater. "Does that mean you like it?"

"Oh, yeah. I like it just fine," he assured her, nodding enthusiastically.

"What about my hair? I thought about having it cut super short, but I chickened out. I could always go back, though."

"No," he said quickly. Judging from the suspicious

lift to her eyebrows, he figured he'd probably said that too quickly.

"Are you sure? It's only hair, you know. It'll grow back."

"Trust me, it looks great this way."

"But does it change the way I look enough?" she asked. "Or will they all look at me and see the same old Gracie?"

"I don't think so. It's a real sexy look, Grace, but it's the changes on the inside that'll matter the most."

"I know," she said. "But it'll take forever for those guys to notice the inside changes if I don't shake 'em up first with changes on the outside. This is just a whack over the head to get their attention."

Travis let his gaze slowly drift down over her body. "You'll have their attention. I guarantee it."

Grace looked down and lovingly rubbed her palm over the glossy tabletop. After the waiter delivered the pie and filled her coffee mug, she wrapped her fingers around it and deeply inhaled the steam before sipping. It was a purely sensual action, and he wondered why he'd never thought of her as such a sensual creature before this. By the time he'd watched her savor each plump red cherry and smile at each rich spoonful of vanilla ice cream, he was grateful she couldn't see his lap.

At last she pushed her empty plate away and accepted a coffee refill. "What time are you leaving for Powell tomorrow?"

"Probably around five o'clock. Mom wants me to be home in time for the Christmas Eve service."

"It's nice you can be with your family."

He shrugged. "Yeah, I guess."

She frowned. "That doesn't sound very enthusiastic."

"I just spent ten months recuperating at home. We nearly drove each other batty."

"But it's the holidays, Travis. If you don't want to be with your family, where do you want to be?"

The worry in her eyes touched him more deeply than any words she could have said. It had been a long time since anyone had cared that much about his feelings. What would she think if he told her he'd rather spend Christmas with her and the boys? It would be a lot more fun to spend the day watching her confuse the heck out of her siblings than listening to his own family snipe at each other.

As if she'd read his mind, she added, "You're welcome to spend the day with us."

He considered the idea for a moment, but fearing she might feel sorry for him if he told her the truth, he forced a smile. "I wouldn't dream of it. I didn't get to see that much of my brother and his family. I'll have a great time with my nieces."

"Are you sure?"

"Yeah," he said with a laugh. "I promised my mom I'd be there. If I don't show up, she'll have the national guard out looking for me."

"I should hope so," Grace said. "You guys just don't appreciate how important holidays are."

Oh, but he did. After only a few weeks at the Flying M, he knew that his own family's version of the holidays would be pale in comparison with what the McBride clan would share. Grace could rant all she wanted about her siblings, but she wasn't fooling him for a second. If she didn't love them all to the depths of her heart, their opinions of her wouldn't mean squat, but she agonized over them.

Someday for fun, he'd have to see how many times he could criticize Jake or Zack or Dillon before she'd come to their defense. Two? Three? Four at the most, and she'd come at him like a mare guarding her foal. Deep down, the McBrides loved and protected each other in ways he deeply envied.

If he ever had kids, he would want the same kind of family for them. Shoot, he wanted one for himself. He didn't know how you went about building a family like that. But Grace did.

Dang woman really had him going now, didn't she? If he didn't watch himself, she'd have him believing in fairies and magic wands and happily ever afters. It was a good thing he was going back to Powell tomorrow. By the time he came back on the twenty-sixth, he'd remember all the reasons he'd never make a decent husband and father.

Whenever he needed a reality check, he could always count on his loving family to give him one.

Chapter Eight

Christmas morning passed for Grace in the usual crazy whirlwind of opening gifts, cooking breakfast and putting the turkey into the roaster and a ham into the oven before the rest of the family arrived. When Jake and the boys went out to feed the stock, she dashed upstairs to shower and get ready to unveil the "new and improved" Grace.

She'd been wearing her old clothes and keeping her ears covered since her shopping spree in Cody, but today was the day she would strike a major blow for independence. By the time dinner was over today, her sibs would have no idea what to make of her anymore. Too bad Dillon and Marsh wouldn't be here to get the full effect.

Even more, she regretted that Travis wouldn't be here, either. He was the one who'd given her this idea and the courage to carry it out. What a shame for him to miss all the fun.

What was he doing right now? He really hadn't wanted to go home, and he hadn't fooled her a bit when he'd insisted on going anyway. There'd been such a bleakness in his eyes, she'd wanted to comfort him, but she feared he would see it as pity and hate her for it.

She swept the sides of her hair up with the silver combs, checked her makeup one more time and smoothed the hem of the new Christmas sweater she'd bought over her hips. It was amazing that a few small changes could make her look so different and feel so much better about herself. Not that she'd looked bad before. She'd just looked too mommyish, too whole-some, too darn naive to be let out on her own.

Now she looked like a grown woman. And her siblings were bound to notice. Pronouncing herself gorgeous, she hustled down the stairs, humming.

Cal and Emma arrived first. Cal hugged Grace, then stepped back and studied her, eyes widened in surprise. "Damn, Gracie," he said, "you look…good. Real good."

"Good?" Emma shot him an incredulous glance before hugging Grace herself. "She looks fantastic." She pointed at Grace's right ear. "I love that. It really suits you."

"Thanks," Grace said. "I like it, too." She took the green salad and relish tray Cal had brought, and stuck them in the refrigerator.

The back door opened again and in walked Alex, her husband Nolan, and their children, Tasha and Rick. Before she took off her coat, Alex shrieked, "Gracie, your hair looks— Ohmygosh, you got your ear pierced, too? And that sweater is gorgeous on you!"

Nolan gave her a thumbs-up sign. "Who's the lucky guy?"

Smiling, Grace set the vegetable casserole Alex had brought on the work peninsula. "I just felt like making a few changes."

"They're good ones, Aunt Alex," Rick said with a wicked grin. Uh-oh, this kid was going to be a heart-breaker before he turned sixteen.

"No kidding," Tasha said. "When do we get to open presents again?"

"As soon as Zack and his family get here and Jake and the boys are done feeding," Grace said. "You and Rick could set the dining room table for me while you're waiting."

The teenagers made the obligatory, oh-yuck faces, but Grace knew that eventually they would do the job. Dillon and Marsh called to wish everyone a Merry Christmas and to announce Dillon and Blair's engagement. The excitement of that call had barely dissipated when Zack, Lori and Brandon arrived.

Sniffing the air, Brandon clapped both hands over his stomach. "Mmm, Aunt Grace, it sure smells good in here."

"Thank you, Bran—"

"Oh, God…" Lori shoved a big glass bowl of fruit salad in Grace's direction and then bolted into the half bath off the kitchen. The unmistakable sounds of some-body losing her breakfast came through the door.

"Ohh, poor Lori," Emma said with a wince.

"Yeah," Alex agreed.

Nolan and Cal nodded. Grace set down the salad and turned to go after her sister-in-law until she heard Zack and Brandon laughing. Whirling around, she scolded the insensitive clods. "What is the matter with you two?

Poor Lori is sick as a dog and you're laughing at her? And why on earth did you make her go out when she must be feeling lousy?''

Zack's smile cut a white slash in the middle of his beard. "She's not sick."

"Could have fooled me," Cal muttered.

Grace glanced from Zack to Brandon and back to Zack, seeing the delighted pride she'd missed the first time. She held out her arms to Zack and hugged him hard. "Congratulations, Papa Bear." She hugged Brandon next. "And you, too, Brother Bear."

Everyone started talking at once. Lori stepped out of the bathroom and blushed a lovely shade of crimson at the standing ovation she received. Zack scooped her up and held her against him, his expression so tender it brought tears to more than one pair of eyes.

When he finally set her back on her feet, Alex chuckled. "You little sneak. So *that's* why you wouldn't drink margaritas with us in Billings. I even asked you once if you were pregnant, remember?"

"I didn't mean to lie to you, Alex," Lori said. "I just wasn't sure yet and I didn't want to get anyone's hopes up in case it was a false alarm."

"It's wonderful news, honey," Cal said.

"You'll be next, Cal," Zack said.

Emma shrugged. "Works for me. If Cal wants to have a baby, I'll even hold his hand through labor."

While everyone was still laughing over Emma's blithe remark, Grace noticed Lori smiling directly at her and tapping the upper part of her right ear. "It looks very chic."

"What does?" Zack asked.

"Grace's new earring," Lori said.

Zack glanced at Grace, then did a double take and

studied her from head to toe, his eyebrows forming the beginnings of a frown. Promising herself that no matter how stupid Zack or Jake acted, she would not lose her temper, Grace shot him a grin and carried the fruit salad to the refrigerator.

"Do you need to lie down, Lori?" Alex asked.

Lori shook her head. "It seems to be a once-a-day thing. I'll be fine now until tomorrow morning."

Jake and the boys came into the mudroom. Alex yanked open the door and blurted out the news about Lori's pregnancy. When the excitement died down again, Grace shooed everyone into the living room to finish opening the gifts from one family unit to another, as well as the big boxes from their parents. They'd better have those gifts opened by the time their parents' call came through, or there would be hell to pay.

By some miracle, Grace managed to get through the presents and dinner without a direct confrontation with Zack or Jake. She'd been receiving some mighty long, hard stares from the two of them, though. And now Cal was doing it, too.

Darn it, she wished Travis was here, and not just because he could lend her some extra courage, either. She simply...missed him. She missed his company, seeing his eyes glint with amusement, hearing the sound of his voice. Not to mention the ever present possibility that he might take it into his head to kiss her again. That alone was enough to add some real zing to a woman's day.

She got up to clear the table and couldn't hold back a laugh when she remembered the appalled expression on Jake's face when Travis had dared to do a little "women's work."

"What's so funny, Gracie?" Zack asked.

"Nothing much, Zackie."

Brandon's eyes widened and one side of his upper lip curled away from his teeth in disgust. "Zackie?"

"She's just bein' a smart aleck, son," Zack assured him.

"I kind of like it, though," Emma said. "Makes you sound kind of...sweet, Zackie. What do you think, Lori?"

"Don't answer that," Zack said.

"Okay, Zackie," Lori replied.

Jake scowled at Grace. "Now, wait a minute. There's no reason to pick on Zack that way. He only called Gracie by the name we've all used for her since she was born. It's just an affectionate little nickname."

Grace gave him a tight smile. Now that people were laughing at one of the guys, he'd had enough. Well, wasn't that just too darn bad? She wasn't about to back off now. "So maybe I want to use affectionate little nicknames for you guys, too. Jakie."

Everyone but Jake, Zack and Cal cracked up. Jake's face turned a dull, reddish color, a sure sign that his temper was hanging by a fraying thread. "Cut that out."

"I will if you will," Grace offered.

The boys were actually whooping now. Grace settled them down with "the look," a scowl Steven swore could peel the hide off an old bull at fifty yards.

"That's enough, Gracie," Cal demanded. "Stop it right now."

Infuriated by his parental tone, Grace turned "the look" on him. "You want a piece of this, Caleb?"

"Take it easy," Alex interjected. "It's not that big of a deal."

Grace gave Alex credit for saying that with a smile,

but it wasn't going to get her off the hook for siding with the guys on this one. "I don't agree. I know you've all done a lot for me over the years, and I appreciate it. But I've done a lot for all of you, too, and I deserve to be treated with the same respect you give each other."

Jake glared at her. "Alex is right. It's Christmas for God's sake, and this isn't the time or place to hash this out."

"Whatever you say, oh wise one, but this isn't over." Grace collected a load of plates and carried them to the kitchen. Emma and Lori followed and took turns hugging her.

"One step at a time," Lori said.

"That's right," Emma agreed. "Just keep working on them and you'll get through those granite heads one of these days."

"I wish I was that patient," Grace said. "But I'm not."

"Wait a minute." Emma leaned closer, studying her face. "That smile looks really evil. What are you planning to do?"

"I don't know yet, but I'm sure something will come to me. And when it does, they're all gonna get it." The telephone rang. Grace crossed the room and answered it. "Yes, thank you, operator." She covered the mouthpiece with her hand. "Go get everyone. It's our Christmas call from the folks."

While Emma was gone, Grace spoke to both sets of McBride parents, who sounded as if they were using a speaker phone. "Hello, Mamas and Papas. Merry Christmas! How are you?" Smiling and nodding, she listened to their replies. Glancing up, she made sure all of her siblings were in the room.

"Everybody's fine here," she said. "We just finished dinner."

As expected, the mamas wanted to know how many people had been at the table. Grace could have kissed both of them. After what her brothers and Alex had just pulled, the opportunity was too golden to resist. "There were thirteen of us today. Why so many? Well, it was just the family."

Grace heard several strangled gasps and when she looked at her siblings again, four huge pairs of eyes, silently begged her to shut up. She smiled sweetly at them. "No, you're right, Dillon and Marsh are in California. So how did we get thirteen? Well, gee, hasn't anybody sent you a wedding announcement?"

She held the receiver away from her ear until the screaming subsided. Then she said, "No, it's not who's *getting* married, it's who already *got* married. Alex was first. Uh-huh. She married Nolan Larson. That's right. And then Zack was next. He's got a ten-year-old stepson, and his wife's expecting another baby next summer. Isn't that wonderful?"

She had to hold the receiver away from her ear again to save her hearing. When the screaming died down, she continued. "Wait, I'm not finished. Cal got married, too. You'll love his wife. She's a mechanic. Uh-huh. And wait'll you see his tattoo. What's that, Mama? Did Jake know about all of this? Of course, he did. He helped plan the weddings. I thought he'd told you or I would've sent a telegram."

Before she could say one more syllable, Jake ripped the phone out of her hand and immediately went into what a political analyst would have called "damage control." Zack, Alex and Cal dragged Grace into the hallway.

"Dammit, Gracie, you know what they're like," Zack snarled.

"I can't believe you did that," Alex said.

Cursing under his breath, Cal jerked his right hand through his hair. "Why the hell did you tell them?"

Grace patted his shoulder as if he were one of her boys. "I only did it for your own good. The mamas would have found out someday that you all got married before they came home. Wouldn't you rather get the hysterics over with while they're still an ocean and a contintent away?"

"That wasn't your decision to make," Zack said.

"That never stopped you," Grace returned with a smile. "And you've made so many important decisions for me, I thought I should return the favor."

"Favor! Dammit, Gracie, we've always covered for each other," Alex said.

"No, you and the guys all covered for each other, but you never missed an opportunity to tattle on me. I always wanted to be one of you, but I never have been and I never will be if you can't see me as an equal. You treated me like a bratty little sister today, and that's what you got. Deal with it."

"You did this for revenge?" Cal demanded.

"That part held a certain appeal," Grace admitted. "But where do you guys get off keeping a secret like getting married from our parents? It's bad enough you didn't give them a chance to come home for your weddings—"

Zack waved a hand toward the kitchen. "If we'd done that, the mamas would have been on the next flight. They would have taken over all the plans and we'd be damn lucky if any of us would even be married by now."

"You're exaggerating."

"Not much. Jeez, would you listen to that?"

In the quiet, Jake's voice carried from the kitchen. "Yes, Mama. Yes, Mama Lucy. We just didn't want to interrupt your trip. Of course I know family's the most important thing in the world. There's not a clinker in the bunch, I promise."

Grace dismissed Jake's troubles with a snort. "You're all big cowards. You're talking about two sweet, loving women who only want us all to be happy. So they tend to get overly emotional at weddings. Big deal. You won't melt if they cry on you. The very least you should have done was tell them you got married and sent them some pictures they could show off."

"Maybe we just wanted to enjoy being married for a while without having to listen to one of their big hoo-ha scenes," Zack grumbled.

"Oh, now I get it," Grace said. "What you're really saying is, if it's easier and more comfortable for you to keep a secret, it doesn't matter if you hurt someone else. Is that what you're gonna teach Brandon and the new baby? Don't worry about honesty, kids. Go for whatever's expedient."

"We'd have told them when we were ready," Zack said.

"Would that have been before or after you picked them up at the airport in Cody? Forget it, big brother. You guys have been playing God with your secrets for too long. You didn't learn a damn thing from what you did to me. Maybe now you will."

"This doesn't just affect us," Cal protested. "Now our spouses and the kids are gonna get caught in the cross fire."

Grace shook her head at him. "The mamas don't

work that way, and you know it. They'll love your spouses. They'll adore their new grandkids. But they'll be furious at you, and you deserve every lecture you're gonna get in English and Italian. That's why you're so upset.''

All three of them looked at their feet. Grace waited to see if they wanted to add anything, and when none did, she went upstairs wondering if she'd just ruined her relationships with her siblings forever. Okay, so maybe she had acted a bit impulsively. And maybe she *did* feel some remorse.

But why should she? Everything she'd said was the truth, and if they'd just been reasonable and listened to her for once... On the other hand, if she'd had another half hour for her anger to cool she probably wouldn't have gone so far. She hadn't expected her bid for independence and equality to be quite this painful. Lord, but she wished Travis were here to help her keep things in perspective.

Travis parked his pickup beside the guest house later that night. Relishing the silence, he just sat there and looked up at the stars. What an odd day. He'd gone home and felt like a stranger. Now he'd returned to the Flying M, and it felt like he'd come home. He'd even brought his blueprints along in case he found the nerve to show them to Grace.

He turned on the dome light, glanced at his watch and grimaced. It was too late to disturb Grace, but he felt too restless even to think about going to bed. Well, maybe he'd check out the action in the barn. He crossed the yard and opened the door.

A light burned in the back, somewhere near the over-size stall they called the delivery room, but he didn't hear anything. Cows could be dang quiet when they were giving birth though, even when they were having trouble. He walked through the building to make sure everything was all right back there.

As it turned out, there was a first-calf heifer who looked big enough to pop out a calf or two any second. She raised her head and looked at him, her red-and-white face perfectly placid. Evidently he didn't look too interesting; she turned away and went back to chewing her cud.

Travis checked the other stalls, but they were all empty. Then he heard a funny little sighing sound and turned around to find Grace, sitting on a small stack of hay bales with her legs stretched out in front of her. Sound asleep, she had a blanket wrapped around her shoulders, a disreputable cowboy hat tipped sideways and the back of her head resting against the rough wall.

A sudden warmth and tenderness filled his chest. She really looked whipped, and unless the light was fooling his eyes, there were dried tear tracks running from her eyes to her chin. Aw hell, what had those brothers of hers done now? They weren't bad guys, really, but they sure were stubborn, and he shouldn't have left her alone to try to make a point with them.

He sat down beside her, slid his arm behind her shoulders and pulled her against him. Her hat fell off as she snuggled her face into the crook of his neck. Gently rubbing her arm and shoulder, he stretched his own legs out and allowed a contented sigh to slip from between his lips.

This felt good to him. Better than good, it felt right. He'd wanted this far more than any wrapped-up presents underneath the tree at his parents' house. He couldn't say when or how Grace had gotten to be such an important part of his days. Only that she had. He gave her a one-armed hug.

Her lips curved into a sleepy smile and she rubbed her cheek against his puffy ski jacket. He kissed her temple. Her smile deepened and a moment later, her eyelids slowly lifted.

"Travis?"

He nudged her head back under his chin "Yeah, it's me. Didn't mean to wake you."

She let out a yawn and shook her head as if to clear it. "'S okay. I need to check on that cow."

"I just did. She's fine. Go back to sleep."

"'Kay." Grace closed her eyes, but she kept on talking. "How was your Christmas?"

"All right. I missed you, though."

That made her smile again. "You did? That's nice. I missed you, too."

"Good. How'd your new earring go over?"

She laughed, but didn't open her eyes. "Like a pregnant pole vaulter."

"That bad, huh?"

"Worse. It wasn't really about the earring, though. We just got into a big hassle." She sniffled and a tear leaked out of her right eye. "I ruined everybody's Christmas."

"All by yourself? I don't believe that."

"Yeah, I did." More sniffles. More tears. "And they all hate me now."

"Want to tell me what happened?"

She nodded, sat up straighter and swiped at her eyes with her knuckles. Then she told him a long, half-garbled story about nicknames at the dinner table and a phone call from her parents. Tears flowed in a continuous stream. When she said she'd ratted out her siblings, he didn't know whether to laugh or cry with her. If she'd been half as furious as she'd been that night in Billings and finally let all that anger loose, God help the others. And now she was beating herself up with guilt.

"Hey, sweetheart," he said. "Give it some time."

"I never should have done that."

"Maybe so," he said. "But then again, maybe not."

"Oh, right." She took the handkerchief he offered, scrubbed her face and blew her nose. "They would've gotten in trouble on their own anyway. I should've let them keep their stupid secrets."

"It's not for me to say in this case, but secrets can be real hurtful. One of 'em I kept blew up in my face and hurt a fine woman, and I'll regret that 'til I die. If I'd just been honest with her, I could've saved us both a lot of grief."

"Your wife?"

"My ex-wife. Her name was Bridget. I never should've married her."

"Why did you?"

"She was pregnant. I figured it was my responsiblity to stand up like a man and support her and my kid. But I didn't love her."

"And you kept that a secret?"

Travis nodded. "She didn't want any part of marrying me at first, but when I told her I really loved her, she gave in. We got married the next week and a month later she miscarried."

"Oh, Travis."

"Yeah." He clasped her hand in his and gave it a squeeze. "She turned to me for comfort and I didn't have any to give her. I was sad about losing the baby, all right, but when I looked at her, all I could think about was leaving.''

''What happened?''

''She figured out what I'd done and gave me a no-fault divorce. Then she got back into her tight jeans and turned into a party girl. Every time I'd come through on the circuit she was out with a different guy, drinking more heavily, looking more dead inside.''

''Couldn't you talk to her? Help her somehow?''

''Hell, I tried lots of times. I even offered to pay for her to go into rehab. But the only thing she ever said to me was that now we were just alike. Footloose and always ready for the next new love to come along. I felt like such a crud, my own party days ended overnight. That's why I'm not a big fan of keeping secrets anymore. When you think about it, letting somebody believe something that's not true is pretty much the same as lying.''

Grace looked away for a moment. ''You're right. My brothers have been making a habit of it. Now Alex has done it, too, and it's not right. So why do I still feel so darn guilty?''

''I don't know. The dust hasn't even started to settle yet. Believe it or not, some good things might come out of this mess.''

''Like what?''

''Like, maybe your folks will learn that when they make such a fuss over something, it makes their kids really uncomfortable. So maybe they'll learn to tone it down.''

Grace laughed. ''And maybe that pregnant heifer's gonna go out and climb a pine tree. Where their children are concerned, our mamas are absolutely unstoppable. As big and tough and stubborn as they are, Jake, Zack,

Dillon and Cal can't stand up to them. When you get right down to it, neither can the papas.''

"Why not?" Travis asked. "That's the part I don't get."

"It's because the mamas are so sweet and loving and they cry like you're breaking their hearts if you won't do what they think is right for you. They could make the Pope feel guilty if they put their minds to it. Then they slip in and out of Italian and you get all confused by the words you can't remember, and you really hate to see them get so upset. I think the guys just adore them too much to disappoint them. We all do.''

"What about Marsh?" Travis asked.

"He charms them," Grace said with a grin. "He gives them just enough of what they want to keep them happy while he goes off and does what he wants. But he's the only one who ever gets away with that.''

Travis chuckled softly. "Sounds like he's quite a guy.''

Grace nodded. "He is. I wish he'd come home more often.''

"He's probably afraid they'll catch on to him and make him stay here.''

Surprise flashed over Grace's face, and then she laughed out loud. "I've never thought of it that way, but I'll bet you're right.''

"That's a nice sound, you know.''

"What sound?''

"Your laughter. I'm glad you found it again.''

"Oh, Travis." She sniffled and took a deep breath as if she might start crying again.

He shook his head at her. When he'd been watching her make the centerpieces, he'd sneaked a sprig of mistletoe from her collection and stuck it into his shirt pocket. He'd tacked it up out here, hoping to catch her alone sometime. Now was as good a time as any. He pointed to the beam overhead.

She looked up, then gave him a misty smile. "How did that get there?"

"Must've been one of Santa's elves," Travis said solemnly. "They're real sneaky little fellas."

"Uh-huh." Her smile widened. Her eyes sparkled with amusement. "That's a pretty high beam for elves. I suspect they had help. Maybe from a big cowboy."

"Yeah, it was probably Jake."

When she laughed, he pulled her closer and framed her face with his hands. "Merry Christmas, darlin'. I've wanted to do this all day."

Chapter Nine

When Travis's mouth settled on hers, Grace felt an infusion of heat in the region of her heart. Oh, wow. This was no ordinary mistletoe kiss. It was a Christmas fantasy come to life. It was skipping all the frogs and going straight to the prince. And in her eyes, Travis was a prince.

She loved his physical strength, loved knowing she aroused him as much as he aroused her, loved his taste and his touch and the way he smelled. She slid her hands inside his coat and tried to tug his shirttail out of the waistband of his jeans. Trapping her hands against his sides with his elbows, he kissed her again and again, delving into the depths of her mouth with his tongue.

"Careful there, sweetheart," he said, he voice low and gritty. "I want you so much, I'm liable to go crazy if you touch me like that."

She nipped at his lower lip. "Maybe I want you to go crazy."

He groaned and pulled her even closer, rocking his pelvis against hers. "I've been thinking about you and me being naked together. Touching each other. Making love with each other."

"Me, too," she admitted. "So much it shocks me."

"Will you come back to the guest house with me tonight?" He pressed his lips to her forehead and she sensed he was holding his breath while he waited for her answer. She smiled at the sweetness of it, and slowly nodded.

His pent-up breath escaped in soft, warm puffs that struck her face. Then he moved back far enough to smile into her eyes. "Thank God. I didn't want our first time together to be in a drafty old barn."

Travis wrapped his left arm around her shoulders. She slid her right arm around his waist. They hurried side by side across the barnyard and entered the guest house by the kitchen door.

Flipping on the light, Travis left her to take off her boots on the throw rug just inside the doorway, walked to the thermostat and turned up the heat. The oil furnace whooshed into life, tossing off a smoky scent that would vanish with time. Shedding his coat, he came back to her, his eyes narrowed with intent, his beautiful mouth pulled taut with restraint, his hands already reaching for her.

She wanted him. Her blood heated. Her body softened in anticipation. An echo of an instinctive, feminine fear of a thoroughly aroused male skittered across her nerve endings, making her shiver. Old doubts rose up to haunt her. She hadn't been woman enough to keep Johnny faithful. Would Travis find her lacking, too?

As if he could hear what was going on in her head, Travis paused and gave her a potent, reassuring smile. "It's all right. I won't hurt you." Though his voice was gruff, his fingertips moved over her cheek in an exquisitely gentle arc.

Unable to meet his gaze, she fiddled with the snaps on his shirt. "I know you won't," she murmured. "It's just…I've only been with one man in my whole life. I want to please you, but I don't think I ever was much good at this."

He slid his fingers into the sides of her hair, tipping up her chin and teasing her lips with airy kisses. "This isn't a test, sweetheart. We'll take it easy."

Nodding, she pasted a smile on her lips, took the hand he held out to her and let him coax her into the bedroom. He switched on a small bedside lamp and turned back to face her. With slow, deliberate movements, he peeled off her coat and draped it over a straight-backed wooden chair sitting beside the rumpled bed.

His eyes widened when he saw her clingy Christmas sweater, and then a slow, seductive smile spread from his lips to his eyes. Taking her hands in his, he held her arms away from her body; his obvious approval made her breath quicken, her breasts tingle. He released her hands and traced her shape from under her arms to her waist and over the curve of her hips, murmuring, "You're beautiful."

He lowered his head and kissed her, gently at first, and then with a growing passion that drove all doubts and insecurities from her mind. There was no past. The future didn't matter. There was only this man and this moment, and she intended to enjoy them with every bit of her body and soul.

Exploring the inside of her mouth with his tongue, he crushed her to him. A groan rumbled out of his throat. Kissing him made her feel drunk, dizzy and wonderfully alive. She grasped his shoulders and held on tight. His hands crept under the hem of her sweater, his palms and fingers kneading the bare flesh at her sides and her lower back, gradually moving higher until his thumbs brushed the undersides of her breasts.

He continued to kiss her over and over, as if he were feeding on her lips. It was her turn to groan. She loved his kisses, but she wanted more. Wanted to feel his palms cupping her breasts, his fingers teasing and caressing her nipples. Well, if she did those things to him, maybe he'd get the idea.

One at a time, she popped open the snaps on his shirt, then gently raked her fingernails across his upper chest, then down over his sides. His skin twitched, the muscles underneath tightening as if he might be ticklish. She felt him smile against her lips.

"Watch those cold hands," he said.

She stroked his abdomen and slid her palms up his chest, burying her fingers in the triangular patch of hair growing there. "They don't feel cold to me."

He shivered, then laughed and caught her hands before she could get him again. "Well, they do to me, and I'm going to have to fix that." Raising them to his lips, he blew on her fingertips. Holding her gaze with his, he took them into his mouth one by one and bathed them with his tongue.

They warmed up, all right. The heat started under her nails and swept up her arms, across her shoulders to her collarbone and straight down her torso to a spot low in her belly. Her knees turned mushy as squashed bananas, and she leaned heavily against Travis to keep herself from melting into a lust-ridden puddle of hormones at his feet.

She was still fully dressed. He'd hardly done a thing but kiss her, and she was almost ready to rip off his clothes and her own, shove him onto the bed and have her way with him if he didn't start moving things along a little faster.

Didn't he know it was cruel to get a woman so excited if he wasn't going to satisfy her? She could feel his impressive hardness through the barriers of their jeans, and after so much kissing and petting, she doubted any man would last long enough to take her over the top with him.

She jerked her hands free and raised them to the back of his neck, pulling him down for a deep, wet kiss that should have made his toes curl up inside his boots. Then she rocked her hips against his, trying to communicate a sense of urgency. He made a muffled sound against her lips. Breathing hard, she pulled back.

"Take it easy, honey." He hugged her against him again and nibbled a wicked, arousing path from her earlobe, down the side of her neck. "We've got all night."

"No, it doesn't have to take that long."

His head came up and he studied her with a perplexed frown. "Doesn't have to?"

The incredulous note in his voice told her she'd said something wrong. She felt embarrassed, but couldn't see the problem. She'd never made love all night with Johnny, not even on their honeymoon. Oh, why hadn't she remembered that before now? She really wasn't any good at this.

"What did you mean?" he asked. "Have I done something you didn't like?"

"No. It's been lovely, but…" She couldn't finish that sentence out loud. It would sound too crude.

"But what?" He tucked her hair behind her ears, while his eyes silently willed her to talk. "This is definitely not the time to keep secrets."

He was right. If they were going to be lovers, he might as well know how she felt about certain things. "I just don't want you to get too excited, you know?"

"Why not?"

"Because then it'll be over too fast, and I'll be unhappy."

Comprehension dawned in his eyes, and he slowly nodded. "Yeah, I can see how you'd feel upset if it happened that way."

"If?" she asked. "Isn't that the way it always happens?"

"I guess it probably happens to most guys once in a while, but it sure doesn't have to happen all the time. And even when it does, there are other ways to please a woman."

"I knew about that, sort of. I mean, I've read women's magazines, and they have lots of articles about improving your sex life, but do people really *do* any of those things?"

"Sure they do. Why not if it makes your partner happy?"

Now, wasn't that interesting? Johnny had never been willing to talk about her needs in bed, much less try anything new, and she'd just assumed other men probably felt the same way. Whenever she'd heard other married women talking about sex, it had sounded as if they hadn't found it to be anything worth fussing over. Besides, she wouldn't have risked asking questions like that of anyone in Sunshine Gap. Her family hadn't liked

Johnny in the first place, and if even a hint of problems in their marital bed had ever leaked onto the grapevine, he never would have heard the end of it. But dammit, how could she have married such a selfish jerk?

"Grace?"

She looked up and thought she saw a hundred questions in Travis's eyes. Oh, jeez. At best, he must think she was an ignorant fool. She certainly did. She didn't have a clue what to say to him, either. She tried to turn away, but he grasped her shoulders and held her there.

"I'm not him," Travis said.

"I know you're not."

"Then trust me enough to let me show you what it's like to make love with me."

She wrapped her arms around herself and looked at her stocking feet. "I don't think that's a good idea right now. I seem to have lost the mood."

"That's all right. Why don't we just lie down and snuggle? I'll set the alarm, so if we fall asleep, you'll still wake up in plenty of time to go back to the other house before anybody else gets up."

Eyeing him doubtfully, she asked, "Wouldn't it be better for you if I just left now?"

He smiled. "I want your body, woman, there's no doubt about it. But I don't mind snuggling. If that's all you want, that's all you're gonna get."

She was mortified over what she'd revealed to this man, but he hadn't laughed at her. The thought of going home to her lonely bed held zero appeal. "Okay."

While he took off his boots, pulled his heavy belt free of his jeans and fiddled with his alarm clock, she folded back the bedspread, straightened the sheets and blankets and crawled in on top of them. She grabbed one pillow and rolled onto her left side. Uh-oh. Big mistake here. The pillowcase smelled just as good as Travis.

The mattress dipped as he climbed into bed behind her. His long legs had no place to go but right up against the backs of hers. His broad shoulders and massive chest blocked most of the light and when he draped his arm around her waist and "snuggled" her bottom and her back against his front, the double bed shrank to the size of a tea bag.

He pulled the bedspread over them. All by himself, he had her surrounded with his heat, his scent and his gentleness. She inhaled a deep, ragged breath, and knew she was a goner.

Travis figured it was going to be one long, hellish night. Having Grace's curvy little rump so close to his groin and her breasts practically draped over his forearm would leave him harder than an ax handle. He wasn't about to kick her out of his bed, though. In fact, after the conclusions he'd drawn about what her marriage must have been like, there was nothing he wanted more than to show her that some guys weren't total pigs.

It looked to be a tough assignment. She was all huddled up in a rigid mass of tension, as if she expected him to jump her whether or not she'd "lost the mood." He laid one hand flat against her back. Impossible as it seemed, she tensed even more.

"It's okay," he murmured. "Relax or you won't get any rest."

She didn't relax, but she didn't pull away, either. Taking that for assent, he gently rubbed her back from her neck to her hips. It took five solid minutes of massage, but muscle by muscle, she finally started to let go. After another five minutes her neck and shoulders were nice and loose, and she was practically purring.

"Where did you learn to do that?" she asked.

"You see a lot of sore muscles on the circuit and we tried to help each other out when we could. A bull rider from Texas gave some of us lessons. Pretty good, huh?"

"Mmm. If you could bottle that, you'd make a fortune."

Laughing softly, he turned off the light, settled in behind her again and put his arm back around her waist. Ah, this was much better. Of course, without the distraction of giving a massage, her nearness had a predictable effect on his body, but for one night he could live with it. Neither of them spoke for a while. Then, out of the darkness, he heard a soft, hesitant voice. "Travis?"

"What, darlin'?"

"What if I changed my mind about making love?"

"You mean you want to now?"

She rolled over to face him. He couldn't see her face, but maybe she needed that. "Yeah. I want to know what I've missed, and I want you to be the one to show me."

"Are you sure? That was just a back rub. No obligations implied."

"I know. That's why I'm asking you to do this for me, too. No obligations implied."

"All right, but you'll have to do one thing for me."

"What's that?"

"Forget what you thought you knew about sex before tonight. You're free to say no to anything, but you're going to show me what you like or tell me what you want."

"That's two things," she pointed out.

"So sue me."

He kissed her while she was still chuckling, and she

responded with a joyful sweetness that made his heart race and his palms sweat just like they had the first time he'd done this. If he messed this up, he would never forgive himself. She sighed and moved closer to him, and his momentary fears vanished. Focusing on her pleasure would help him delay his own, and even at his worst, he would do better than that idiot who'd left her frustrated and unhappy for so long.

Deepening his kisses, he slowly unbuttoned her pretty sweater, lavishing her soft skin with caresses, concentrating on her neck, shoulders and upper chest. She plunged her fingers into his hair and nudged his head in the direction of her breasts. He obliged her, smoothing both sweater and bra out of his way. If she noticed, she didn't object.

He wished he could turn on the light and see her facial expressions as well as the luscious curves he was touching and tasting, but he didn't want to jar her out of this moment. Judging by her sighs and moans, he was doing pretty well working by feel alone. She tugged on his hair until he took her nipple into his mouth and laved it with his tongue.

She tasted like warm, dark honey, and she was so sensitive there, her hips arched right off the bed. Moving on to her other breast, he swept his hand over the indentation at her waist, then slid his fingers down inside the waistband of her jeans, stroking her belly, barely grazing the curls where her thighs came together. She writhed and moaned, giving him such clear nonverbal cues, he didn't need any verbal ones to give her what she wanted.

He loved it. Loved her responsiveness. Loved knowing she trusted him enough to give her body into his care.

Slipping her jeans and panties down her long, smooth legs, he kissed his way across her torso to her belly-button and swirled his tongue around inside it before caressing her intimately with his fingertips. Oh, man, she was moist and ready for him now, but he wasn't going to interrupt the proceedings to find a condom, or take any chances that she wouldn't be completely satisfied after making love with him. No way.

He parted her soft folds repeatedly, coaxing her most sensitive flesh out of hiding. Her breath came in harsh, choppy little pants now, and the skin between her hip-bones heated beneath his lips. She dug her heels into the mattress and raised her pelvis in time with the movements of his fingers, driving him deeper inside her with every stroke.

Moving back up her body, he nuzzled her breasts again while maintaining the rhythm with his fingers. "That's it, darlin'. You're almost there and it feels good, doesn't it?"

Yes, yes, she *was* almost there, but it felt better than good. More like stupendous. Fabulous. If there were words to describe these incredible sensations, she didn't know them. His deep, gravelly voice caressed her ears, as his clever fingers teased and stroked fire through her body.

Were those bizarre little whimpers actually coming out of her mouth? She didn't care. Her only goal was to cling to his voice while she finished this wild ride he was giving her. Now he'd gone back to suckling her nipples and the fire flowed in both directions, consuming her with a delicious heat she couldn't resist.

"Oh, yeah, darlin'," he said. "Let go now. I'll be right here to catch you, so just let go."

Something inside her obeyed, and it was like falling

off a cliff backward, seeing rainbows of colors on the way down and landing on a soft, shimmering pool of water. For a moment she went under and floated in a world of sensation so pure and golden, it nearly made her weep at the beauty of it. Gradually she rose to the surface and Travis was there, holding her, kissing her, praising her as if she'd just done the most wonderful thing in the world.

But he had it all turned around. He was the one who'd been wonderful. Oh dear. He hadn't even...and he was kissing her again, and she needed to catch her breath. Clasping the sides of his face, she tore her mouth free.

"Wait a minute," she said.

"What is it?"

"Turn on the light. Please." She heard a click, and then a sudden bright flash blinded her. She raised one hand to shade her eyes, and gradually a big dark shape materialized beside her.

"Is something wrong?" he asked.

She still couldn't see his face clearly, but he sounded so worried, she had to smile. "No. This is the rightest it's ever been for me, but what about you? I mean, I really don't want you to be left out of the fun."

Finally his face came into focus, and she found herself looking up at a smug, yet delightfully wicked grin. He slowly trailed one hand from her neck to her knees, detouring to caress her curves in between. "I had lots of fun."

She trailed her own hand down his chest, teasing the bare skin under the open front panels of his shirt. Smiling at his moan of pleasure, she explored the hard ridge of flesh trapped behind the zipper of his jeans. "Don't you think you're overdressed for the occasion?"

He cleared his throat. "Yeah. You're right. Sure is hot in here all of a sudden."

They were both so eager to get him out of his clothes they kept getting in each other's way and ended up in a laughing tangle of arms and legs. The job eventually got done, however, and she couldn't help being fascinated with his naked body. His upper body had well-defined, iron-hard muscles that looked better to her than a body builder's. His lower body was nothing less than a work of art.

She'd never thought about the leg muscles it would take to stop a young, healthy steer running full out. Obviously, it took quite a few, and they all looked gloriously powerful. Even his butt had sculpted muscles on it. She was used to seeing big, strong, good-looking men with their clothes on, but if the world of advertising ever caught Travis in the nude, she suspected steer wrestling might become as popular as football or baseball.

Touching him tentatively, she traced the long, ropy muscles from his ankle to his knee to his thigh. They flexed and rippled under his skin and he groaned softly when she moved on. She wrapped her fingers around his manhood and caressed it with gentle strokes. "Tell me what you like."

"You're doin' fine." He sucked in a harsh breath and tipped back his head, making the sinews in his neck stand out. "Real fine."

Smiling, she became bolder and discovered the joys of pleasing a man who occasionally groaned or muttered earthy comments, but clearly enjoyed everything she did. She felt powerful and aroused and sexy in ways she hadn't known she could. Finally he announced he couldn't take any more fooling around and playfully rolled her onto her back.

Kissing her deeply, he ran his hands all over her, then produced a condom from the night stand. When he was ready, she eagerly reached for him and when he slowly entered her, she wrapped herself around him and held on tight. She couldn't imagine a better fit, physically or emotionally.

If the first time had been a wild ride, this one was sheer magic. The sensations were the same, but a hundred times more powerful because she knew he felt them, too. It was a horizontal dance, slow and sensuous one moment, hot and fast the next, and always, they moved together through the ancient choreography that led them to a shattering peak of satisfaction.

He fell into that shimmering pool with her and held her safely in his big arms until they surfaced again. Exhausted, but absolutely happy and satisfied, she draped one arm across his chest and gave him a sleepy smile. "It wasn't just me with a problem, was it?"

"No, sweetheart. It wasn't your problem at all."

Travis pulled her closer, knowing she was falling asleep and savoring the moment until he began to feel the chill in the air. He reached down and dragged the jumbled covers over them. After taking one last look at Grace's peaceful face, he switched off the light.

Lying there in the darkness with her in his arms, he realized the feeling of coming home he'd experienced earlier hadn't had anything to do with returning to the Flying M or parking by the guest house. That had only been a rehearsal.

This was the real thing. Holding and kissing and

making love with this woman gave him all those feelings of belonging he'd craved his whole life. Suddenly he understood the power the McBride women held over their families.

Chapter Ten

Grace awoke in Travis's bed before the alarm went off. She lay there in the dark for a moment, enjoying the warmth of their shared body heat and reliving the thrill of his lovemaking. If she had her way, she'd stay right here all day. Unfortunately that was not an option.

Real life was about to intrude and there was no way she could stop it.

She slid out of the bed, located her clothes and left the room. Shivering and covered with goose bumps, she yanked on her clothes in the hallway, then crept into the bathroom. She washed her hands and face at the sink, trying to avoid looking at herself in the mirror for fear of what she might see. Curiosity won out, however, and the woman staring back at her was a stranger.

Her hair was a crazy tangle of curls. She had a hickey on the side of her neck and a whisker burn on her jaw. Her lips were red and slightly swollen. And her eyes held a sultry, wanton look of satisfaction that kicked up a horde of ambivalent emotions.

She turned away, shook her head to dispel the image and hurried to the main house. Back in her own bedroom, she put on her robe and curled up in the big old rocker she'd bought secondhand when Riley was born. She'd done some of her best thinking in this chair. If ever there was a time for serious thinking, this was it.

Though she wasn't entirely comfortable with what she'd done last night, there was no sense in beating herself up over it. She honestly didn't regret making love with Travis. He'd treated her with great care and respect, taken her to amazing heights and proved that she wasn't the hopelessly cold fish Johnny had once claimed she was. Besides, she'd always been so disappointed with sex, she'd wondered for years why everybody else seemed to be in such a twitter over it.

Well, now she knew. And it felt wonderful. She felt wonderful. The whole blessed world felt wonderful. At another time in her life she might have thought she was falling in love, but she knew better than to read too much into any sexual encounter no matter how stupendous it had been.

If she wasn't falling in love, however, she had to wonder at her real motives for making love with Travis. Yes, she found him extremely attractive. She enjoyed his company and felt flattered by his attention. But it would take more than that to justify going to bed with him. It should, anyway.

But then, on second thought, why should it?

With the notable exception of marrying against her family's wishes, she'd spent her whole life playing by the so-called "rules." She'd been a "good" girl before marriage and a faithful wife afterward, and what had been her reward?

A cheating husband who hadn't been willing to teach his virgin bride about the joys of sex and then blamed her because she didn't want to do it all the time. And a family who thought she was too immature to make her own decisions. If not for her sons, she would have said the past fourteen years of her life had been nothing but a waste. The "rules" simply hadn't worked for her.

So maybe it was time she stopped playing by them. When she'd told Travis there were no obligations implied in his making love to her, she'd meant no obligations for him. But if there were no obligations for him, then there shouldn't be any for her, either.

What a concept.

Could she, Grace McBride Kramer, actually have a passionate affair with a man and walk away unscathed? Why not? Guys did it all the time and lightning didn't strike them dead.

She cared about Travis and she believed he cared about her, but love didn't have to be a part of this. She wasn't hurting anyone, wrecking a marriage or breaking up a family. She wouldn't get pregnant or risk contracting a sexually transmitted disease. If she and Travis were discrete enough, nobody would ever know what they did when they were alone. He would be moving on when Dillon came home, so she wouldn't even have to see him when the affair ended.

By golly, this could work. And it could be a lot of fun. She already knew she was going to do it. It had taken her so long to find out she actually liked having sex, she wasn't about to give it up any time soon.

Travis would have to cooperate, but that shouldn't be a problem. But then, men were such perverse creatures in general, nobody but God ever knew what they'd take into their fool heads to do. Well, she'd just have to wait and see.

After Christmas she didn't have time to worry about much of anything but the increased pace of the calving operation. Most of the cows managed to have their calves out in the pastures on their own, but there were always a few that had problems. To make matters worse, the weather stayed lousy with frigid temperatures, high winds and deep snow, all dangerous conditions for the newborns.

The men ran the delivery room in the barn, but she was in charge of the neonatal nursery in the house. Barely a day or a night went by when she didn't have at least one calf tucked into a box with a blanket and a hot water bottle in front of the kitchen fireplace. The tiny Herefords needed plenty of attention and bottle feedings just like human babies did.

Then they lost three cows to birthing complications and Grace's life became a continuous round of mixing buckets of calf formula and teaching the orphans to drink from a pop bottle with a rubber nipple attached. The calves always fought the process, gagging and spewing formula everywhere until they figured out eating was a good thing. Besides doctoring and cleaning up after the calves, she had to do her usual chores, keep the humans fueled with hot, nutritious meals, provide them with warm, dry clothes to wear and make sure the boys did their homework.

Stealing time to be alone with Travis became a major challenge, but those were the moments that kept her going when she didn't think she could take one more day of this birthing marathon. At least they could always count on the kitchen clearing out whenever he helped her do the dishes.

Night after night as she cleared the table, put away leftovers and stood at the sink scrubbing pots and pans the crazy man made a game out of sneaking kisses and caresses under the cover of a dish towel. He called it kitchen foreplay, and while her own skills were improving she readily admitted he was the undisputed champ. One night toward the end of January he came up behind her, set an empty serving bowl on the counter with his left hand, wrapped his right arm around her waist and nibbled on her left shoulder, all at the same time.

"Stop that," she scolded, laughing and twisting her neck to block his access.

He kissed the other side of her neck, licked her earlobe and then gently blew on it. "You don't really want me to," he whispered. "Do you?"

She let her head fall back against his chest, closed her eyes and murmured, "No, Travis. Please don't. Stop, I mean."

She reached behind herself and caressed him through his jeans. He uttered a soft groan and moved out of her reach. In a moment he was back with a crumb-filled brownie pan and another sensual attack. He made washing dishes so much fun, she was giving serious consideration to disabling the dishwasher.

Jake walked in at a particularly inopportune moment and stood there scowling at them. Travis left her to bring a load of glasses from the table. Keeping a perfectly straight face, he said, "Get your mind out of the gutter, will you? Grace got a blob of soap in her eye and I was helping her get it out."

Muttering to himself, Jake stomped off to his den.

Travis sidled up to her and nuzzled her ear. "Gonna visit me tonight, Ms. Grace?"

"Sure you're not too tired?" she asked.

"Tired? Me?" He flexed his arm and shoulder muscles and beat on his chest like Tarzan, then clomped around in a hilarious imitation of a ballerina's pirouette. "Lady, you're lookin' at a veritable dynamo of stamina and strength."

"In that case, I'll be out after I make the midnight barn check. How does that sound?"

"Sexy. But then you always sound sexy."

She was about to turn into his arms and kiss him when Riley's plaintive voice cut through the atmosphere. "Are you ever gonna get done with those dishes, Mom? I need help with my algebra. I don't get these stupid word problems."

Grace's heart sank. She'd hoped they wouldn't need a study session tonight. It wouldn't be so bad if she remembered how to do algebra, but she always had to read the book and work through the examples before she could help Riley. The energizing glow of anticipation of making love with Travis evaporated, and she suddenly felt exhausted.

Travis gave her shoulder an encouraging squeeze. "Hey, I'm pretty good at math, Riley. I'd be glad to give you a hand if you don't mind a substitute for your mom."

Riley's face brightened. "That'd be great, Travis. Mom tries, you know, but she does it sorta backward."

"Thanks a lot, Riley," she said, pretending indignation.

Laughing, Travis and Riley thundered up the stairs. Grace smiled and shook her head. It was a darn good thing she wasn't taking her relationship with Travis seriously or she'd be hopelessly confused by now. On one hand, she would love him dearly for his thoughtfulness and for the easy way he related to her boys. He seemed to enjoy their company as much as they enjoyed his.

On the other hand, she'd be worried about his ability to turn off his arousal in a split second and act as if everything were dandy, when she knew darn well that his heart was pounding just as hard and fast as hers was. But, since she wasn't taking this relationship seriously, she could ignore any character flaws he might have. What a pleasure it was, simply to relax and enjoy his inventiveness both in and out of bed.

The alarm barely started to buzz when Grace smacked the button that turned it off, sat up and swung her legs over the side of the bed. Travis reached out and rubbed the small of her back, smiling into his pillow when she let out a jaw-cracking yawn and relaxed into his touch. He ran his palm the length of her naked spine and massaged the base of her neck.

"Wish you didn't have to go," he said.

"Me, too," she whispered. "But I do, so go back to sleep."

"Come over here and give me a kiss first."

"If I do that, I'll wind up back in the bed with you, and neither one of us will get any more sleep."

He gripped her shoulder, tipped her over backward and zoomed in for a deep, lazy kiss. "So, who needs sleep?"

She planted a hand on his chest and pushed him away. "You do, Sullivan. Behave yourself and let me find my clothes before I freeze. Jeez, no wonder Grandma always wore those flannel nighties in the winter. I think I'll get one."

Imagining Grace in some shapeless, floor-length nightgown covered with little flowers made him chuckle. "Yeah, that'd be real fetching."

She switched on the bedside lamp and turned on him with a pout. "You wouldn't want me anymore if I wore one?"

"Are you kidding?" He caressed her waist, her hip, the sweet curve of her bottom. "I'd want you if you wore a potato sack to bed. Besides, I'd have you back out of it in two minutes or less."

Grabbing his hand before he could get any friskier, she stood up and moved away from the bed. "Yeah, yeah."

He braced himself up on one elbow and enjoyed watching her wiggling into her panties and bra. "You think I couldn't? Care to make a little wager on that?"

She tugged a turtleneck over her head, then climbed into her jeans and switched the light off again. "I think you can do just about anything you put your mind to. Now, go back to sleep. I'll see you in a few hours."

He heard her moving through the little house, pulling on her boots, then letting herself out the back door. A deep sense of loneliness washed over him. Rolling onto his back, he stacked his hands behind his head and gazed into the darkness.

In spite of all the hard work, crazy hours and tension between Grace and her family, the past month had been a happy time for him. Weird as it sounded, even to him, he'd loved the whole shooting match—taking care of cows and calves day and night, making love with Grace at every opportunity and grabbing a meal or a few hours of sleep in between. It was exciting and fun, and he wouldn't have changed a thing.

After all, what did he have to complain about? Great

food? Working with folks he respected? A sweet, beautiful woman who was not only willing, but eager to explore the pleasures of the flesh with him? Without even hinting at a commitment? Not hardly. A man would have to be stark raving nuts to complain about that.

But on the other hand, he kept feeling that something was missing in their relationship. It wasn't really time to be trotting out the *L* word or the *M* word yet, but for some strange reason, he was starting to feel like a... Well, for lack of a better word or phrase, a *kept* man.

Oh, he knew that was pure nonsense. He was earning his keep, his pay and then some, and he should be grateful that Grace wasn't in any rush to throw her rope over his head and tie him down. It gave him a chance to do the chasing and wooing for once. Only problem was, he didn't seem to be very good at being romantic.

He tramped a big heart in the snow outside her kitchen window and put their initials in it, and when she saw it, did she throw her arms around his neck and kiss him? Hell, no. She just gave him a big grin and said, "Oh, that's so sweet. Thanks, Travis."

Sheesh. He'd felt like some bashful high school freshman giving the head cheerleader a flower or a box of chocolates. The same thing happened when he left a note in her favorite coffee mug. And when he drove all the way to Cody, bought her a plant with pink flowers all over it and snuck it up to her room.

He'd even sunk low enough to write a little poem about her cinnamon rolls, for God's sake, and hide it under her pillow. He figured it wasn't worth publishing, but he'd worked darn hard on it and even managed to get in a few double entendres that were real clever if he did say so himself. And there came that same big grin and another, "Oh, that's so sweet. Thanks, Travis."

She acted so damn perky when she said that, she might as well have petted him on the head and scratched behind his ears. He couldn't tell if she honestly thought he did goofy stuff like that for women all the time, or if she was being intentionally dense. But why would she do that?

Grace wasn't a mean woman. She wasn't the kind of woman who'd have a fling with a guy she really didn't care about, either. But dammit, he was beginning to feel like all she wanted was his body, and she really didn't give a rip about his heart or his mind.

It was almost enough to make him believe in that karma stuff he'd heard about from a little gal he'd met down in Santa Fe. Some people might think there'd be a certain kind of cosmic justice if Grace never loved him the way he was starting to love her. He'd sure learn firsthand how Bridget had felt when she'd figured out his big secret.

Hell, his dear ex-wife had even predicted that he would. If he remembered correctly, her exact words had been, "Someday you'll meet a woman who won't just fall at your feet, and be all impressed with your fancy belt buckles, Travis. She'll see right through you and when she does, you remember what I'm telling you now. Payback's hell."

Even the thought of that happening gave him the willies. But it wouldn't happen. He'd make sure it didn't. How? Well, he just would, that's all. He'd work harder on his wooing, be more direct about his intentions so she couldn't misunderstand what he was trying to do. And somehow he'd prove to her that he intended to be a solid citizen, not traipse around the country like a saddle tramp anymore.

Yeah, that was it. Maybe he'd even show her the blueprints he'd brought from his parent's house on Christmas Day. Then she'd know he had something worthwhile to offer her and the boys. That was bound to help her see him in a new and more serious light. Wouldn't it?

Aw, hell. He flipped over the pillow and punched it a couple of times before settling back down. Grace wasn't going to be impressed by his big dreams. He wasn't even sure he had the brains to build a dude ranch, much less operate one as a profitable business. But then her soft words came back to him.

I think you can do just about anything you put your mind to.

Did she really mean that? Yeah. She did. She was real good at taking some ordinary thing everybody else took for granted—like a pine cone—and seeing its potential rather than how ordinary it was.

She did that with people, too, and in her own subtle way, she was a source of encouragement for everyone around her. Including him. Especially him. Just thinking about her and imagining her face made him want to be a better man than he'd ever been before. With her help, maybe one of these days he would be.

The vicious cold broke during the first week in February and they finally saw the daily number of calves being born start to drop. When the weekend arrived, Cal brought out some food prepared in his restaurant to give Grace a break. Zack and Alex spent the nights at the ranch and took turns checking on the cows during the night. Lori took Riley and Steven home to spend the weekend with Brandon.

Jake went to bed early, vowing to catch up on some much needed sleep. Travis had gone to the guest house right after supper, and undoubtedly was doing the same thing. Grace thought about going to bed, but knew she was too restless to try.

She wished she could have some girl talk with Alex, but Alex and Zack obviously were staying out of her way. It had been weeks since the debacle on Christmas Day, and Grace found their continued aloofness discouraging and infuriating, but there was nothing she could do about it.

She didn't feel like cleaning or cooking or making anything. She couldn't sit still even if there was something decent to watch on TV, which there probably wasn't. It was so unlike her to feel at such a loss for something to do, she thought at first that she might be coming down with a cold or the flu.

After pacing from one room to another for the better part of an hour, however, she realized she was lonely. Dammit, she wanted to be with Travis tonight, but she shouldn't disturb him, and she shouldn't advertise her relationship with him to any more family members. Of course she shouldn't.

Well, tough. She wasn't playing by the "rules" anymore, was she? She went into the kitchen, grabbed a metal tin that had once held packets of cocoa mix and filled it with cookies she'd baked yesterday.

Yanking on a coat in the mudroom, she grabbed the tin and quietly let herself out the door. If the guest house was dark, she would leave the cookies in the barn for Zack and Alex, then go on back to the main house. She crossed the snow-packed yard in near-record time, smiling to herself when she spotted lights blazing from the kitchen windows in the guest house.

Knocking, she wiped her feet on the mat. A moment later Travis opened the door and stared at her as if he couldn't imagine why she would be there. Maybe this wasn't such a good idea, after all.

"Grace?"

"It's me, all right. Mind if I come in?"

"Oh. Sure." He stepped back out of the way and rubbed one hand down over his face. "Sorry. Guess I'm not too with it right now."

"Were you sleeping?"

"No. Just dreaming."

"Travis, have you been drinking?"

Laughing, he shook his head, took the tin and opened it, then stuck a cookie in his mouth and waved one hand toward the table. Taking that as an invitation, Grace hung her coat on one of several hooks beside the door and crossed the room.

"Didn't you want to spend some time with Alex and Zack tonight?" he asked. "I thought if I cleared out, you guys might be ready to start making up with each other."

"They're still not talking to me, Travis." Her voice broke and she felt the sting of tears at the backs of her eyes. He came to her and slung one arm around her shoulders. She took a deep breath and forced herself to go on. "So I came to see you instead." She glanced at the table. "But if you're busy..."

"I'm never too busy for you. I was just looking at some plans."

"Really?" She glanced toward the table. "They look like blueprints. Are you going to build something?"

His smile looked a little pinched, but it eased the ache

in her heart over Alex and Zack's stubbornness. It also intrigued her. She'd never seen him act the least bit nervous, but he was now.

"Yeah," he said. "I've been working on this idea off and on since I left home the first time, and I'm finally ready to do it."

"Do what?"

He hesitated, then took her elbow. "Come take a look."

He nudged her into the chair he'd obviously been using and stood behind her. She looked at the cardboard tube on the windowsill, the paper spread over the table, the cups and salt-and-pepper shakers used to hold down the corners. He hadn't been kidding about how long he'd been working on this. The edges were worn and stained. The drawings were covered with erasures, and he'd plastered sticky notes everywhere.

She smiled up at him. He shoved his hands into his front jeans pockets and hunched his shoulders just enough to give away the tension he obviously was trying to hide. Ooh, interesting.

"I'm not much of a draftsman," he said.

"It communicates," she said. "Want to tell me about this dude ranch?"

"It's just a lodge and some cabins."

Yeah, and it's only your life's dream. "Do you have a particular piece of land in mind for it?"

"Not yet." He shifted his weight from one foot to the other and jabbed his index finger at the plans. "When I find the right one, I'll hire an architect to get all the dimensions just so. And a nice sketch of what it's going to look like."

"That's a good idea."

"I thought so. Well, now you've seen it, and I don't

want to bore you with the details.'' Leaning over her, he reached for the plans.

She slapped both hands down on top of the paper. ''I'm not done looking at it. I *like* details. Remember?''

''Yeah, sure, but—''

She inclined her head toward the other chair. ''I want to know more. Frankly, I think you'd be good at running a dude ranch.''

Sitting on the edge of the chair, he looked touchingly surprised and pleased with her compliment. ''You do?''

''Why wouldn't I? I don't know what your money situation is, but you've got everything else going for you.''

''Like what?''

''What's going on here?'' she asked. ''It's not like you to go fishing for compliments.''

He shrugged. ''I don't want compliments so much as an honest appraisal of my strengths and weaknesses. You know what I mean?''

She nodded. ''But, Travis, I'm not exactly sure I could be impartial when it comes to you.''

''Ignore that for a minute and be real blunt. Why do you think I'd be good at this? Give me some concrete reasons.''

''Okay. You know how to do almost all the jobs on a ranch, and if there's something you don't know, you have plenty of folks you can ask. You're good with animals. You like people and you're a pretty likable guy yourself. That's important. You've even got a claim to fame. That's always a good draw.''

His shoulders relaxed slightly and his smile looked more genuine. ''That's a good start. What else?''

''You can be real entertaining when you put your mind to it. You're not afraid to get your hands dirty.

Shoot, I don't know what else until you tell me more about what you have in mind."

"I want a nice little place where people can come and relax and really get away from it all."

"Will you allow children to come?"

"Of course. What kind of an idiot wouldn't allow kids on a ranch?"

She laughed at his automatic indignation. "Not everybody likes kids, Travis. Especially screaming toddlers and teenagers with attitudes. Some places specialize in catering to honeymooners, senior citizens, couples who intentionally never had kids or couples who just really want to get away from their children—"

His scowl cut her off. "Okay, I see your point," he grumbled. "But that's not what I want for the Diamond S."

"The Diamond S?" She said it a couple of times, just to see how it felt rolling off her tongue. "That's a good name and a good brand. I like it."

"Thanks. Me, too."

"Tell me what you want the Diamond S to be like," she said.

He looked off into the distance, giving the impression that he could see this place quite clearly in his mind. "I want it to be a family place, where parents can get away with their kids and nobody, including a boss or a mother-in-law, can interrupt their vacation time together unless they can convince me it's a life-or-death emergency. No phones for the guests. No faxes. No televisions, radios or computers."

She loved the way his hazel eyes glowed when his enthusiasm for his plans started pumping. "Go on."

"I want my customers to feel like guests, but they should also be able to work right along with the hands if they want to, take riding lessons, camp out under the stars, go fishing at the lake, toast marshmallows, sing around a campfire, do crafts…. You know, all that camp stuff that's so much fun and nobody ever has time for anymore.'' He shot her a sheepish grin, then shook his head. ''I suppose that sounds dumber than—''

''It doesn't sound dumb at all. There are lots of families who need exactly those things you're talking about. From what I've been seeing in the newspaper and on TV, good quality time together is mighty hard to come by for most families these days.''

''Well, I know I've got to have a solid program to offer if I want to pull in the folks who have enough money to keep me in business,'' Travis said. ''But I'd like to offer some sick kids and some disadvantaged kids a chance to get away and play cowboy for a week. I'm gonna use some of my old rodeo contacts to finance that. Maybe Dillon and his gal can shake some money loose in Hollywood, too.''

Grace felt as if her heart had tipped sideways in her chest. Lord, but he was a dear man. If she wasn't very careful, she could fall in love with him. She didn't want to think about that right now, however.

''Oh, you old softie.'' Leaning across the table, she planted a loud, smacking kiss on his mouth. ''It's a great plan, Travis.''

''Glad you like it. Now I've got one more question I want to ask you.''

''What's that?''

''The Diamond S is my dream now. How'd you like to help me build it?''

Chapter Eleven

Grace blinked in surprise. "What did you say?"

Travis laughed out loud, and she realized her mouth was hanging open. She closed it, then shook her head at him. He laughed again before rephrasing his question for her.

"How'd you like to help me build the Diamond S?"

His eyes were absolutely serious now, and behind his smile, she detected an edge of vulnerability, as if telling her this was his dream wasn't already a sneaky enough way to get past her defenses. But if she helped him build it, she would invest so much of herself, she'd become a part of it and she would fall in love with him in the process. She sputtered and hemmed and hawed, but the best refusal she managed to come up with was, "Oh, I couldn't."

"Why not?" he asked mildly. "I'm not asking you to do it for free, you know. I'd pay you—"

"I wasn't thinking about that," she said. "But now that you mention it, I already have a job right here and it's really full-time. I could give you a couple of hours here and there, but that's about it."

"That's all I'd need at the start."

"Look, Travis," she said. "I've met a few folks in the business, but I don't really know anything about running a dude ranch. What is it you think I can do for you?"

"Everything."

She huffed in exasperation. "You'll have to be more specific than that.

"All right." He took a minute to think about it, then continued. "What I need the most is someone who can help me organize the whole project."

"You can do that yourself."

"Not really. It's easy for me to visualize what I want the ranch to be like in general, but when it comes to breaking it down into individual steps I can work with and follow through on, I get lost."

She heaved a mental sigh of relief. He might not realize it, but he'd just given her an out. "That's only a matter of making a list and prioritizing it. Anybody can do that. It's no big deal."

He got up, wandered to the refrigerator and brought back a couple of beers. "For those of us who don't see what items need to go on the list in the first place, it's a huge deal." Handing her one, he slowly shook his head. "You're not giving yourself enough credit again, Grace. You're wasting special talents you should be exploiting."

"I like what I'm doing just fine."

"Are you sure about that?"

"Of course," she said. "Why wouldn't I be?"

"Because you've never done anything else. You have nothing to compare it to."

"And here I thought you respected my work."

"I do," he said. "But I also think you're past due to try something different. Wouldn't you like to take on a brand-new challenge?"

Until this moment she hadn't thought so. But now that he mentioned it, a new challenge sounded exciting. She'd always wanted to share something like this with Johnny—a goal they could work toward together, celebrating each new accomplishment as they completed it. Unfortunately Johnny hadn't had the vision, the ambition or the stamina to take on such a daunting task.

But this dream of Travis's—starting a whole new enterprise that could become a business for future generations to carry on—that was special. You'd work your rear end off, but when you finally had it up and running, you'd really have something worthwhile. And it would be your own.

There would be no one else to blame if things went wrong. But if things went right, no one else would take the credit, either. Talk about temptation. Any second now, he was going to sprout red horns and a forked tail. Still, she wanted to know more.

"Why a dude ranch, Travis? Why not just a regular one?"

"Because I know myself too well," he said. "I like ranch life and I don't mind doing the work, but I get bored and moody if I get locked into a routine for too long. What I loved best about the circuit was seeing new places and meeting new people all the time. A dude ranch would give me the extra stimulation I need without traveling eleven months a year."

She had to admit that made sense. Last summer she'd

been surprised to learn she enjoyed having the movie company at the Flying M. Life had become much more interesting and exciting when she didn't know every single thing that was likely to happen each day.

"So, what do you think?" Travis asked.

"I don't know," she said. "How are you planning to finance this thing?"

"That's my problem," he said. "Before I break ground on anything, though, I'll have all the backing I need. You know you want to help me, Grace. I can see it in your eyes."

"It's an interesting idea," she admitted. "It would be fun to plan something like this and then watch it take shape, but…"

"But what?"

"But, as I've pointed out, I have a full-time job. I also have two boys to raise, and I don't want to disrupt their lives. I'm really not free to pick up and go off somewhere to help you build your dream, no matter how much it appeals to me."

"So, I'll have to find a good piece of land somewhere around Sunshine Gap."

"You'd locate it here just to get my help?"

"Damn right, I would," he said. "And it shouldn't be that difficult. This is perfect country for it. Then you can help me whenever you can spare a couple of hours."

Alarm bells and flashing lights went off in her head. She'd counted on him leaving the area once Dillon came back. She glanced away and cleared her throat. "It's not that simple, Travis."

"Sure, it is. It'd probably be better for you and your family if you tried a different job for a while."

"What do you mean?"

"You never really left home, Grace. You've lived and worked on this ranch all your life, even when you were married. I think it might help the others to see you as an adult if you get out on your own, or at least work for somebody else for a while."

She nodded thoughtfully. The wretched man certainly knew how to push her buttons, didn't he? He expected her to give in and do what he wanted, too. The expectation was right there in his eyes as clearly as if he'd tossed a challenge right in her face. Well, it wasn't going to be quite that easy.

"I'm not ready to make any long-term commitments right now," she said. He gave an exasperated little grunt that made her smile. She swept one hand across the blueprint. "But if you'll come over here and explain more of the details, I'll help you look for the land."

"And make lists for me?"

"Only enough to get you started. You're really going to have to learn how to do that yourself."

"Yeah, yeah. Whatever you say."

Before she could scold him for his attitude, he got up and came around to her end of the table. She got up as well, intending to give him her chair, but he swept her into his arms, started to hum, and waltzed her around the small kitchen until she was breathless and laughing.

"What was that for?" she asked.

"You've been looking so serious and sexy over there, I couldn't help myself."

He kissed her then, with the exuberant passion of a truly happy man. There was nothing to do but kiss him back, and then one thing led to another and the next thing she knew they were buck naked and making love on the rug in front of the small fireplace in the living room. She lay in his arms afterward, staring into the flames and stroking his sweaty chest while he stroked her hair and her back.

Each time it was more exciting, more satisfying. If he kept taking her to paradise, how was she ever going to resist him? Maybe a better question to consider at this point was, did she really *want* to resist him?

In all honesty, no, she didn't. But for all she knew, this could be all he really wanted from her. This and her ability to make lists. She smiled to herself and rolled her eyes in amusement.

Did she make lists? Hell, yes, she did. Grocery lists, chore lists, wish lists, lists of important phone numbers, lists of errands to do the next time she went to Cody, lists of lists she needed to make. For her, a list was nothing less than a survival tool, but nobody besides Travis had ever noticed their importance.

Chuckling, she turned toward him and forgot everything but the joy she found in making love with him. She might be flirting with disaster, but she was willing to take the risk. She couldn't bear to give him up just yet.

Travis drove down the middle of the gravel road, watching for a Realtor's sign in the overgrown brush on his left while Grace peppered him with questions for another one of her never-ending lists. He'd created a monster with that conversation, but he'd do whatever it took to keep her involved in his project. This was the fifth afternoon they'd gone out looking at parcels of land for sale, and he was having the time of his life.

"What kind of rock are you planning to use for the fireplace in the lodge?" she asked.

"I don't know yet." He shot her a grin.

She gave him back a dubious look that clearly said he'd better be figuring it out and fast, then turned back to her list. "Do you have any idea which architect you want to use?"

"Not yet."

"How about a contractor?" she asked. "Or are you going to try to do everything yourself?"

"Could this wait just a little while, darlin'?" he said. "I'm afraid I'm gonna miss the sign if I don't pay close attention. Should be right along here somewhere."

"Okay." she said. "I'm driving you crazy, aren't I?"

"No more crazy than I'm driving you," he said with a shrug. "You want me to speed up. I want you to slow down. I figure when we find our compromise point, we'll move along together as well as Pete and Repete, and we'll have it just about right."

Laughing, she pointed toward his side of the road. "There it is."

A comfortable silence settled into the pickup's cab while he drove deeper into the foothills. From the corner of his eye he saw Grace automatically bracing her feet against the floorboards, her bottom against the seat and clamping her jaws shut to avoid biting her tongue when they approached crater-size pot holes. What a woman.

While the road went from pretty darn bad to truly terrible, the country outside the windows opened up, becoming wilder and rougher by the half mile. His heartbeat cranked up a notch, and he craned his head, trying to see everything at once. The property they were going to look at included fifteen thousand acres. If all of it looked this good...oh, man, this could be it.

The mountains to the west carved chunks right out of the sky with their jagged granite peaks. A small river, still iced over in spots, twisted between parallel rows of willows. Where there was water, some kind of grass was possible, even probable unless the snow cover was completely disguising the true contours of the land. At last the road turned into a narrow, muddy lane that curved through an aspen grove.

Past the small, slender trees, they topped a rise, and both of them sucked in a deep, excited breath. Spread out before them was a flat meadow surrounded by clusters of cottonwoods, backed up by rows of towering pines. Travis braked to a stop and climbed out of the pickup, hoping his shaky knees would hold him up. Grace climbed out on the other side and silently stood there, her head turning this way and that. Her glowing eyes finally gave him the courage to speak.

"Grace? Are you seein' what I'm seein'?"

"Yeah. I think so."

By some wordless agreement, they met at the front of the pickup. A thick, pristine layer of snow dazzled his eyes until he raised one hand to shade them. Even then, everything looked Christmas-card soft and fluffy. He could hear the river gurgling to the north. That was a fishing river if he'd ever seen one. It would be a huge asset for a dude ranch. As would the spectacular view of those mountains. Lord, they just soared right up to heaven.

"Is it big enough?" Grace asked, her voice as hushed as if she were in church. "The meadow, I mean."

He answered in kind. "I think so. We'll have to pace it off to be sure. Get the water tested. And the second this snow melts, I'll bring a horse out here and ride the whole property, just to make sure there's not something bad we can't see, like a toxic waste dump."

She grabbed his arm. "Oh, Travis, don't even think

of that. No one would defile something this beautiful, would they?''

He patted her hand until she eased her grip enough to let blood flow into his arm again. ''I sure hope not, darlin', but I've got to be sure. Is it close enough to the Flying M for you to make the commute?''

''For this place, I'd drive a lot farther. But we're really only about fifteen, twenty miles away, and it's not like this road's ever going to have much traffic.''

''We'll have to get some work done on the drive that branches off the county road. That thing's a menace.''

''I'll put it on the list.''

Her smug grin begged for a kiss, so he had to oblige her. If it hadn't been so darn cold, it would have been fun to take the kiss to its logical conclusion, but he contented himself with a quick, sweet one this time. Taking her hand, he started pacing off the meadow's rough dimensions. By the time they'd returned to their starting place, he'd made his decision, no matter what might be under that snow.

He felt seduced by the sensations assaulting him from every direction, but it was a good, even a pure kind of seduction. His heart swelled with such complex emotions, he'd never be able to figure them all out or express them. Not that he really wanted to. Some things were better left unanalyzed.

''You really want it, don't you?'' Grace said, still in that hushed voice that seemed so right for the majesty of this setting.

Oh, yeah. He wanted it with every atom in his body, every breath in his lungs, every bit of yearning in his soul. If a benevolent God ever allowed him to hold the title to it, he never would try to tame it. He would nurture this land with as much care and tenderness as he would give his own child. Throat too tight to speak, he met her gaze and nodded.

Her eyes shone with the very same yearnings he felt, and he realized that a huge part of what made this spot seem so magical to him was having this particular woman standing beside him. He wasn't falling in love with her now. He'd already fallen as hard as a man could fall and live to tell about it. She was the only woman he would ever want to share his life and this place with him. And if he blurted that out, he knew with absolute certainty that she would bolt like a panicked horse.

He cleared his throat. "Yeah, I want it. What do you think?"

"I think we should buy it."

"We?" he asked.

She pursed her lips for a moment, then nodded emphatically. "We. I don't want to be an employee anymore. I want to be a partner."

His heart hammered his rib cage when she said *partner*. Jeez, was she reading his mind or what? Smiling at her, he said, "That could probably be arranged."

"Probably? No dice on that one, Sullivan. I want a partnership, with a say in how this place is built and run. I have some money."

Damn. For a minute there, he'd dared to believe she was talking about the *M* word. Disappointment stabbed through him, but he refused to let her see it. A business partnership wasn't a bad place to start. A smart man could build on that. If he had enough patience.

"I really don't need money," he said. "But just for the sake of argument, how much are you talking about?"

She shrugged. "I don't know for sure. My share of

Johnny's life insurance money was pretty hefty, but I've never spent a dime of it. Jake's been investing it for me. I'd guess he's probably doubled it by now. And what do you mean you don't need money? It'll take a small fortune to get this ranch started.''

After a moment's hesitation, he explained his financial situation. Her eyes widened in surprise, then glinted with amusement. ''Well, you're right. You don't need my money. Of course, the price of writing a list just tripled.''

''Hey, I'd rather have you as a partner than an employee any day, but I don't want you to put your whole nest egg into this business. If it fails—''

''It won't, Travis. It'll take a few years to get it running and see a profit, but we can't miss unless we really work at messing up the whole thing.''

''That's the way I see it, too,'' he said. ''And we'll work out a partnership agreement we can both live with. So, where do we start?''

She crossed her arms over her chest and glanced away from him. ''I'm not sure, but you know who could really help us get going? Jake. He knows all about permits, leases, insurance and all that kind of stuff. We should probably have him do the negotiating on this land for us, too. We want it too much and any seller with half a brain will see it right off.''

''You're right about that one,'' Travis said with a laugh.

She continued as if he hadn't spoken, her voice growing huskier with every sentence. ''We should talk to Cal, too, about zoning regulations in the county. I doubt we'll have a problem with it, but he'd know for sure. Zack could help us find a good string of saddle horses and pack animals. And Alex could dream up some easy skits to entertain our customers.''

Pausing, she gulped and swiped a hand under her eyes. ''Of course, if I'm involved, none of them will want any part of helping the Diamond S.''

''You miss them, don't you?'' he said, wrapping his arm around her waist.

She nodded, then sniffled. ''Yeah.''

''I'll bet you twenty bucks they're all missing you as much as you're missing them.''

''You'd lose. I thought that by now at least one of them would have talked to me about Christmas Day, but nobody has so far. I guess we're all going to act like strangers for the rest of our lives.''

''That's silly, Grace. You could always go talk to them one at a time.''

She shook her head and sniffled again. ''No way. If I do that, I'll be giving in and they'll call me Gracie 'til I die.''

''At least they'd be talking to you,'' Travis pointed out. ''Wouldn't you like that better than carrying on with this stalemate or whatever it is you're all doing to each other?''

''No. If they make the first move, I'll be thrilled to meet them halfway. But this time, dammit, they need to come to me.''

''What if you're expecting more than they can give?''

A couple of tears ambled down her cheeks and dripped off her chin. ''Then we'll all just have to live with it. But don't worry about the Diamond S. I'll find out whatever we need to know.''

Travis gave up trying to argue with her. They climbed back into the pickup and drove back to the

Flying M. Grace remained quiet and withdrawn, and it hurt Travis to see her agonizing over the loss of her family's affection and support. Dammit, this stupid rift had gone on long enough. If Grace wouldn't budge, maybe one of the others would.

The next day when they were out feeding, Travis brought the subject up with Jake. Jake listened intently while Travis told him what Grace had said.

Sadly shaking his head, Jake said, "Hell, Travis, we're all upset over what happened, too. She went a little overboard, but we've all taken a hard look at how we've treated her, and we understand why she felt so frustrated with us. And it's not that we don't want to apologize to Gracie. I'm mean, Grace. That's right. Grace. Grace. Grace."

"Then why don't you?" Travis demanded. "All she needs to hear are two little words. *I'm sorry.* Can't one of you manage to give her that much?"

"You'd think so." Jake's laugh had no humor behind it. "I guess we're all scared to death we'll say something wrong again and wind up alienating her even more than we already have."

"Well, you've got to do *some*thing. This is eating her alive," Travis said.

"We know that," Jake said. "It's eating us alive, too. But who asked you to interfere? You're not her husband. Hell, you're not even her fiancé."

"Not yet, but I'm going to be as soon as I can get her to say yes. I'm in love with her, Jake."

"What about the boys?" Jake asked.

"They're great kids." Travis said. "I think they'll accept me all right, as long as I don't try to throw my weight around too much. What do you think?"

"They like you well enough. As long as you make Grace happy, they'll be happy, too."

"And what about you and the others, Jake? Am I going to have to fight you every damn step of the way, or will you accept me as a brother-in-law?"

"What do you love about her?"

"Everything," Travis said, without the slightest inclination to flinch. "Her generous heart. The way she nurtures everybody. Seeing her face light up when she's making something for somebody. Watching her with her boys and feeling all the love she pours out on them. I even love how much she loves all of you jugheads, who don't appreciate her half enough."

Jake winced, then winked at Travis. "Hoo, boy, have you ever got it bad."

"Yeah, I know. Ain't it great?"

Laughing sincerely this time, Jake clapped him on the back so hard, he nearly fell off the hay sled. "You any good at basketball?"

"Used to be back in high school. Why? What's basketball got to do with me and Grace?"

"Nothing, but we can always use an extra man for our town league games."

"So, do I have your support to marry Grace or not?" Travis said.

"We're all just like Riley and Steven," Jake said. "You make Grace happy, we'll be happy, too."

"I'll do my best. Now, have you got any ideas how we can get Grace and the rest of you together so you can work this out?"

Jake drew in a long breath and scanned the horizon before he nodded at Travis. "Yeah. The volunteer fire department holds a Valentine Ball every year, and everybody goes. You get Grace to that dance, and we'll take it from there.''

"You'll be subtle, though, right?" Travis asked. "You won't gang up on her or anything."

Jake shot him an indignant frown. "Hey, we've got a little class in this family. You just do your part and let me worry about the rest."

Chapter Twelve

Travis was up to something. Grace glanced at the kitchen clock, hiked up the scooped neckline of her red dress for the tenth time and wondered if the stick-on bra cups and the skinny spaghetti straps on this slinky little number were going to be strong enough to corral her cleavage if Travis got rambunctious on the dance floor. And where the heck was he?

He was already ten minutes late and she wasn't the type who loved to make an entrance, even if she was making one on the arm of the handsomest man in town. Which she undoubtedly would be tonight.

The thought made her heart thud and her toes curl up inside her shoes. She knew that she and Travis made a striking couple, and it would be fun to see the surprised faces on a few of Johnny's girlfriends when ''poor Grace Kramer'' walked in with such a good-looking man. Even so, she had doubts about the wisdom of going to the Valentine Ball.

The whole darn family would be there, and who knew if they could all manage to be polite to each other for four whole hours? The last thing she ever wanted to do was to provide Sunshine Gap with any more free entertainment from the McBride family. Should she stay home?

She could always send the volunteer fire department a cash donation to ease her conscience for not showing up. But then Jake, Zack, Alex and Cal might decide she was too chicken to face them in public. No way. She wouldn't give them that much satisfaction. Not that she was looking for a fight, of course.

Maybe this dress was too much. Or too little. But anything went at the Valentine Ball. She could just wear a nice winter dress or even jeans if she wanted to. And now she'd officially gone over the line to obsessing, but she was too far into this snit to stop herself.

She turned toward the back hall stairway, but paused when she heard the thunk of a car door outside. A *car* door? Not a pickup? Where would Travis get a car?

The storm door opened and shut, and then she heard a quick rap on the mudroom door. She hurried to open it, and there he was, all dressed up in black slacks, a crisp white shirt, a gray, Western-cut sports coat and a bolo tie with a small, beautifully detailed silver bull-dogger on the slide. He carried his dress hat in one arm, a plastic corsage box in the opposite hand.

"Holy smokes." He let out one low, rough whistle. "You look beautiful, Grace. Think I'd better go strap on a six-gun to make sure no other guy tries to make off with you."

The approval in his eyes as he came closer told her

that as far as he was concerned, she'd chosen the perfect dress. Other than her own, his was the only opinion that mattered. Her insecurity vanished, and she smiled at him.

"Thanks. You look pretty darn good yourself."

He set his hat on the table and brought the corsage to her, along with a whiff of that wonderful cologne he'd been wearing the night she'd met him in Billings. So much had changed between them, it was hard to remember how awkward and shy she'd felt back then. He leaned down and kissed her cheek, then opened the box and slipped a cluster of small red roses and baby's breath onto her wrist.

"Oh, that's so sweet," she said. "Thanks, Travis."

He gave her an odd, nearly hostile look, but it passed in an instant. While she pinned a boutonniere onto his lapel, he asked, "Where are the boys?"

"Jake took them into town. They'll spend the night at Alex and Nolan's house with their other cousins and two hulking senior football players to keep them in line. Alex cons a couple of her students into baby-sitting for extra credit every year."

"Well, shoot, who's gonna take our picture?"

Uh-oh. She'd never seen one of her brothers willingly have his picture taken. Travis really *was* up to something. She knew he wouldn't tell her what it was if she asked, so she didn't ask. "We'll take the camera with us and get Emma or Lori to do the honors. How does that sound?"

"Like a plan." He offered her his arm. "Ready to go, pretty lady?"

She tucked her hand into the crook of his elbow. "As I'll ever be, Mr. Sullivan."

He escorted her out the back door, down the steps

and out to the car she'd heard earlier. Only it wasn't
just any car. It was her dad's beloved, fifteen-year-old
luxury sedan that only left the protection of the garage
for special occasions. Speechless, she stood there staring at it, until Travis helped her into the passenger seat,
hurried around to the driver's side and climbed in. Then
he gunned the engine and roared off down the driveway
like an eighteen-year-old boy taking his girlfriend out
on a hot date.

When she'd stopped laughing, Grace asked, "How'd
you get the keys?"

"I knew you'd get all prettied up, and I didn't want
to bounce you around in my pickup. So I just asked
Jake if he had a car we could borrow tonight, and he
handed the keys right over."

"He did?"

"Yup.

"Gee, I hope he's not coming down with something."

Travis's laughter filled the sedan with the golden
glow of intimacy that stayed with them all the way into
town. For all his rough edges when he was out working
at the ranch, he certainly knew how to play the attentive
gentleman, and she loved every blessed second of it. By
the time she walked into the bar at Cal's Place on
Travis's arm, she felt relaxed and happy. With Prince
Charming hanging around, even Cinderella could afford
to let down her hair and boogie.

Emma took their tickets at the door and gave Grace
an exaggerated wink. "Wow. Don't you two look
smashing?"

Grace leaned down and gave her sister-in-law a hug.
"Yes, we do." She straightened up, then grinned at the
explosion of red hearts, golden cupids and white stream-

ers haphazardly plastered all over the room. It was just corny and tacky enough to be fun. "Who was on the decorating committee this year?"

"On it?" Emma snorted with laughter and held up both hands. "Honey, you're looking at it. So what do you think? Isn't it grand?"

"It's perfect, Emma. Absolutely perfect."

Cal joined them then. Since he was doing his snooty maître d' bit, Grace had no choice but to allow him to escort her to a table for two convenient to the dance floor. When he'd seated them and taken their drink orders, Cal stepped back and studied her. "You look wonderful, Grace. I hope you have a real good time tonight."

He left before she could reply, but she smiled at his back. He hadn't apologized, but he *had* called her Grace and wished her a good time. It was an opening for future conversations, and at this point, that was all she could hope for. Travis took her hand and kissed it, then linked their fingers together and rested them on his thigh.

Old friends and neighbors dropped by their table, offering greetings and angling for an introduction to Grace's "new fella," or "man friend," or "handsome date," depending on who was asking. Of course, some of the men recognized his name. Once the word got out that a former rodeo champion was in their midst, the traffic around their table dramatically increased and Travis wound up autographing a whole stack of cocktail napkins. While he was occupied, Zack came around to Grace's side of the table and held out his hand to her.

"Would you like to dance, Grace?"

Though his tone was light, his eyes were utterly serious, and she wondered how long he'd had to practice to make her name roll off his tongue so easily. After only a second's hesitation, she accompanied him onto the already crowded dance floor. He didn't say much, but when he delivered her back to the table, he kissed her cheek and gave her hand a squeeze, and she knew that another closed door had been left open.

Travis leaned close and murmured, "Everything okay?"

She smiled. "Just fine. Are you finished with your adoring fans?"

"I sure hope so. Do you want to dance or just sit here and make out for a while?"

"Dance."

He heaved a huge sigh of disappointment, then took off his jacket and hung it on the back of his chair. After rolling up his sleeves, he took her hand and pulled her to her feet. "All right, but I hope you've got comfortable shoes on."

The evening sped by in a flurry of dancing with each other, changing partners and finding each other again. She talked and laughed and flirted, thoroughly enjoying herself. This must be how it felt to be the belle of the ball.

During a break between sets she encountered Alex coming out of the ladies' room. Alex rocked back on her heels in surprise, then gave her a tentative smile. "It's good to see you, Grace. That dress looks fantastic on you."

"Thanks," Grace said. "And thanks for including the boys in your baby-sitting arrangements."

Alex's eyebrows rose and temper flared briefly in her eyes. "We're still family, and nothing will ever change that. I'll see you later."

Smiling to herself, Grace watched Alex hurry away, practically bristling with irritation, then stepped into the rest room. When she came back out, the band had started the last set, traditionally made up of slower, more romantic songs. Eager to dance again with Travis, she hurried back to the table, but he wasn't there. She studied the crowd of dancers, hoping to spot him. She felt a tap on her shoulder, and turning, found herself face-to-face with Jake.

"Travis is waltzing with Miz Hannah," he said, referring to the elderly retired school teacher who worked as a part-time hostess at Cal's restaurant on the other side of the building. "When she found out he was one of Dillon's rodeo buddies, there was no stopping her."

"That's sweet of him," Grace said.

"Will I do as a substitute, Grace?" Jake asked. "Just for one dance?"

Even big, bad cousin Jake was calling her Grace now? She didn't know whether to kiss the stubborn cuss or clutch her heart and fall over in a dead faint. She settled for smiling at him. "You'll do just fine."

He dutifully steered her around the dance floor. Though his sense of rhythm wasn't great and anything more complicated than the most basic steps was beyond him, Jake did the best he could. Like Zack, he didn't say much, but she knew this was as close to an apology as she was ever likely to get from him. Considering his temperament, Grace recognized the dance for the peace offering it was, and gladly accepted it.

When Travis returned to claim her for the next song, Grace kissed Jake's cheek. He released her hand with a smile and she danced away, feeling better than she had since Christmas Day. She gave herself up to the music and let Travis sweep her into a dreamy, romantic trance. The gaudy hearts and cupids, her family and the other dancers faded from her consciousness until there was nothing left that was real, but Travis's eyes, his strong arms holding her and the intimate movements of the dance.

Skipping the usual round of goodbyes when the set ended, he found her coat and hustled her out to the car. She slid to the middle of the front seat, resting her palm on his right thigh while he drove back to the ranch. A sizzling, sexual energy pulsed in the air between them. In the muted light from the dashboard, she saw him smiling to himself, and for a moment, she thought he looked a little smug.

"What are you smiling at?" she asked.

"Nothin' much." He shot her a wicked grin, then turned his attention back to the road. "I'm taking the prettiest woman at the dance home with me, and if I'm real good, I just might get lucky."

Laughing, she shook her head at him. "Oh, you think so, huh? And why would you think that?"

"Well, it seemed like she had a pretty good time at the Valentine Ball," he said.

"Yes, she did," Grace agreed.

"And, she seems pretty happy right now."

"Yes, she is."

"Any particular reason?" he asked.

"Besides having the most handsome man and the best dancer at the ball as my date?"

He chuckled. "Yeah, besides that."

"I think this problem with my family might be starting to work out. Nobody called me Gracie tonight."

"Hey, that's great. I know it's been troubling you a lot."

"Some," she admitted. "But I don't want to think about them right now."

"What do you want to think about?"

She squeezed his thigh and murmured directly into his ear, "How soon I can get you naked."

Travis tromped on the gas pedal. The car shot forward, sending Grace into peals of laughter. She'd barely regained control of herself by the time he parked beside the guest house and shut off the engine. He got out, walked around the car and helped her to her feet, then kissed her senseless.

Sliding an arm behind her knees, he swept her up against his chest and carried her inside. She wrapped her arms around his neck and rested her head against his shoulder.

"I've got a surprise for you, darlin'," he said. "Close your eyes until I say you can open them."

Chuckling, she scrunched up her eyes like a little kid. He carried her into the living room and set her on her feet. Taking her coat, he kissed the tip of her nose, then pressed on her shoulders, guiding her down onto the sofa.

"Don't move," he said. "And keep those eyes shut, no matter what you hear, okay?"

"Okay." She drew the word out, voicing her doubts about whatever he planned to do even while she agreed. She heard the scratch and hiss of a match being struck, the crackle of kindling catching fire, a rattle that might have been ice cubes hitting a bucket, the distinctive pop of a champagne cork. Good grief, he must be setting up one heck of a seduction scene.

"Hurry up, Travis," she said.

He reassured her with a kiss on her lips, then she heard him hurrying around again, and she imagined a cartoon character zipping here and there, trying to get everything just right. Finally, she heard him take in a deep breath, then blow it out.

"You can look now," he said.

"After all that thumping around, I'm not sure I have the nerve," she said.

He sat down beside her, stretched his arm across the seat back behind her shoulders and coaxed, "Come on, Grace, open up."

Teasing him, she slowly opened her eyelids and scanned the contents of the small coffee table in front of her knees. Oh, Lord, she'd expected a bottle of wine, a little box of candy, *maybe* some candles, but he'd gone far beyond that. Too far.

It wasn't just a bottle of wine, it was champagne, complete with an ice bucket and two slender flutes decorated with curling red ribbons. A ripple of unease rolled up her spine.

It wasn't a little box of candy, it was one of those two-pound, heart-shaped numbers high school boys bought for their steady girlfriends. There were candles all over the place, fat ones, tall ones, short ones, heart-shaped ones. Her stomach clenched into a hard lump.

There were red roses. Two dozen at least, in a big, crystal vase. And a small, velvet box from a jeweler in Cody. The air became so thick, her lungs hurt. She clasped one hand to her chest and pressed her back farther into the sofa cushions.

Travis looked at her expectantly, the pleasure in his eyes dimming with every second she remained silent.

"My goodness," she said, uttering a nervous little laugh that made her cringe inside. "You've been, uh, busy."

He glanced at the table as if he thought something might be missing. Obviously, he'd hoped she would be surprised and thrilled. She felt shocked and overwhelmed. She couldn't just hurt him, for heaven's sake.

"This is so sweet of you," she said. "Thanks, Trav—"

Cutting her off with a snarl, he surged to his feet and scowled down at her. "Don't, Grace." Cursing under his breath, he raked one hand through his hair, then waved at the gifts he'd laid out for her. "This isn't sweet, dammit. And neither am I."

Unwilling to let him tower over her, she stood up. "Don't yell at me. I can see my reaction isn't what you wanted, but I never asked you to go to so much trouble."

He inhaled loudly, and she could see him struggling to control his temper. "It wasn't any trouble," he said quietly. "I liked doing something nice for you for a change."

"It is nice," she said. "And I appreciate it. I just didn't expect you to do so much."

"Why not?"

"Well, the Valentine Ball is fun, but it's still just a little country dance. It's not that big of a deal."

"This isn't about the Valentine Ball, and you know it." He waved at the coffee table. "I'm trying to tell you something here, but you're not getting it."

"I get the message." She hated the defensive tone in her voice, but couldn't entirely get rid of it. "Maybe I don't want to hear it."

"Don't want to?" Travis huffed at her. "I think you're scared to."

"Whatever explanation works for you is fine with me. You're not going to get to me with word games."

"I'm not playing any games. Dammit, Grace, I love you. I'm *in* love with you. And I think you're in love with me, too."

His words burned a hole in her gut. Aw, jeez. Of all

the guys in the world she could have had a fling with, she'd figured he would be the last to say these things to her and act as if he really meant them. She wrapped her arms around herself. "No. I like you. I respect you. I care about you. But love you? I don't think so."

He moved closer to her. "Horse apples."

"Don't push me." She held up her palms as if she could ward him off with them. "I'm not ready for this."

"You said that about kissing me, and you went ahead and did it. Now we've been lovers for six weeks. What's left not to be ready for?"

"Having great sex and falling in love are two different things."

"Maybe for some people, Grace." His crooked smile tugged at her heart. "But not for you."

She looked away from his smile. "Because I'm a sweet, naive widow from the sticks?"

He shook his head, and she told herself it was a patronizing gesture, as was his tone. "Because you put your whole heart into everything you do, whether it's cooking breakfast or pulling a calf or making a Christmas centerpiece for some lady you never met. You're not just going through the motions with me."

She stepped back. "Don't tell me what I feel or don't feel. We had a wonderful time together tonight. Why don't we enjoy the champagne, eat some chocolate, make wild, crazy love and just leave it at that?"

"It's not that easy."

"It can be, if you'll let it."

He grasped her upper arms and she felt a fine trembling in his fingers, as if he were fighting an urge to shake some sense into her. When he spoke, his voice was rough. "No. I can't pretend I'm only having great sex with you anymore. And I can't pretend I only want you to be my business partner. I love you, Grace, and I want you to be my wife.''

Though she'd been arguing with him, Travis thought he'd been making progress with Grace—until he said the word *wife*. The second that four-letter word came out of his mouth, she jerked herself out of his hold and even in the candlelight, he could see her face go pale.

''I told you a long time ago that I was never going to get married again,'' she said. ''Weren't you listening?''

''Sure, I was, sweetheart.'' Her eyes practically snapped with anger, and he reminded himself to can the endearments for a while. ''But never's a long time. We all say things like that when we're hurt, but we don't really mean it.''

''I did. Marrying Johnny was the biggest mistake I ever made, but I learned from it, and I'm not going to make it again.''

''That was years ago. You won't make the same mistake again because you've grown up and matured.''

''Yes, I have, but you're the only lover I've had besides Johnny,'' she said. ''I don't really know enough about men yet to make that kind of a choice.''

''It's not like choosing a brand of toothpaste,'' he said indignantly. ''You can't just go try out a whole bunch of different guys and then pick your favorite.''

''Says who? Almost everybody I know has dated lots of different people. I'm a little behind, but I'll catch up.''

''Just for the sake of conversation, how many guys are you planning to sleep with?''

''I don't know. How many women have you slept with?''

"That's none of your business. And it's not the issue."

"I agree, but you seem to be awfully interested in it."

Travis closed his eyes for a moment. Dillon was right. The woman was going to drive him to drink. Heavily. "That's because I plan to marry you, Grace. I want to be the last man you ever sleep with. Haven't I satisfied you so far?"

"It's not that. You know you're a wonderful lover, Travis, but I don't want another husband."

"Hey, I'm not your first husband," he grumbled. "From what little you've said about him, I don't think I'm anything like him. Being married to me would be a whole different experience."

"That's supposed to guarantee it would be better?"

He jammed both hands into his hair. "I can't believe I ever thought Dillon was stubborn."

"That's right. The woman won't do what you want, so now you call her names. Gee, where have I heard this before?"

Her sarcasm lit his fuse. "Oh, come on, Grace, you're not going to go out and sleep with ten men so you can choose the best one. You're just arguing out of sheer stubbornness now. It's no wonder your family was afraid to talk to you since Christmas. If it wasn't for me, you would've carried on this stupid feud for months, and you'd all have been miserable for what? So you could score some ridiculous point?"

Her cheeks flushed, her nostrils flared and her eyes narrowed to mere slits. Her voice came out low and deadly. "What are you talking about?"

Oh, man, what had he done? What had he said? He knew better than to let his stupid mouth get out ahead of his brain, but he'd been mad enough to eat nails. He should've just backed off and given her more time instead of trying to make her see reason. She would've come around eventually. Maybe.

She stepped closer, her fingers curled into fists. "What did you do, Travis?"

"Nothing that didn't need to be done."

"You talked to them, didn't you? You went behind my back and you sold me out."

"It wasn't like that, Grace."

"Like hell, it wasn't. You told them I was upset and asked them to make the first move. Didn't you?"

He couldn't look into her big, wounded eyes and lie to her. But he didn't think he could get any words out of his throat at the moment. He settled for nodding.

"Dammit, I told you my feelings in confidence. You had no right to pass on what I said. You had no right to interfere—"

"Sometimes, when you're right in the middle of something, you can't see it as clearly as someone who's not so involved," he interrupted. "Jake and the others were just as upset as you were. What difference does it make who blinked first?"

"If I have to explain it, you just wouldn't get it. But now, everything nice that happened with them tonight doesn't count."

"That's childish, Grace. I did what I did for your own good."

She shook her head as if she couldn't believe what he'd just said. When she spoke, her voice was so low and controlled he had to strain to hear it, but it scared the living hell out of him all the same. "For my own good? Where on earth did you find the damn gall to say that to me?"

Chapter Thirteen

"What's so bad about that?" Travis asked. "I was only trying to help—"

"Oh, please." She placed one hand on her forehead as if she felt dizzy, and he prayed she wasn't angry enough to have a stroke. He stepped forward, preparing to catch her if necessary, but she jerked her hand down and shook her head at him. "Spare me your lame excuses. You sold me out and that's the end of the story. I have to leave now."

He blocked her path with his body. "No, darlin', you can't. Not when you're so upset."

"Upset? You think I'm just upset?" She turned back to the coffee table, picked up one of the champagne glasses and hurled it at the cheery fire burning in the fireplace. It shattered on impact. She smiled as if she'd found the crash immensely satisfying. "Honey, that's what started this whole damn mess. Other people keeping secrets from me and then trying to justify it...."

She paused and pitched the other glass at the fireplace, smiling again when she got the same result. "By telling me it was for my own good, and they were only trying to help."

"You're talking about your brothers?"

"Duh. Like they haven't told you everything by now?"

"Nobody's told me anything about what started this feud," Travis said. "That's the truth, Grace."

"Then you men must all be just alike under the skin, because you sound like my brothers and you think exactly like them."

"Look, I'm missing some pieces of the puzzle here. Why don't you tell me what secrets you're talking about?"

"It's humiliating."

"So?" He swept one hand over the coffee table, then looked back at her. "I'm feeling pretty humiliated myself, right now. At least let me understand what I did that was so wrong."

Mashing her lips together, she glanced away from him and crossed her arms over her breasts, clasping the opposite elbows with her hands. Her skin looked so pale against the red of her dress, she seemed fragile. She took a couple of deep breaths, then looked at him again.

"All right," she said reluctantly. "I guess you deserve that much."

"Gee, thanks." If she caught his sarcasm, she ignored it, which was probably just as well. He really didn't want to give her a chance to detour into a pointless argument. He gestured toward the sofa. "Why don't we sit down?"

She shrugged then returned to the sofa and sat at the far end. "I don't know why this is so hard to say," she said. "It's not a unique story. It's not even unusual. It's just really humiliating when it happens to you."

"When what happens?"

"When your husband cheats on you with half the women in town, and you find out everybody knew about it but you."

"Ouch," Travis said. "But I thought your husband died five years ago, and you're still acting like it's something that just happened."

Her mouth twisted in a parody of a smile. "To me, it is. I didn't know anything about it until Dillon finally caved in and told me the truth just before I went to Billings."

"Last December?" Travis asked.

"Yup. All my brothers knew, and not one of them had the decency to tell me. They let me shoot off my mouth about what a great husband and father Johnny was all over town, and never said a word."

"I don't get it," Travis said, shaking his head in confusion. "Your brothers are all stand-up guys. Why would they do something like that?"

"They were protecting me *for my own good.*" She raised an eyebrow at him, as if she expected him to say something. But what could he say? "That's their story, anyway."

"There has to be more to it than that, Grace. Give me the whole picture."

"You want the whole picture?" She got up and paced to the fireplace and back. "Dillon was home from the circuit healing up from something. A shoulder separation, I think. One night he played cards with Jake, Zack and Cal in the back room at Cal's Place. When they came outside, they saw Johnny's pickup parked down the street, so they decided to go see what he was up to. Did I mention that they all hated him?''

''No, you didn't,'' Travis said.

''Well, they did. My folks did, too, and so did Uncle Gage and Aunt Mary. If they all would have just shut the hell up in the first place, I probably never would have married Johnny.'' She sat down again and uttered a bitter laugh. ''But hey, I was seventeen when I started dating him and I was rebelling against everything, especially all of that baby-of-the-family garbage. Eventually it turned into one of those you-and-me-against-the-world situations.''

''The harder they pushed you to dump him, the more you defended him.''

''Exactly. It was awfully exciting and romantic, and the night we graduated from high school, Johnny and I drove across the border to Idaho and got married. Considering all of the flak I knew I was going to get, I was absolutely determined to have a successful marriage. God knows I tried.''

''What happened?''

''I don't know all the details. I don't even know when he started to cheat on me or why. But that night my brothers were playing cards, they literally caught him with his pants down, sitting in the front seat of his pickup with the town tramp straddling his lap.''

''Aw, jeez,'' Travis muttered, aching for all the pain she must have suffered when she'd finally heard all of this.

''Do you remember when I wouldn't kiss you in Billings?'' When he nodded, she asked, ''Did you ever wonder why?''

''I just figured you didn't know me well enough.''

"I probably didn't, but it sure wouldn't have stopped me if I hadn't spent half the morning at the doctor's office being tested for sexually transmitted diseases."

Her eyes glistened with tears, but she pressed on, her voice growing more ragged with every word. "I was afraid to kiss you for fear of passing on something that Johnny might've picked up and passed on to me. I know now that I probably couldn't have passed on anything dangerous with just a kiss, but back then I was so horrified with the whole idea, I didn't want to take any chances."

"Are you all right?"

Grace swiped at her eyes and nodded. "Yeah. My tests all came back clear, or I never would have made love with you. I guess that's one of the benefits of living in the boondocks. We don't have as much exposure to all the diseases you'd be sure to run into in a big city. We didn't back then, anyway. Which is probably why it never occurred to my idiot brothers to worry about it."

Neither of them spoke for a moment. Travis figured they both needed a breather, but finally he asked, "So, what happened that night your brothers caught your husband with the other woman?"

She got up and paced some more. "According to Dillon, Johnny was drunk, and when he saw four McBrides looking in the windows at him, he panicked. He shoved his girlfriend out and tried to drive off."

"He probably thought they'd beat the tar out of him."

"And they probably would have." Grace snorted in disgust. "But, as it turned out, Dillon was the only one who managed to get into the pickup. He said he tried to talk Johnny out of driving, but he wouldn't pull over.

He missed a curve and they had the wreck. Johnny died. Dillon's face got all torn up. End of story.''

"I'm sorry, Grace.''

"Yeah, me, too.'' She sighed wearily and flipped her hair behind her shoulders. "I didn't know Johnny was unhappy with our marriage. That sounds like a stupid cliché, but it's the truth. When I found out he'd been cheating on me for God only knows how long, I was so angry with him, if he hadn't already been dead, I probably would have killed him myself. Now, I feel more sorry for him than anything else. He really wasn't a bad man. Just a weak one.''

"But you're still angry as hell at your brothers.''

She nodded. "They're all strong, honest men, and I deserved better than that from them. Dammit, they're my family. They should have told me the truth right away.''

"Did they ever say why they didn't?'' Travis asked.

"They figured I had enough to cope with from becoming a widow and having two little boys to take care of. They didn't want to hurt me any more than I already was hurting. No matter how many times I ask that question, it always comes back to the idea that they did it for my own good.''

"You don't believe that?''

"No. I think they just didn't want to see me cry anymore. Not knowing the truth was never in my best interests. Besides leaving me wide-open to any diseases Johnny might've given me, and letting me make a fool of myself in public, they deprived me of any chance to learn from my own mistakes.''

"What do you mean?''

"They all knew he was cheating long before that night. That was just the first time they'd ever caught him at it. If they'd just said something to me when they heard the rumors…maybe Johnny and I could've worked things out. I would've been a better wife and he would've been a better husband. And he'd still be alive.''

"You don't know that, Grace."

"No, I don't." She shook her head, came back to the sofa and sat down again. "And thanks to them, I never will."

"Aren't you ever going to forgive them?"

"I'm trying to. But to be honest about it, having one man I loved betray me was bad enough. To find out all five of my big brothers—who were my heroes—did, too, makes it damn hard to trust men, period."

"I thought there were only four there that night," he said.

"There were. But with something that serious, they would've told Marsh. And he kept their secret, too."

She looked at him then. Really looked at him. He didn't know what she saw in his face, but she gave him a fierce frown and shook an index finger at him. "For God's sake, Travis, don't even think about feeling sorry for me. I hate that so bad, it makes my skin crawl."

"I wouldn't dream of it. I feel sorry for your brothers."

"Why? They're all convinced they did the right thing."

"No, they're not. They might tell you that to save their own pride, but losing your trust and respect has got to be a real blow. They're all going to be miserable until you forgive them."

"I forgave Dillon before he left," she said softly. "He already paid a huge price for what happened that night, and he did finally break their damn code of silence. But I don't know about the others.''

"Maybe you just need more time.''

"Maybe. Changes don't happen very fast in our family. I thought we were getting somewhere tonight, but since they all think I caved in... Well, we've already covered that territory.'' She crossed her arms over her waist and studied him for a moment. "I really thought you were different, but you're just as sneaky and dishonest as they are.''

"That's not fair,'' he protested. "I never hid any big secrets from you, and I never told anyone you'd caved in. In fact, I said you felt sad about what happened at Christmas, but you didn't feel you could make the first move. They did the rest on their own.''

"You still went behind my back, Travis. Because you knew I wouldn't like what you were doing.''

"But I didn't know all this other history. If I had, I never would have talked to Jake or anybody else.''

She folded her hands in her lap and silently studied them until he thought he would explode with impatience. "I'd like to believe that, but I can't continue to make excuses for people. You've already proved you have the same instincts my brothers do. If I married you, you'd just try to run my life the way they always have. And if I wanted to do something you didn't agree with, there's no telling how far you'd go to save me from myself. Well, thanks, but no thanks.''

Unable to sit still any longer, Travis crossed the room, grabbed a chunk of wood from the wood box and added it to the fire. "Dammit, Grace, that's not true.''

Holding up a hand like a traffic cop, she interrupted him. "All I know, is that I need to be able to trust the people around me to be honest and straightforward with me, even if it's not easy or convenient. And I don't trust you to do that anymore.''

He turned back to face her. Anger and pain roughed his voice. ''Man, you're tough. A person doesn't even get to make one mistake with you?''

''Not when it involves hiding the truth.''

''Well then maybe it's time you stopped hiding the truth from yourself.''

''What are you talking about?''

He took a deep breath. ''I'm talking about that big fat lie you told me five minutes ago.''

''I didn't tell you any lies.''

''Oh, yeah? What was that garbage you tried to feed me about not knowing Johnny was unhappy in your marriage, and everybody in town knew he was cheating on you, and you supposedly didn't?''

Her hands curled into fists and her voice rose to a near shout. ''I didn't know, dammit. Haven't you heard that the wife is always the last to know?''

''Yeah. And it's called denial. You knew, all right. You sure knew your sex life didn't work.''

She jerked back as if he'd hit her. ''I can't believe you're actually going to stand there and throw that in my face.''

''I'm not throwing it in your face,'' he said, struggling to rein in his temper. ''I'm being honest and straightforward with you. I'm saying that at some level, you knew what Johnny was up to. You wouldn't let yourself see it or admit it, because if you did, then you'd have to do something about it.''

''You are so full of beans.''

''Think about it and you'll know I'm right. You denied the whole thing so you wouldn't have to confront him or divorce him, or admit to your family that you'd fouled up your whole life. And now you're doing the same thing with me. I know you love me, Grace. You just won't admit it, because then you might have to do something about that, too—like, take a risk, or admit that you know damn well you can trust me, or maybe even marry me.''

"You're all mixed up, Travis. First I'm in denial about Johnny, then about you? One thing doesn't have anything to do with the other.''

"Sure it does. It's the same damn defense mechanism. Any time you're faced with something that scares you, you stick your head in a sack and pretend the problem doesn't exist. If you won't even admit the truth of what's going on around you, why do you expect the people who love you the most to do it for you? That's the lesson you needed to learn from all of this, Grace.''

Tears trickled down her cheeks and she wiped them away with her fingertips, all the while shaking her head at him. Much as her pain ripped at his heart, he couldn't quit now or she might never face the truth.

"Stop blaming your brothers for following the lead you gave them," he said, "and start accepting your own responsibility for what happened before and after Johnny died.''

"You don't know—"

"Oh, darlin'." He reached a hand toward her but she batted it away. "You think I haven't done my share of denying the truth? Well, I have, and admitting it was the hardest thing I ever had to do. But that's how people really grow up.''

Grace inched her way past him and backed into the kitchen. "Well, thanks for sharing," she said. "It's been quite an evening, and I'm leaving now.''

He handed over her coat, sighing inwardly when she

put it on without letting him help and hurried to the back door. "I'll drive you back to the house," he said.

"No, I'm fine" she said quickly. "I won't hurt Dad's car driving it across the yard."

He held up both hands to show her he was giving up for now. "Okay. We'll talk more tomorrow?"

She mashed her lips together again, the way she always did when she was fighting tears. Then she shook her head with a finality that chilled his blood. "No, Travis. You may be right about a lot of what you said, but I'm not ready to be the kind of woman you need. You come on up to the house for your meals, but as far as I'm concerned, there's really nothing left to say."

"Dammit, Grace," he said, but before he could think of what else he could say to convince her otherwise, she was gone.

He turned back to the small living room, his chest aching, his throat hard and tight with a lump in it that had to be the size of a softball. Gazing at the things he'd gathered on the coffee table for her—the flowers, the champagne, the candy, the velvet box—he felt as if each was a chunk of his heart that was going to get as busted up as the wineglasses in the fireplace if he didn't figure out where he'd gone wrong tonight. And what he could do to fix it.

He didn't like the thought of letting her go off anywhere alone when she was so upset, not even to the main house. But maybe it was for the best. A little time and space could help a person find a new perspective on her problems. Or, it could just give her an opportunity to dig deeper into the position she'd already chosen—that she couldn't trust him and she never wanted to marry again, anyway.

Aw, but that would be such a waste. They could be

so good together. He didn't even have to shut his eyes to imagine her and the boys building the Diamond S with him, welcoming guests, sharing that special piece of God's creation with folks who had to work hard to find a park just so they could see a lousy tree. She would find as much satisfaction and delight in that as he would dammit, if only he could make her see...

Make her see? And there it was, just like she'd said, his own damn part of this problem. He cursed under his breath, then did it again right out loud. He'd thought he was beyond this. Thought he was more "evolved" than her brothers, that he could tolerate differing opinions and feelings better than most of the guys he knew. Hah!

Put him under a little emotional stress, let him fall in love and feel that edgy, uncertain tangle of emotions when he didn't get an immediate commitment, and he reverted right back to his upbringing. He'd always resented the way his dad had figured out what everybody else was supposed to think and feel, and then found a way to punish anyone who dared to oppose him. It had driven him away from home, and now he'd done the same damn thing and driven Grace away from him.

There may have been a time in human evolution when that kind of unquestioning obedience had helped the species survive, but it just didn't work that way anymore. He didn't have any right to tell Grace what she should think and feel. If she said she wasn't ready for this kind of discussion, then he should've accepted that and backed the hell off.

But he hadn't. It had taken him so long to find a woman he could love with his whole heart, he'd been scared to death of losing her unless he got his brand on her. It was as simple as that. The question now was, what could he do to fix this mess?

The answer was as obvious as it was frustrating. Nothing. What Grace ultimately decided to do wasn't up to him now. It was up to her. All he could do was shut his mouth and pray she would decide to give him one more chance. That was all he needed to get it right. One more chance.

That was when he heard the roar of a pickup engine tearing out of the ranch yard. He rushed to the back door, then sprinted for the main house. Aw, jeez. He'd known Grace wouldn't do anything reckless with her dad's precious car. But her pickup was a whole different thing. It was just big enough and beat-up enough that she wouldn't be too worried about putting another ding or dent in it, and she'd been so upset, she could do almost anything. He should stop her. Go after her.

By the time he reached the house, she was gone again, and he had no idea which direction she'd taken. He stood there, breathing hard, wondering if he should go find Jake, then slowly shook his head. Jake would only do what he himself wanted to do, which was use her safety as an excuse to bring Grace back home where he could keep an eye on her. And she would believe that he'd sold her out again.

He had to show more faith in her than that. Above all else, she was a loving mother. She wouldn't risk orphaning Riley and Steven. No way in hell.

So it was back to waiting, and he would wait however long it took for her to decide what she really wanted, even if it killed him. In the meantime, there was one person in her family he could talk to and ask advice from. Maybe, if he found a new perspective for himself, he wouldn't screw everything up all over again when Grace returned home.

Chapter Fourteen

After aimlessly driving the back roads around Sunshine Gap for two hours, Grace realized she was even more confused than when she'd left the Flying M. It was almost three o'clock in the morning. Her shoes pinched her toes and she was sick to death of this slinky red dress. But she couldn't go home. Not yet.

Not until she got her head back on straight.

No matter how much she told herself that logically and rationally, she'd done the right thing in breaking off her relationship with Travis, her gut instinct kept telling her she'd just made the biggest mistake of her life. But how could that be? Considering the awful things he'd said, she couldn't see why he even thought he wanted to marry her in the first place.

The big jerk had made her sound like some kind of a nutcase. She hadn't known about Johnny's cheating, dammit. She *hadn't*.

Well, she'd known he was restless sometimes. And she'd known he liked to flirt with other women, but that had just been Johnny's way. He'd been so handsome and charming, other women had often flirted with him, even when she'd been sitting right next to him. What red-blooded man wouldn't have responded to some degree? She'd never dreamed he would take it so far as to break his wedding vows. Had she?

Lord, she'd been over it and over it, and she never got the same answer twice. So maybe it was time to take one reasonable thing he'd said and get someone else's perspective on the situation. But whose? She'd neglected too many of her friendships outside the family to trust anyone else.

Jake, Zack and Cal were out. She was almost as confused about her feelings for them as she was about her feelings for Travis. She didn't want to pull any of her new in-laws into a hassle. Dillon was gone. That left Alex.

Grace turned back toward town. She might not like what Alex had to say, but she did trust Alex to shoot straight. Now she only had to figure out a way to wake Alex without disturbing all those nosey children.

Fifteen minutes later, she parked in front of Alex's big old house. The lights were all off, but the stars and the moon provided enough illumination for Grace to find Alex's bedroom. Grabbing a handful of small rocks, she pitched them at the window until she saw a face appear and an arm wave. She reached the front porch at the same time the door opened and Alex poked her head through the opening.

"Grace?" she whispered. "What's wrong?"

"You said we were still family," Grace said. "Can we talk?

"Of course." Alex stepped back and pulled the door wide-open. "Come in. The kids are all upstairs." She led the way into the living room and waved Grace toward one end of the sofa. "Want something to drink?"

"Something cold would be nice," Grace murmured.

Alex went into the kitchen and returned a moment later with a can of diet cola in each hand. She handed one to Grace, then sat on the sofa's middle cushion, angled herself toward Grace and pulled her bare feet up under her long nightshirt. Her unquestioning willingness to listen nearly undid Grace's composure. In spite of their differences, she'd missed Alex, who had always been more of a sister than cousin.

Stalling for time, she asked, "Have you heard from the mamas?"

Alex took a sip, then chuckled softly. "Only twice. You were right about getting the hysterics over before they came home, by the way. The last time they called, we actually had a conversation."

"I'm glad," Grace said.

"Me, too." Alex grinned wickedly. "But I'm still counting on Zack and Lori's new baby to provide the ultimate distraction."

"If that doesn't do it, nothing will," Grace agreed.

"Okay, so now we've chitchatted. What's up?"

Grace popped the top of her can and drank until the tightness in her throat eased. "I want you to put all the family stuff aside for now, and just be my friend."

"All right. I'll do my best."

Once Grace started telling Alex what had happened with Travis, the words and the tears poured out of her like milk from an overturned glass. Alex handed her a box of tissues and asked an occasional question, but for the most part, she simply listened.

"Do you see why I'm so confused?" Grace asked, mopping her face for what felt like the twentieth time.

Alex nodded. "You've got about three different issues all mixed up together. I think you'll make more progress if you take them one at a time."

"What do you mean?"

"First there's you versus the six of us. Then there's you and Johnny. And finally there's you and Travis." Alex laughed softly and shook her head. "Tell you the truth, Grace, it's confusing me, and it's my own theory."

"Well, keep trying. Sooner or later, it's bound to make sense to one of us."

"Okay, somehow, I think you've got Travis tangled up with some anger that doesn't belong to him. He didn't know all our history. His talking to Jake wasn't meant to sell you out and I don't believe that he did. The message I got loud and clear from Jake, was that if we wanted to have our relationship with our sister back, we'd damn well better shape up and treat you like an equal."

"Really?" Grace said.

"Yeah. Once we all cooled down from Christmas, we could see what you were saying and we knew you had a point. I never thought about you feeling left out because you were the youngest until you said what you did about us covering for each other, but never for you. We all felt terrible about that, but we didn't know how to fix it. An apology seemed too easy."

Grace rolled her eyes and huffed at Alex. "It would've been a pretty good place to start."

"I know. And we would've gotten around to it eventually, but Travis just sort of goosed us into hurrying up. I'm glad he did.'' Alex misted up and Grace passed her the tissues. "I've missed my best girlfriend.''

"Yeah, me, too. Now stop bawling and tell me what you meant about me and Johnny.''

"You want me to be honest?''

Grace shrugged. "Probably not, but do it anyway.''

"All right.'' Alex took a deep breath. "I know you loved Johnny, and in spite of his infidelities, I think he loved you and the boys. But I also think he was weak and immature, and since he died, I think you've built him up into this perfect guy that he really wasn't.''

"I agree,'' Grace said. Alex's eyes bugged out and her mouth dropped open. Grace leaned over and tapped on her chin until she closed her mouth again.

Alex blinked. "You do?''

Grace offered a sad smile. "Since Dillon told me everything, I've started remembering some of Johnny's faults. I just never wanted to admit there were any problems. Especially not to any of you guys.''

"Because you thought we'd judge you?'' Alex asked, clearly surprised again.

"Yeah. You guys always seemed like you had it all together.''

"Jake's about the only who would've had any room to talk about having a successful marriage.'' Alex sighed and shook her head. "Don't you remember what a sweetheart I married the first time out? Brad was meaner and more immature than Johnny was. Jill took off when Dillon got hurt in the wreck. And Billie hated Zack so bad when she left, it's a wonder he ever got to see Melissa again. Cal wasn't married then, but he came close to marrying someone he didn't love. And Marsh took off and left the only woman he's ever really loved behind. See what I mean?''

"Now that you mention it, some of you guys didn't do any better than I did. Why didn't I ever see that before?"

"Because we're all so involved in keeping our own heads above the water, and so concerned about what everyone else thinks of us, we don't have much time or energy left to be judging anyone else. Just take it for granted that all the rest of us wanted, was for you to be happy."

Grace grabbed the tissue box and wiped away the next round of tears. Lord, if she didn't stop this, she was going to drown. But somehow, these felt like healthy tears, the kind that healed old hurts.

"There's one other thing about Johnny, Grace."

"What's that?"

"It's time to let him go."

"I did that already," Grace said.

"No, you didn't," Alex said. "You're still comparing every guy you meet to him and expecting they'll all be just like him."

"How do you know I'm doing that?"

"'Cause I did the same thing," Alex said. "Until Nolan opened my eyes."

"It's really different being married to him?"

Alex nodded without hesitation. "It's so wonderful being married to him, I could kick myself for all the time I wasted treating him like a pal. There *are* some wonderful men out there, Grace. You just have to be willing to believe that. So let Johnny go, and get on with your life."

"And do what?" Grace asked. "Marry Travis?"

"Not unless you really want to," Alex said.

"Now that surprises me," Grace said. "I thought you really liked him."

"I do. I think he'd make you a great husband, but I'm not the one who'd have to live with him. You are. I think you need to figure out a few things before you make any kind of a decision about Travis."

"Like what?"

"Like whether or not you really want to have a man in your life at all."

Grace rolled her eyes, then clasped one hand to her chest as if her heart were suddenly racing out of control. "You mean I have a choice about that?"

Laughing, Alex fired a throw pillow at her. "You're a strong woman, Grace. You don't need a man to take care of you, so decide what you need and want to make you happy first. Do you want to be attached or unattached?"

"Okay," Grace said. "What else do I have to figure out?"

"If you do want to share your life with a man, you need to know what qualities you expect him to have."

"That sounds about the way I'd pick out a new car."

"Men are a lot like cars, but you tend to keep the good ones longer," Alex said with a grin. "But getting back to the subject, once you figure out what you want in a man, then you look around and see if any guy you're interested in comes close."

"How close does he have to come?" Grace asked. "You know how slim the pickings can get around here. What if nobody meets the criteria?"

"Nobody's going to be perfect. You just have to figure out your minimum standards of what you're willing to tolerate. If the guy's going to drive you nuts because he picks his teeth or doesn't use enough soap and deodorant, or the boys hate him, dump him."

"You didn't do all of that with Nolan."

"I didn't have to with Nolan. We were practically married in every way but the sex and the ceremony before we finally admitted there was an attraction between us. This isn't a process you should hurry. When in doubt, wait."

"You're not going to tell me what to do this time, are you?"

Alex smiled sympathetically. "Not if you want me to treat you like an adult. This is your decision to make, Grace."

Grace climbed to her feet, grumbling, "You picked a hell of a time to start listening to me."

"Yeah, wouldn't you know?" Alex said with a chuckle. She stood up as well and held out her arms. Grace hugged her, feeling a familiar sense of affection and peace when Alex hugged her back.

"You go make your decision," Alex said. "And don't worry about what the rest of the family will think or say. We love you, and whatever your side turns out to be, we'll be on it."

Pulling away, Grace nodded, accepted the box of tissues Alex offered and walked to the front door. Alex followed her. "Want me to keep the boys for you all day tomorrow?"

Grace shook her head. "They've got chores and 4H. It'd help if you could send 'em home with Zack and Lori, though."

"Okay. Go home and get some sleep. It'll all look better when the sun comes up."

Grace agreed and climbed into her pickup, but the last place she wanted to go right now was home. Alex had given her a lot to think about. She might as well go burn off another quarter tank of gas and think about some of it.

* * *

Promising himself that he and Grace would have a good laugh over this someday, Travis cleaned up the broken glass, dumped the flat champagne into a snowdrift beside the back steps, left the candy and flowers on the coffee table and put the ring box back into his duffel bag. Then he poked around in his wallet, his luggage and his pickup until he found the scrap of paper with the phone number Dillon had given him in case of emergency. He set a pot of coffee on to drip and dialed the phone.

It rang twice on the other end before a deep, definitely cranky voice answered. "Yeah?"

"Dillon?" Travis said.

"Yeah. Who the hell is this, and do you have any idea what time it is?"

"It's Travis. Sorry I woke you, but I need to talk to you."

"Travis? What's wrong? Anybody hurt?"

"No, calm down, buddy," Travis said. "I just need some advice."

Dillon sighed in what sounded like heartfelt relief. "Okay. Let me go somewhere I won't bother Blair."

"Want to call me back?"

"Nah. Her phones are cordless, so you can wander all over the place with 'em. This should do it. What's up?"

Travis explained what had happened with Grace, feeling more stupid with every word he said. Finally he just shut up and waited in agony for Dillon to start calling him names. To his surprise and gratitude, his old buddy replied with more than a hint of sympathy in his voice.

"Oh, man. She's a tough one. You ever break through all that hurt Johnny dumped on her, you'll have yourself one great little wife," Dillon said. "But you're gonna have one hell of a time gettin' her to let you come that close now."

"You got any ideas how a guy would go about doing that?"

"No quick or easy ones. If you really love her, you're gonna have to be prepared to be in it for the long haul."

Travis suspected he knew what Dillon had in mind, but he asked anyway, "What do you mean?"

"You can't go away so she can pretend you don't exist. You know, the old out of sight, out of mind thing? Don't let her do that," Dillon said. "But on the other hand, don't crowd her. The absolute worst thing you can do right now is back her into a corner. You're gonna have to wait until she comes to you. Think about taming an abused horse and act like that."

"She's not a damn horse, Dillon."

"She'd be a sight easier to handle if she was," Dillon said, "but the same basic principles apply. If I were you, I'd go ahead and get started on that dude ranch and just casually let her know what you're doing and let her curiosity do the rest. By the way, welcome to the family."

"How can you be so sure this'll work?" Travis asked.

Dillon laughed, a low, rough sound that made Travis smile in spite of his worries. "Hell, you don't think it was an accident Jake and I ran into you in Cody that day, do you?"

"You guys set me up?" Travis yelped.

"I wouldn't go so far as to say that. We just figured you and Grace would be a good match."

"Did you set up that trip to Billings, too?"

"Nope. That one really was a coincidence, but it just

goes to show how right we were about you and Grace. All you needed was a chance to spend some time together and bingo.''

''But Jake warned me to keep my hands off her,'' Travis said.

Dillon laughed. ''Did it make you *want* to keep your hands off her?''

''If I answer that, you'll probably break my nose the next time you see me,'' Travis grumbled. ''But you guys are downright evil. No wonder she gets so crazy when she thinks you're manipulating her. Chances are damn good you are.''

Dillon was silent for a moment. Then he said quietly, ''Yeah, and we know it's got to stop. You have my word from here on out we'll mind our own business, but for God's sake, don't ever tell her we had anything to do with getting you together. That's one secret you'd better take to your grave.''

''I hear you. Thanks, Dillon.''

''For the advice or for gettin' you together with Grace?''

''Both.''

''You're welcome,'' Dillon said. ''Just remember one thing.''

''What's that?'' Travis asked.

''Knowing my sister, she's probably gonna put you through sheer hell, but in the end, she'll be worth every bit of it and more.''

''Tell me something I don't know. Now, kccp your big, fat nose and Jake's to yourselves. Good night, Dillon.''

Travis hung up the phone with Dillon's chuckle still echoing in his ear. He looked around the small kitchen, debating what he should do next. Ultimately, one piece of advice Dillon had given him stood out above the rest.

Don't crowd her. The absolute worst thing you can do right now is back her into a corner.

It went against every hunting instinct he possessed, but Travis decided to heed that advice and give Grace a little time and space. Besides, he had a few issues he ought to hash out with his own family. A couple of days apart might even be good for both of them, but it had about as much appeal as kissin' a dead skunk.

When the first gray fingers of dawn started to invade the eastern horizon, Grace pulled into the Sunshine Gap Community Cemetery. She parked as close to Johnny's grave as she could get and sat there for a moment, wondering if she'd lost her mind. There were at least five inches of snow out there, and she still had on her slinky red dress and dancing shoes.

She hadn't been here since Dillon had told her the truth. What would it hurt if she waited long enough to go home and put on some jeans, a sweater and a pair of boots? She could bring all of the stuff she associated with Johnny out here and burn them on top of his grave, or—

No. He'd broken her heart and shattered her trust, but she didn't want vengeance. He was still the father of her children, and for that reason alone, she needed to maintain a respectful attitude toward him. Riley and Steven needed to think well of their dad in order to think well of themselves, and she would do anything to make sure that happened.

She should go home and grab a few hours of sleep before she had to fix breakfast, but the urge to stand at Johnny's grave again was irresistible. This was the only time of day she could count on having the privacy to say what she needed to say. Climbing out before she lost her nerve, she hissed at the icy sting of snow closing in around her feet and ankles.

Memories assaulted her as she slogged her way down the row of headstones. The day Johnny had started school at Sunshine Gap High School. The first time he'd smiled at her and made her heart flip over. The first time he'd kissed her and awakened all those sweet yearnings inside her. His sincere delight when the boys were born. The hideous day she'd stood in this cemetery, watching in shock and disbelief while Father Joe spoke the words that would take Johnny away forever.

The good times. The bad times. The times when she'd felt completely alone, even while he slept beside her. The images and emotions swirled through her mind until she reached the foot of Johnny's grave. She stood there for long, aching moments, studying the gray marble stone bearing his name and the dates of his birth and death. Gradually, a sense of his presence filled her.

"Hi, Johnny," she said softly. "It's me."

She paused, half expecting to hear his reply. None came, of course, but she nodded as if he'd returned her greeting, anyway.

"It's been a while since I've been here, and I guess you know the reason why. You hurt me, Johnny. You hurt me real bad in all the places a woman can hurt. I've been so mad at you, I've hated you. That's hurt me, too, but I don't want to hurt anymore."

The damn tears were back. Impatiently dashing them away with the backs of her hands she went on. "I'm sorry you weren't happy with me, but you know something? I wasn't real happy with you, either. Too bad I didn't admit that earlier and save us both a lot of pain.

You might still be alive if I had. Maybe that's what I've felt so guilty about all these years. Why I turned you into Saint Johnny. You'd have laughed at that idea, wouldn't you?''

She looked toward the east. Now there were pale golden rays creeping into the grayness, promising a new day. Perhaps, a new life?

''Anyway, you died so unexpectedly and I was still so stunned when we buried you, I never really got the chance to say goodbye to you. That's what I came here to do this morning. I loved you. I'm going to believe you loved me at one time. But I'm going to let you go now.''

Her knuckles ached, and she noted with surprise that her fingers had curled in on themselves, as if, in spite of her words, some part of her still wanted to hold on to Johnny and her girlish dreams of happily ever after. She forced herself to release her fingers and shook them hard until they were loose and floppy.

''Yeah, that's it. Wherever you are, Johnny, I forgive you, I wish you well and I'm letting you go. I'm forgiving myself, too. We were young and stupid, but we've paid enough for our mistakes. It's time we both moved on.''

The sun peeked up over the edge of the horizon, bathing the land in a colorful sunrise that felt like a benediction. Feeling as if a crushing weight had been lifted from her shoulders, Grace smiled and directed a brief prayer of gratitude toward heaven. Then she turned away and hustled back to her pickup as fast as her frozen feet and soggy shoes would allow.

She started the engine and switched on the heater. Well, Alex certainly had been right about that much, she thought, rubbing her hands together in front of the heat vents. So what else was she supposed to do? Answer those questions.

She put the pickup in gear and headed for home. Answering the first question was easy. Did she want to share her life with a man or not? Yes, she did. As irritating as men often were, they added a lot of spice to a woman's life. Hers had been too bland and boring for too long.

The second question wasn't quite so simple. What qualities did she want this man to have?

"A sense of humor would be nice," she said. "He has to love kids—especially mine. And my kids have to like him. He needs to have some goals and ambition. He can't be afraid to get his hands dirty or work hard, but he does have to use soap and deodorant."

She steered around a chuckhole the size of a tractor wheel and grinned wickedly as she continued to list Mr. Right's qualities. "He has to be a good lover. It wouldn't hurt my feelings any if he could dance. He has to be strong enough to stand up to a McBride temper—even mine."

There was one more quality for the list, and compared to all the others, it was the most important one of all. In fact, she could live without some of the others, but this was her rock-bottom, bare minimum requirement in a man. She was almost afraid to speak the words out loud for fear of jinxing herself, but when she turned into the Flying M's drive, she finally got them out.

"He has to love me as much as I love him."

Did she know anybody who came close to fulfilling her list of requirements? Did cows like hay? Did kids make noise? Did the mamas make great spaghetti sauce?

Laughing out loud, Grace stomped on the accelerator and tore up the lane, coming to a shuddering halt in her usual parking space. The barnyard was deserted. Her dad's car still sat in front of the main house. She glanced at the guest house, and felt her breath catch at the base of her throat and her heart drop clear down to her knees.

Travis's pickup was gone.

Chapter Fifteen

She found Jake in the kitchen, glaring at the coffee-maker. He looked up when she came in, doing a double take when he saw she was still wearing her dress from last night. If his expression was anything to judge by, the poor thing probably looked as bedraggled as she felt.

"Good morning, Jake," she said, hanging up her coat in the hall closet.

"'Morning," he said. "Mind telling me where you've been?"

"Driving around most of the night," she said. "I was at Alex's house from about three to four. Then I drove around again some more and ended up at the cemetery to say a final goodbye to Johnny. Anything else you want to know?"

The anger in Jake's eyes softened when she mentioned the cemetery, but his voice remained gruff. "You all right?"

"Yeah." She crossed the room, nudged him aside and started making the coffee. "I finally got some things settled with him. I suppose you think I'm crazy now."

Shaking his head, Jake gave her a wry smile. "Not hardly. When Ellen passed on I could hardly get through a day without stopping by to have a talk with her."

Surprised that he would speak of his wife's death at all, Grace reached up and squeezed his shoulder. "Did you ever say goodbye to her?"

He shut his eyes, as if even the thought of doing such a thing caused him pain. "No," he finally said, opening his eyes again. "I figured a shrink would tell me I should, but I never felt the need, so I didn't. Is that what you did this morning?"

She nodded. "And I feel better now. Freer."

"Good." He moved to the cupboard and got out a pair of mugs. "What brought all of this on?"

"A fight with Travis."

Jake's eyes widened in surprise. She knew he hadn't expected her to admit to any such thing, but it was time for them to forge a new relationship, too. After a second, he asked, "Want me to go find him and beat the living hell out of him for you?"

She laughed at his bland tone. He might as well have asked her if she wanted an apple. "Not this time, thanks. I need to talk to him, though. Have you seen him today?"

"He left about an hour ago. Said he had some things to settle with his folks and he'd be back tomorrow night."

"He definitely said he's coming back?" she asked.

"Uh-huh." Jake grinned. "If it makes you feel any better, he looked like death warmed over."

"No, that doesn't make me feel better." She felt tears backing up behind her eyes again, and shook her head, trying to hold them back. "I hurt him. And I'm afraid I've really blown it this time."

"Want to tell me what's going on?" he said quietly

"Yeah. I could really use a big brother's advice. Just remember you only get to give it to me this time because I asked for it."

Jake grinned, then opened his arms wide. She hugged him tight, sighing when his arms engulfed her. "Okay, hon. What's this all about?"

"I promise I'll tell you as soon as I get a shower and some clean clothes." She kissed his cheek, then dashed up the stairs to change.

By the time she came back down dressed in jeans, a sweater and her old hiking boots, she was shocked to find Jake standing at the work counter with a pancake turner in one hand, a stack of buttered toast and a paper-towel-covered plate ready for the skillet full of sizzling bacon.

"Why you old sandbagger," she said.

He grinned. "I'm not quite as helpless in a kitchen as you think I am. Ellen taught me a few things before she died so I wouldn't starve."

Hearing that didn't surprise Grace. She remembered Jake's wife fretting about his ability to go on with his life when it became clear that she was losing her battle with breast cancer. Grace smiled sadly at him. "Been holding out on me, eh?"

"Yeah. It wasn't fair to you, but when the folks left on their trip and you and the boys moved back into this big old house, you seemed to need a territory that was yours. And you're so much better at cooking than I am, it seemed silly not to let you do it all the time.''

She shook her head at him. ''You were right. I needed to be needed then. But now that I know what you're capable of, all bets are off.''

He whipped up some scrambled eggs, and they sat down to eat. Grace told him how she'd rejected Travis's proposal. Jake listened and pondered, and when he offered a suggestion, she clapped her hands in delight and rushed to the phone. As she'd expected, Alex's husband, Nolan Larson, readily agreed to help.

After breakfast, Jake and Grace went out to feed. When they returned to the house, Lori drove into the yard and the boys jumped out of the minivan. Lori chatted with Grace through the open window.

''So, did you and Travis have a nice time last night?'' Lori asked, inclining her head and making faces toward the boys in a way that warned Grace to be careful about Nosy Parkers.

''Mm-hmm,'' Grace replied.

''Did you get anything…interesting for Valentine's Day?''

''Sort of. But nothing's definite,'' Grace murmured.

''You will call me later….'' Lori said.

''If there's anything worth reporting.''

Lori narrowed her eyes and said in a solemn tone, ''You'll call me anyway.''

Grace grinned. ''Yes, master. Anything you say.''

Lori made a face at her and drove away. Jake had gone somewhere, but Grace hadn't noticed where. Riley and Steven went into the house with her, chattering about their night at Aunt Alex's house and how they'd driven the big football players crazy. Steven's impressions of their baby-sitters made Grace laugh and wish Travis were here to share the fun with her.

Steven finally ran out of stories and went upstairs to change into clothes more suitable for doing chores. Riley hung back, glancing around the kitchen with a perplexed frown.

"What is it?" Grace asked.

He glanced away and stuck his hand in his front jeans pockets, hunching his shoulders slightly. "Nothin', Mom."

"Come on, Riley," she said. "You were looking for something. What was it?"

"It's just...Uncle Nolan gave Aunt Alex a bunch of flowers and candy, and Brandon said Uncle Zack did the same thing for Aunt Lori, and I was sorta wonderin' if Travis might've given you something."

Oh, dear. How was she supposed to handle this one? She didn't want to give him too much information, but she needed to know for sure how he and Steven felt about Travis. So maybe that was the right approach.

"How would you feel if he had?" she asked.

Riley backed away, hands in front of his chest as if he feared she might try to hug him. "It doesn't matter, Mom. It would have been cool, but if he didn't, well, I didn't mean to make you feel bad or anything. I just wondered, is all."

"It's all right, honey. Why do you think it would be cool if he had?"

Riley hunched his shoulders even more and his cheeks turned a shade of pink that would have mortified him if he'd seen it. "I don't know, it's just...Travis is such a cool guy, you know? Me and Steven really like him a lot."

His voice cracked. He took a deep breath and struggled on, his eyes big and imploring her to understand. "I mean, we don't even hardly remember our real dad, and our uncles are all pretty decent to us, but it's not like having your very own dad."

"And you'd like to have Travis for a stepfather."

Riley nodded. "It would be okay. Do you think it could happen?"

"I like Travis a lot, Riley," Grace said.

He jerked his head to one side in an impatient gesture that was pure male McBride. "Well, what's that mean?"

"It means I can't promise you anything because it's not all up to me, but there is a possibility that we could get together some day."

"Really? What kind of odds are we talking here? Fifty-fifty? Eighty-twenty? What?"

"You can't quantify something like that," she said with a laugh. "It's kind of an all-or-nothing deal."

"Duh, Mom. But how do you know there's a possibility? Huh? Huh? Did he give you something for Valentine's Day?"

"Candy and flowers and champagne," she said, deliberately leaving out the jewelry box.

"No, sh—kidding?"

She gave him a reproving look, just to let him know she knew what he'd been about to say. He grinned and waved it away. "So, what did he say?"

"I'm sorry, honey, but some things are private," she said. "And I'm afraid the evening didn't end too well. We had a disagreement—"

"About what?" Riley demanded.

"Riley—"

"Well, *jeez*, Mom, that Wade guy was interested in you last summer and you ran him off. And Travis is way cooler than Wade, so I don't want you to mess this up. If you want, I'll go talk to him for ya.''

''No,'' Grace said. ''Absolutely not. This is strictly between Travis and me. Do you understand me?''

He gave her a grudging nod. ''You know, Mom, sometimes I don't think you even like guys very much. But I'm a guy, and so is Steven, and when you get all huffy with Uncle Jake or Uncle Dillon or one of the others, well, then I have to wonder if you even like us. Me and Steven, I mean.''

''Riley, I love both of you very much, and I love your uncles very much. People can get on each other's nerves a lot sometimes and still love each other.''

''So, is that what happened with you and Travis last night?''

''Not quite, but I'm hoping we'll be able to work this out. I'm glad to know you and Steven like him so much. I would never want to bring anyone into our family you boys didn't feel okay about.''

''Travis is cool,'' Riley said, as if he hadn't already said that several times. ''He's real patient when he's teaching us how to do stuff. And I think he really likes us, ya know?''

''Well, of course, he does.'' Grace slung an arm around Riley's neck and ruffled his hair before kissing his forehead. ''What's not to like about you guys? You're just so adorable.''

''Ugh, Mom!'' Laughing, Riley ducked away from her and sidled out of her reach. ''Should we go talk to him right now?''

''He's not here right now.''

''Where'd he go?''

''Home to Powell for the weekend. He'll be back tomorrow night.''

"Tomorrow night?" Riley said. "We have to wait *that* long to find out?"

"Probably even longer," Grace said. "You can't hurry these things, honey. You've got to take your time."

"Yeah, yeah. But do you love him, Mom? I mean, you don't have to marry him just for us."

"I wouldn't do that," she said. "It's important to me that you like him, but when I marry Travis Sullivan, you can bet your new saddle that I love him with all my heart."

Travis left Powell after supper on Sunday night, feeling better about his folks than he had in more years than he wanted to remember. Of course, the McBrides didn't hold any exclusive rights to the supply of stubbornness; he hadn't solved all of his problems with his parents by any means. But he'd made a good start. Knowing that even a relationship as strained as theirs had always been could heal given enough honesty and time, gave him hope that he still might be able to heal his relationship with Grace.

Unfortunately his good feelings began to fade as he got closer to Sunshine Gap. By the time he turned off the county road at the Flying M, his guts felt as if somebody had tied them into one big, hard knot and his fingers ached from gripping the steering wheel tighter than necessary. The lights were all on at the main house, and there were several vehicles parked beside it he recognized as belonging to other family members.

Damn. He wanted to see Grace, but not with all those other people watching. If she started crying when she saw him, Jake, Zack and Cal were liable to pound him into the ground first and ask questions later. He drove on to the guest house.

To his surprise, the porch light was on. The kitchen light was on, too, and a thin column of smoke spiraled from the chimney. He grabbed his duffel bag and hurried inside. His nose twitched at the aroma of fresh coffee and he spotted an ink pen and a document with a blue paper cover lawyers sometimes used, sitting in the middle of the kitchen table.

Pulling off his boots, he set them on the mat, hung his coat and hat on separate pegs and poured himself a mug of coffee. He carried it to the table, sat on one of the straight-backed chairs and pulled the document close enough to read. It started off with a bunch of legalese gobbledygook, but after a few minutes of working at it, he finally was able to decipher enough of the party-of-the-first-part and party-of-the-second-part lingo to figure out this was a partnership agreement. A partnership agreement between him and Grace.

He sipped his coffee and turned to the second page. The next section involved the purchase and operation of the Diamond S. While it all sounded fine as far as he could tell, he felt disappointed that it was all so dry and legal. So businesslike.

Taking another sip, he turned to the third page. More of the same jargon here and more on the fourth page. Snorting in disgust, he took a healthy gulp from his mug and turned to page five.

He skimmed the first three paragraphs, and was about to toss the stupid thing across the room, when his eye caught a mighty odd phrase for a legal agreement. *Foot rub*.

"Foot rub?" He reached for the coffee cup again, skimmed the page a second time, found the phrase and felt an urge to smile as he read, "The party of the first part—" which was him "—agrees to give the party of the second part—" which was Grace "—a complete foot rub on demand for as long as this agreement shall be in effect."

"The party of the second part agrees to bake fresh cookies and cinnamon rolls for the party of the first part at least once a week until such time as he hollers 'Uncle.'"

Travis laughed and shook his head. "Yeah, like that's gonna happen some day soon." The agreement became even more entertaining. He was not allowed to criticize or shout at Grace, but she was allowed to "correct his behavior" in any way she "deemed beneficial for the health and continuation of the relationship."

Getting into the spirit of the thing, Travis grabbed the pen and drew bold black lines through that clause. The next three were equally ridiculous, but the fourth one made his heart lurch, then race like a steer in a rodeo arena, who thinks that *this* time, he'll finally outrun that stupid horse.

"Following a wedding at a mutually agreed upon date, the party of the first part promises to deliver to the party of the second part, half of the genetic material necessary to produce a minimum of two children, with an option to renew for no more than two additional children, should the first two prove to be as incredibly lovable as the party of the first part is to the party of the second part."

He stared at that paragraph until his vision blurred and he realized he'd been holding his breath. He let it go, took in fresh oxygen and read the paragraph again. Damn. It still said what he'd thought it had. His vision blurred again, but this time he felt an unfamiliar tingling at the backs of his eyes.

Blinking hard and fast, he sniffed, then cleared his throat and slowly turned to the last page. He found only one clause there.

"The party of the second part requests a written reply from the party of the first part within seven days from the date printed below."

Grace had scrawled her name and today's date across the bottom of the page, and there were blank spaces reserved for his own signature. He got up, yanked on his boots, shoved the pen into his shirt pocket and folded the partnership agreement in half. Carrying it in his right hand, he slammed out the door, muttering, "Written reply? Seven days? Like hell."

Steven skated on his stocking feet to the doorway from the back hall and hissed, "Pssst! Mom! Pssst!"

Annoyed to have her conversation at the kitchen table with Emma, Lori and Alex interrupted, Grace said, "What is it, Steven?"

"He's comin' right now," Steven said.

Grace's heartbeat stuttered, then picked up speed. "Who? Travis?"

"Yeah," Steven said. "Riley saw him from his bedroom window. He says Travis is walkin' real fast and he's carryin' that blue paper thingy Uncle Nolan brought."

Alex started humming the theme from *Jaws*. Emma elbowed her in the ribs. Lori just smiled and patted Grace's suddenly cold hand. From Riley's description, Travis could be angry or eager, Grace thought, praying for the latter, half expecting the former.

The back door banged open, she heard three heavy

steps and then the kitchen door swung open. Travis strode across the room to Grace's chair and tossed the agreement on the table in front of her. Her heart sank, she felt sick to her stomach and she couldn't stand to meet his gaze. Oh, God, his hands were balled up into fists. She'd only meant to reopen the door she'd slammed in his face on Friday night, not start another painful argument.

"Grace," he said.

Shaking her head, she focused her gaze on her own hands, clasped tightly together in her lap. She tried to speak, but no sound would come out of her throat.

"Grace," he said again, his voice softer and carrying a hint of entreaty. "Honey, please, look at me."

She shook her head again, fearing she would bawl all over him if she did what he wanted. She'd been waiting for him for hours, secretly fearing he wouldn't come back at all, and her whole family had showed up to offer their help and moral support. She'd had such high hopes....

He went down on one knee and cupped his right hand around her chin, coaxing it up with gentle, but insistent pressure. When she finally looked into his eyes, she saw an intense emotion, but it wasn't anger. The rest of the room, the house, the whole dang world faded from her consciousness until all she could see or hear was Travis. She could tell he wanted her to say something, anything, but she had no clue how to form an intelligent response.

She cleared her throat. "What is it, Travis?"

He framed her face with his big hands. "The partnership agreement was cute, but I need more than that from you."

"W-wasn't it clear?"

Gently stroking her cheeks with his thumbs, he

slowly shook his head. His voice was deeper, rougher than usual. "I understood what it said, but I need to *hear* the words from you. In plain English. Do you love me, darlin'?"

She nodded. His chuckle tugged a smile from her own lips. "I need to hear the words. That means you have to talk out loud."

"Oh. Okay," she said, meeting his gaze head-on. "I love you, Travis, with my whole heart and soul."

The smile that spread across his face erased the seething fear in the pit of her stomach. "And you'll marry me?"

"Yes."

"What changed your mind?"

"I finally figured out I had to separate the past from the present, and I stopped comparing you to my brothers and expecting you to be like them or like Johnny. Then I described my perfect mate, and he turned out to be you. A very wise woman helped me do that."

"Remind me to kiss her when I get a chance."

"I might, but you have to kiss me first."

"I'll get there, don't worry. Do you think Riley and Steven will accept me?"

She smoothed a windblown lock of hair off his forehead. "I have it on good authority that won't be a problem."

His eyes widened in obvious surprise. "You talked about us with them?"

"Some. Riley actually started the conversation. I think they both love you almost as much as I do."

"Wow." He blew out a gusty sigh, grinned and shook his head. "That's amazing. I can't believe how lucky I am already, but did you mean what you said in the agreement? About the other babies?"

"Well, the numbers are negotiable, but I'd love to have babies with you. If you're game."

His eyes glinting with wicked delight, he puffed out his chest and drawled, "Well, I'll sure give it my best shot."

Gurgling with laughter, she looped her arms around his neck. "That's all I'll ever ask of you."

He pulled her close and settled his mouth over hers, sealing their promises to each other with a kiss so sweet and passionate she felt as if her bones were starting to dissolve. It went on and on, and she plunged her fingers into his hair and held on for dear life. She would have been completely content to let the kiss go on forever, but finally, he pulled back and rested his forehead against her.

It was then that she heard the catcalls, hoots and applause, and realized that her entire family had just witnessed what should have been an extremely private moment between her and Travis. Breathing hard, she returned Travis's smile. "Can you please make them all disappear?"

"Don't think so, honey, but I can make us disappear. Will that do?"

"That would be wonderful."

He scooped her off the chair and carried her out the back door, ignoring the razzing from the family. Once they were outside, she kissed his cheek.

"If you marry one McBride, you automatically get the rest of them," she said. "Do you mind?"

"Not a bit. I'd take on all of your siblings, your boys, your in-laws and even more to spend my life with you."

"What more is there?"

"Seems to me I've heard a lot about your mamas lately."

"The mamas!" Grace smacked her forehead with the heel of one hand. "Ohmygosh, Travis, we've got to get married right away. Before they get home."

"But I thought the others were in big trouble for doing that."

"They are, but they were right to do it anyway. Believe me, we either get married now or we'll still be tangled up in arrangements next year at Christmas." She shuddered, then added, "And I might have to wear ruffles. You might, too."

"Those are my only choices, huh?"

"I'm afraid so," she said. "What do you say?"

"Let's find a priest!"

Epilogue

A week later Travis and Grace stood before the local priest in the big living room at the Flying M. Their families occupied rows of folding chairs behind them. Everybody was all dandied up for the occasion, and Travis thought they'd created a real nice celebration, considering how fast they'd put this wedding together.

"Travis, you may kiss your lovely bride."

Travis smiled at Father Joe, winked at his young best man and his even younger groomsman, then gathered Grace into his arms and kissed her gently. To his way of thinking, he'd provided the rest of those rowdy McBrides with enough entertainment for one marriage, so he intended to behave with a little decorum at his wedding. When he started to move away, however, Grace raised her hand to the back of his head, and with a decidedly wicked twinkle in her eyes, pulled him down for a deeper, steamier kiss.

Before he knew it, he was lost in the hazy magic of her luscious mouth. He vaguely heard Riley and Steven giggling, Father Joe clearing his throat, his dad and brother chuckling. Travis didn't give a rip. If he kissed this woman forever, he would never get enough of her, but he sure as heck intended to spend the rest of his life trying.

The front door suddenly crashed open, breaking the spell of the kiss. Travis steadied Grace with his hands and looked back over his shoulder in time to see a pair of middle-aged, raven-haired beauties dressed in stylish suits and high heels step over the threshold. It had been a long time since he'd last seen them, but he'd never forgotten Lucy and Mary McBride. After one look at the priest, Travis in his black, Western-cut suit and Grace in her pretty blue-and-white wedding outfit, the women started to scream and cry and make big, dramatic gestures with their plump hands and arms.

"Gracie, what on this earth are you doing, you bad, bad, girl? Are you trying to break my heart?" the woman on the left cried.

"And who is this man to take our darling girl away without even having the decency to beg her papa for her hand? Father Joseph, I demand that you annul this marriage immediately."

While the women marched across the room, ample bosoms trembling with indignation and bracelets jangling angrily with every step, Travis glanced at Grace. "Are we in big trouble now?"

"Uh-huh," Grace whispered. "But their bark is worse than their bite. Just don't show any fear."

To Travis's amusement, Grace bravely put herself between him and the approaching women. Even in their high heels, they only came up to her shoulder, but she managed to convey a proper sense of respect.

She hugged the woman on her left. "Mama, I'm so glad you made it in time for the reception." She hugged the woman on her right. "And Aunt Mary, you look so wonderful. It's easy to see your trip was wonderful. Come and meet my new husband. This is Travis Sullivan."

Both women turned their glittering black eyes on him, and he suspected that, given the opportunity, they would have strung him up naked and upside down over a cook fire for committing what they obviously perceived to be a terrible sin against them. Well, he'd met a few mamas like them in his day.

Smiling, he held out a hand to each of them, and when they gave him their hands in return, he raised them to his lips and lightly kissed the backs of their fingers. "Grace has told me so many wonderful things about you and her papas, it's a real pleasure to meet you, ladies. I sure can see where she gets her beauty."

The one Grace had called Aunt Mary raised an eyebrow at Mama, and some silent message passed between them. When they turned back to him, however, the fierce glitter in their eyes was less pronounced, and a ghost of a smile lurked at the corners of their mouths. Breathing out a silent sigh of relief, he caught his father's eye and motioned him to bring the family over.

Travis gave the ladies what he hoped was his most charming smile and presented his family when they arrived at his side. "Ladies, this is my beautiful mother, Mrs. Louise Sullivan and my father, Mr. Mike Sullivan, my brother Luke, his wife, Debbie and my adorable nieces, Nikki and Carrie."

Stepping back beside Grace, Travis let his family distract the McBride women for a moment. "How am I doin' so far?" he asked Grace, speaking out the side of his mouth.

"Wonderful," she said. "You're almost as good as Marsh, and that's saying something."

"Only almost? Well shoot, I'm just getting warmed up here. By the way, where are the papas?"

Grace chuckled. "Outside waiting for the screaming and crying to stop. They'll wander in in a few minutes."

"Are they going to want to take me apart, too?"

"I doubt it. You just saved them a small fortune in wedding froufrous."

"I don't even want to know what those are," Travis said. Then he turned back to the mamas. Lord, but they were a lively and a lovely pair.

"So, Mr. Travis Sullivan," Aunt Mary said. "What makes you think you're man enough to be a good husband for our Gracie?"

"Well, gee, ma'am, all I know is that I love Grace with my whole heart and I love her boys and I'll do everything in my power to make 'em happy," Travis said.

"Then why didn't you wait for her parents to come home before you married her?" Mama asked.

"To tell you the absolute truth, ma'am," he said, "I'm not old yet, but I'm not a real young fella, either. And, well, we weren't sure how long you'd be gone, and Grace and I really want to have more babies just as soon as we can. I know it was awful selfish of us not to wait, but I hope you can forgive our impatience."

While the mamas beamed gorgeous smiles at him, Grace elbowed him none too gently in the ribs. "Now, you've done it," she muttered. "We've got nine months and counting to produce the first child."

He wrapped his arm around her waist and pulled her close to his side. "That's all it usually takes, isn't it?"

Ignoring him, Grace smiled at the mamas. "Travis is right. We do want to have more babies *eventually,* but the real reason we wanted to hurry our wedding along, is that you have a huge wedding to plan in just a few months, for Dillon and his fiancée, Blair DuMaine. They want to get married here at the Flying M, but Blair will be awfully busy promoting the movie."

Mama placed one hand over her collarbones. "We're to plan a wedding for a big movie star? Us?"

"A lot of it," Grace said. "Blair's cousin Hope will be arriving within the next month to help you. She's going to stay right here at the house so you'll have plenty of time to talk and plan. Isn't that wonderful?"

A groan came from the back of the room and Travis looked up in time to see the color drain out of Jake's face, leaving him a pasty shade of white. Wondering what that was all about, Travis saw Zack, Cal, Alex and Emma closing in on Jake, all talking and laughing at the same time. They made so much noise, the mamas looked in their direction and suddenly remembered they had more new in-laws and grandchildren to meet.

They kissed Travis's cheeks and hugged and kissed Grace, then hurried off to join the others. Grace and Travis said goodbye to his family and hugged the boys before slipping out the open front door. They found Grace's father and her Uncle Gage chatting outside the barn.

After visiting with them for a few moments, the older men good-naturedly waved the bride and groom on their way. Grace and Travis climbed into his sparkling clean pickup. She slid across the seat and fastened the middle safety belt while Travis fired up the engine. Grinning at her, he said, ''Ready to go build some dreams, Mrs. Sullivan?''

''You bet, cowboy,'' she answered, leaning over to kiss his cheek. ''Let's get out of Dodge while the gettin's good.''

* * * * *

Return to Whitehorn

Look for these bold new stories set in beloved Whitehorn, Montana!

CINDERELLA'S BIG SKY GROOM by Christine Rimmer
On sale October 1999 (Special Edition #1280)
A prim schoolteacher pretends an engagement
to the town's most confirmed bachelor!

A MONTANA MAVERICKS CHRISTMAS
On sale November 1999 (Special Edition #1286)
A two-in-one volume containing
two brand-new stories:

"Married in Whitehorn" by Susan Mallery
and
"Born in Whitehorn" by Karen Hughes

A FAMILY HOMECOMING by Laurie Paige
On sale December 1999 (Special Edition #1292)
A father returns home to guard his wife and child—
and finds his heart once more.

*Don't miss these books, only from
Silhouette Special Edition.*

Look for the next **MONTANA MAVERICKS** tale, by
Jackie Merritt, on sale in Special Edition May 2000.
And get ready for
MONTANA MAVERICKS: Wed in Whitehorn,
a new twelve-book series coming from Silhouette Books
on sale June 2000!

Available at your favorite retail outlet.

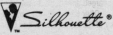

If you enjoyed what you just read,
then we've got an offer you can't resist!

Take 2 bestselling love stories FREE!

Plus get a FREE surprise gift!

Clip this page and mail it to Silhouette Reader Service™

IN U.S.A.	IN CANADA
3010 Walden Ave.	P.O. Box 609
P.O. Box 1867	Fort Erie, Ontario
Buffalo, N.Y. 14240-1867	L2A 5X3

YES! Please send me 2 free Silhouette Special Edition® novels and my free surprise gift. Then send me 6 brand-new novels every month, which I will receive months before they're available in stores. In the U.S.A., bill me at the bargain price of $3.57 plus 25¢ delivery per book and applicable sales tax, if any*. In Canada, bill me at the bargain price of $3.96 plus 25¢ delivery per book and applicable taxes**. That's the complete price and a savings of over 10% off the cover prices—what a great deal! I understand that accepting the 2 free books and gift places me under no obligation ever to buy any books. I can always return a shipment and cancel at any time. Even if I never buy another book from Silhouette, the 2 free books and gift are mine to keep forever. So why not take us up on our invitation. You'll be glad you did!

235 SEN CNFD
335 SEN CNFE

Name	(PLEASE PRINT)	
Address	Apt.#	
City	State/Prov.	Zip/Postal Code

* Terms and prices subject to change without notice. Sales tax applicable in N.Y.
** Canadian residents will be charged applicable provincial taxes and GST.
  All orders subject to approval. Offer limited to one per household.
  ® are registered trademarks of Harlequin Enterprises Limited.

SPED99   ©1998 Harlequin Enterprises Limited

Back by popular demand!

CHRISTINE RIMMER
SUSAN MALLERY
CHRISTINE FLYNN

prescribe three more exciting doses of
heart-stopping romance in their series,
PRESCRIPTION: MARRIAGE.

Three wedding-shy female physicians discover
that marriage may be just what the doctor
ordered when they lose their hearts to three
irresistible, iron-willed men.

Look for this wonderful series at your favorite retail outlet—

On sale December 1999:
A DOCTOR'S VOW (SE #1293)
by **Christine Rimmer**

On sale January 2000:
THEIR LITTLE PRINCESS (SE #1298)
by **Susan Mallery**

On sale February 2000:
DR. MOM AND THE MILLIONAIRE (SE #1304)
by **Christine Flynn**

Only from
Silhouette Special Edition

Silhouette®

Visit us at www.romance.net   SSEPM

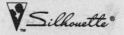

Start celebrating Silhouette's 20th anniversary
with these 4 special titles by
New York Times bestselling authors

Fire and Rain
by Elizabeth Lowell

King of the Castle
by Heather Graham Pozzessere

State Secrets
by Linda Lael Miller

Paint Me Rainbows
by Fern Michaels

On sale in December 1999

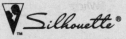

Celebrate Silhouette's 20ᵗʰ Anniversary

With beloved authors, exciting new miniseries and special keepsake collections, **plus** the chance to enter our 20ᵗʰ anniversary contest, in which one lucky reader wins the trip of a lifetime!

Take a look at who's celebrating with us:

DIANA PALMER

April 2000: SOLDIERS OF FORTUNE
May 2000 in Silhouette Romance: *Mercenary's Woman*

NORA ROBERTS

May 2000: IRISH HEARTS, the 2-in-1 keepsake collection
June 2000 in Special Edition: *Irish Rebel*

LINDA HOWARD

July 2000: MACKENZIE'S MISSION
August 2000 in Intimate Moments: *A Game of Chance*

ANNETTE BROADRICK

October 2000: a special keepsake collection, plus a brand-new title in
November 2000 in Desire

Available at your favorite retail outlet.

Where love comes alive™

EXTRA! EXTRA!

The book all your favorite authors are raving about is finally here!

The 1999 Harlequin and Silhouette coupon book.

Each page is alive with savings that can't be beat!

Getting this incredible coupon book is as easy as 1, 2, 3.

1. During the months of November and December 1999 buy any 2 Harlequin or Silhouette books.

2. Send us your name, address and 2 proofs of purchase (cash receipt) to the address below.

3. Harlequin will send you a coupon book worth $10.00 off future purchases of Harlequin or Silhouette books in 2000.

Send us 3 cash register receipts as proofs of purchase and we will send you 2 coupon books worth a total saving of $20.00 (limit of 2 coupon books per customer).

Saving money has never been this easy.

Please allow 4-6 weeks for delivery. Offer expires December 31, 1999.

I accept your offer! Please send me (a) coupon booklet(s):

Name: _____

Address: _____ City: _____

State/Prov.: _____ Zip/Postal Code: _____

Send your name and address, along with your cash register receipts as proofs of purchase, to:

In the U.S.: Harlequin Books, P.O. Box 9057, Buffalo, N.Y. 14269
In Canada: Harlequin Books, P.O. Box 622, Fort Erie, Ontario L2A 5X3

Order your books and accept this coupon offer through our web site
http://www.romance.net
Valid in U.S. and Canada only.

PHQ4994R